D1247142

Blue Feather
and Other Stories

Also available in Large Print
by Zane Grey:

The Lone Star Ranger
Shadow on the Trail

ZANE GREY

Blue Feather
and Other Stories

CONNECTICUT STATE LIBRARY
LIBRARY DEVELOPMENT DIVISION
LIBRARY SERVICE CENTER
WILLIMANTIC, CONNECTICUT

G.K.HALL&CO.
Boston, Massachusetts
1988

GRE
LARGE
PRINT

Copyright © 1934, 1954, 1961 by Zane Grey, Inc.
Copyright © Renewed 1962 by Zane Grey, Inc.

All rights reserved.

"The Horse Thief" was originally published under the title
"Outlaws of Palouse" in Country Gentlemen Magazine.
"Quaking-Asp Cabin" first appeared in the American
Weekly. "Ohio's Writer of the Purple Sage" by Edwin A.
Bauer is reprinted by kind permission from The Sohioan,
October 1960.

Published in Large Print by arrangement with
Harper and Row Publishers, Inc.

British Commonwealth rights courtesy of
Dr. Loren Grey.

G.K. Hall Large Print Book Series.

Set in 18 pt Plantin.

Library of Congress Cataloging in Publication Data

Grey, Zane, 1872–1939.
    Blue feather and other stories / Zane Grey.
       p. cm.—(G.K. Hall large print book series)
    ISBN 0-8161-4700-0 (lg. print)
    1. Western stories. 2. Large type books. I. Title.
[PS3513.R6545B56 1988]
813.52—dc19
                                               88-21694

Contents

Blue Feather

I

In the midst of the great desert rose a tremendous wall of stone, upon the ramparts of which stood the citadel of Taneen, chief of the Rock Clan.

Under the gold-banded, black-fringed table mountain, to the north and east, yawned an abyss of gorges, the unknown, the place of cliffs and shadows, through which rolled and thundered the red river of the gods. To the south stretched the wasteland—the long weathered slope leading down to bare ridges and colored buttes, out over the gray flats, and onto the dunes of clay and the white-shrouded distance. On the west side lay a shallow valley where patches of bleached grass and sere fields of corn stood out starkly from the green cedars.

Taneen paced to and fro on his stone-fenced terrace. A dry hot wind fanned his troubled face. It blew from the west. It bore evil tidings—that the rains would not come. The preceding year had been dry; the winter

3

snows had been scant; and now the springs were failing, the streams running low, and the waterfall Oljato trickled like thin wind-swept grasses over the ledge.

These omens haunted Taneen. They re-called the beginning of the twelve-year drought, which in the end had dispersed the starving clans of the Sheboyahs to the four winds. The rains had come again with fruit-ful seasons, bringing back prosperity and happiness to the little people of the rocks. Taneen could look afar, with eagle gaze, to see on a distant craggy height the citadel of the Wolf Clan; and farther still, dim in the purple haze, a dark spur that marked the home of the Antelope Clan. Other clans were scattered far to the westward.

That summer no brave runner had yet crossed the hot, waterless sands and rocks with messages to Taneen. All was not well with the neighboring clans.

Taneen turned to gaze from his terrace down the many-stepped descent over the lit-tle brown dwellings with their dark, eyelike windows, down to the center of the strong-hold, where the domed granaries and cir-cular cisterns stood under the protecting arch of the great wall, and still farther down to

4

the faded green squares and gray ovals of the playgrounds.

But the young braves of the Sheboyahs were not indulging in games this hot day. They lolled in the shade of the walls, or lay asleep inside the cool houses. Naked children swarmed like lazy ants on the courts and terraces. Only the squaws and the maidens were at work, grinding, baking, weaving, carrying, moving in and out of sun and shade. Taneen's Rock Clan had grown populous again, for which gift of the gods he was grateful and proud. But there seemed to be a shadow creeping over them.

He went below to the council chamber where his medicine men convened much of late, obsessed with their interpretations of the signs of the times, with their incantations to their guardian spirits.

A sacred fire of cedar fagots was burning on the east side of the chamber, where the door looked toward the sunrise. In the center of the floor a fine covering of wind-blown sand had been laid, and upon this space Declis, the painter, was sifting colored sands of white and copper, of blue and green and ocher. Old Benei, the star-gazer, was chanting. Clodothie, the chief medicine man of the clan, leaned on his staff with gaze of doubt and fear fixed upon the fourth inmate of the chamber. This was Dageel, the idiot of the tribe, a pink-eyed, red-haired, deformed young brave hideous to behold. He was hated and feared by all the Sheboyahs.

"What is he doing now?" demanded Taneen, aghast.

"Listen," replied Clodothie impressively.

Dageel, bending over the sand painting, was jabbering wild and whirling sounds, meaningless and fearsome to the chief. He made strange and violent gestures; he expelled a puffing breath, such as would be emitted by a watching deer.

"He tells of the First People, who came from animals," translated the medicine man. "Of the time when it was always night, of the coming of the sun, and then of water over all the land."

Taneen silenced the priest with a gesture of impatience. "What of this hot west wind?" he queried darkly.

"O Chief! It is the herald of more dry years," replied the medicine man sonorously, with a slow spreading of his clawlike hands. "Our corn did not ripen. Our melons parched on the vines."

"Give orders that my people conserve their

grain and water. We shall not starve. Meanwhile you priests shall invoke the rain gods. You will seek council from your spirits, to learn what sacrifices we must make, what ceremonies will appease."

"O Chief, it is written! Return Nashta to her outcast clan!" thundered the priest.

Taneen shrank as from an inward stab.

"Wise man, you should know it is also written that my child Nashta, Daughter of the Moon, remains hidden from daylight with the Rock Clan forever," intoned Taneen imperiously.

"Your sin will be visited upon your people," said the priest.

"Be it so. She is my blood, my pride. Nashta is innocent, as is her mother. The fierce Antelope Clan would destroy her, the daughter of their queen."

"Then the devouring drought will come as before, like a swarm of grasshoppers that denude the land."

Taneen stood silent, watching the sand-painter.

"The ice will creep back upon us . . . or the land will be dark again . . . or the water will rise to the tallest treetop."

"No. Taneen does not believe. The ice

and night and flood belonged to the time of the First People."

"Aye . . . But O Chief! If there were a first people so there shall be a last. A race that will make us slaves. Clodothie sees them in the shadows. Their voice is as the thunder of the red river."

Taneen believed this prophecy to be true. He had heard it in the whispers of the wind through the cedars. Even the rock walls waited for the echo of the footfalls of the future. The earth, the sky and the stars remained in eternal fixity, but all living creatures changed. Each clan of the Sheboyahs lived on their rocky height in mortal dread of the unknown. Their old sages squatted beside the fires in the kivas and handed down to the younger generations the legends of the tribe—how the fathers of their fathers fought and overcame the First People, and how their progenitors battled with man before he was man. There were stealthy steps on the trail of the Sheboyahs. The time was not far distant when there would be justification for the old chiefs' custom of building their dwellings on the unscalable cliffs. Had not the Badger Clan vanished strangely off the far escarpment to the south?

Taneen left the chamber of the priests and

repaired to his terrace where once more he leaned on the parapet to gaze with clouded vision over the lowlands.

The searing wind brought hot fragrance of the dry earth, the sand and cactus and cedar, the endless area of stone. On all sides, only that one to the west gave any hope of life. He could not endure that smoky northern abyss from whence at intervals rose a sullen roar. And the white-palled wasteland of shifting sands on the south only augmented his dread. Yet these regions seemed indeed to be insurmountable barriers for those vague hosts that threatened his people. Gray and lonely and monotonous sheered away the cedared valley to the west, solemn and stark under the noonday sun, a wide path to the other clans of the Sheboyahs, yet weirdly formidable at this hour.

The chieftain's gaze shifted to the shadow under the grand arch of the wall that flanked the end of the citadel below. Here, deep in a recess of the rocks, lay the kiva that hid Nashta, Daughter of the Moon. The light of day had never fallen upon this maiden's beautiful face. The secret of that kiva was held inviolate by the Rock Clan. Only the medicine men, and old women of the tribe, and the maiden attendants bound to secrecy, knew of the presence there of Taneen's child, by the queen of the outcast Antelope Clan. Nashta, Daughter of the Moon, whose skin was white as snow! Taneen's hold upon his tribe was no stronger than that precarious secret. There was catastrophe in the air. Whispers of the departed Sheboyahs came with the swallow's rustling flight. The chief's great love for the outcast queen was greater than that for his people. He would cherish Nashta, her daughter, even though through that bond he brought about the doom presaged by the priests.

Taneen liked not the desolate surroundings, nor the significance of the elements. Grieved and tortured, he sought the cool shade of his thick-walled house.

At sunset the medicine men brought to Taneen a runner from the Wolf Clan. Caked with dust and sweat, this brave carried strange tidings. The Antelope Clan was no more. The angry gods had destroyed them. Clouds of smoke rose above their citadel, and long rows of carrion birds sat upon the walls. The approach to their fastness had been broken away by powers beyond the ken of the sages of the Wolf Clan.

"Taneen, take heed," cried Clodothie, his

voice filled with foreboding, "lest your people suffer the same accursed fate."

The chief did not hear. Between deliverance from mortal foes and the death of a woman still beloved, he stood racked to the very soul. Seeking the darkness, he lay wide-eyed and afraid. But the torture was for earthly loss of the dusty-eyed woman who had outlawed her people for love of him.

A low, sand-shifting wind moaned in the clefts of the rocks. Taneen heard and felt that he was not alone. Then soft, moccasined footfalls on the terrace attested to mortal activity, the tryst of braves and maidens who dared forbidden love, even as he had dared in the days of his youth. A nighthawk shrilled a bitter cry. At last in the dead hours silence lay like a heavy mantle over the citadel. Then Taneen stalked forth upon the terrace.

A pale moon gleamed down upon the innumerable facets of rock. The gorge to the north resembled the night, menacing, mystic, waiting. Those whom Clodothie called the First People might be there in the blackness. But Taneen was certain only of a monstrous beating heart in the oppressive silence. The air had cooled and he breathed deeply. It was the midnight hour of vigil that Taneen seldom missed, and never when the moon soared high. Pale forms moved noiselessly, like spirits, out of the shadow of the great arch. Taneen watched them, his heart full to bursting. Nashta, with the star-maidens, her attendants, was stealing out to bathe in the moonlit pool below the citadel.

The austere summer days dragged on. Taneen's high priests, for all their lore and boasted influence with the gods, failed to bring the rains. Rabbits and antelope left the valley. The Sheboyahs fell back upon their store of grain. The springs sank lower. Oljato no longer slid its pale lacy waterfall over the precipice. But the great pool under the wall, shaded from the thirsty sun, held to its shimmering level.

The mysterious fate of the Antelope Clan ceased to dominate the harangues of Taneen's medicine men. Jealous of their power and doubtful of their strength, they bent all their efforts into prayers for rain.

One day Taneen proved to himself that he still retained the keenness of eye which in his youth had been compared to that of the eagle. Far down on the ragged red slope he made out a moving dot. He watched from his terrace. The object might be a sheep or a cougar, but he thought it was a man, and therefore kept his counsel. The black speck moved, enlarged, vanished to reappear, and was always climbing. The time came when Taneen's fears were justified.

He called for his hunters, those of the clan who were farsighted. They came and looked long in silence.

"A tall man!"

"He is not a runner."

"Aie! From the north."

The braves came singly and in groups; the squaws left their tasks to line up along the ramparts; the medicine men heard and stalked forth to see. When the stranger appeared in plain sight on the slope below the base of the cliff, all the Rock Clan crowded the walls, the terraces, the roofs. The hour seemed momentous.

The stranger waved something that flashed in the moonlight. The gesture was friendly. Only the medicine men did not take it so. The maidens were in a flutter of excitement. Taneen waved an answer which was a gesture of welcome. Then old men, squaws, braves and the maidens followed their chief, and a long fluttering line of waving hands and arms could be seen along the parapets.

This visitor had the spring of a deerstalker in his stride. He came on. He climbed with no sign of weariness. He reached the first flight of cut steps in the ragged cliff. These he surmounted as one used to steep walls. Only those watchers who leaned over the ramparts could see him now. Low guttural murmurs flowed back to those behind.

Taneen saw the stranger halt at the second flight of cut steps. His upturned face flashed in the sun. He called aloft in a ringing voice. It was an unknown tongue that silenced the wondering onlookers! Then this daring visitor essayed the second stairway, soon to pass from view under the wall.

"Let down the ladders," commanded Taneen.

The priests made loud and wailing protest. But the chief waved them into silence.

"Bring him before me," ordered Taneen.

The high priest Clodothie raised his gaunt arms to heaven and from his cavernous chest rumbled a dolorous lamentation. It was the end. Taneen was about to receive the serpent into their midst.

Strong-armed braves slid the long spruce poles down over the parapet. Little cross-pieces were bound on these poles for rungs. A brave of the Rock Clan could run up these ladders like a squirrel. It remained to be seen if this visitor could mount the walls.

The silent crowd thronged twenty deep at that point, and waited breathlessly.

Taneen paced his terrace, erect and haughty, true to the nobility to which he owed his heritage; but the lament of his high priest rang like a knell in his ears.

Presently a shout went up. The stranger had surmounted the walls. Taneen turned to see the throng open to make way for a splendid striking figure of a man, striding forward between the priests. They brought the stranger before Taneen, silent, no doubt awed by his majestic presence. Taneen lifted his right hand high and voiced the welcoming words of his clan.

The visitor imitated the chief's gesture and replied in a language which none there understood. He was a head taller than the tallest brave of Taneen's clan. Round his eagle head and raven hair ran a beaded band, from which projected a long, graceful blue feather. His handsome face was of a markedly lighter shade than that of any brave of all the clans Taneen remembered, and its tinge of red was equally slight. His eyes, of a dark, piercing gray hue, held the secret of a great power. Taneen estimated his age to be under thirty years. His magnificent torso was naked to the waist. Below, he wore a short divided garment of buckskin, held in place by a braided girdle. From this hung a flint-headed tomahawk. Moccasins and leggings of buckskin, worn ragged, completed his attire. He carried a long bow, and at his back a quiver of arrows.

"Whence come you?" queried the chief, with slow signs correlating his question.

The stranger understood, for he answered by a sweep of his long arm to the north, indicating a far country beyond the chasms that no Sheboyah had ever crossed. He spoke again, and his speech, illustrated by signs made with his weapons, and his strong hands applied to his body, made plain that he was a hunter, that in the chase he had become lost, and had wandered across the gorges, starved and sore distressed.

Taneen indicated his watching braves, the shy-eyed maidens, the squaws, all his clan, and queried again with further sign.

"Your people?"

"Nopah!" replied the stranger, and touched the blue feather that crowned his raven hair.

"Blue Feather," interpreted Taneen, to his gaping listeners. "Taneen makes him welcome. Give him food and drink."

To the stern high priests Taneen said,

"The Clan of the Rocks cannot change its creed because famine is abroad in the land. Or because there is a creeping cloud on the horizon. Taneen does by this strange visitor from a new people what he would ask for one of his own sons."

With glad acclaim the young braves surrounded Blue Feather to lead him away down the terraces, followed by the whispering, murmuring maidens.

While the summer waned Blue Feather idled with the braves in the cool shade of the walls or under the brush sun shelters. He let it be known that he was content to tarry there until the cold winds of autumn would temper the heat of his long journey back to his people.

Meanwhile he learned the language of the Sheboyahs. Quick and intelligent, he soon mastered the scant vocabulary of the Rock Clan, meeting difficulty only with the words that had many meanings, each of which depended upon the intonation with which it was spoken.

Blue Feather was a trusted spy of the great Nopahs, a tribe from a far country. They were warriors and not tillers of the soil. Nothis Toh, their chief, having destroyed the little people of the cliffs beyond the vast chasms of the red river, had turned his fierce eyes toward the corn growers, the grain grinders of the caves. Blue Feather's work was manifold. It was to make friends with this most populous Rock Clan of the Sheboyahs, to take stock of their possessions, their defenses and the approaches to their citadel, to deceive the medicine men and lastly to corrupt the braves by the subtle arts and games and herbs of which Blue Feather was master, and to work his wiles upon the young women so that they would fall into his power.

In all, the Rock Clan totaled two thousand members. A third of these were able-bodied men. Taneen's fortress appeared impregnable to attack from the outside. The wily Sheboyahs had chosen a great unscalable crag, from which height tribe after tribe could be repulsed. Only through strategy and surprise, through treachery within the citadel, could Taneen be overcome. The huge circular bins were bursting with grain, the cisterns were full, and the deep pool of water under the arch would not fail that year. Taneen could withstand a siege longer than even the Nopahs might sustain one.

From some untraceable source, Blue

fly a seventh race in one day," replied the victor haughtily.

The defeated braves and their backers argued for a competition on the morrow, that they might recoup their losses. Blue Feather agreed to race, but only provided the stakes were larger. Then while he rested the braves indulged in their favorite games. One in particular attracted Blue Feather. In the center of a circle there had been imbedded a post of petrified wood so that about three feet of it projected above the ground. The top of the post was round and polished so smoothly that it shone in the sunlight. A long pole and a small hoop constituted the other implements needed for this game. From an established line the hoop had to be tossed or rolled, by the aid of the pole, and the object of the game was to put the hoop over the post. Blue Feather admitted the dexterity necessary to excel at this game, and resolved to come out in the dead of night to perfect himself at it. His plot called for the winning of all their games before he introduced those of the Nopahs.

That afternoon and night news of the race on the morrow and the size of the wagers went from lip to lip all over the citadel. It augured well for Blue Feather's plan to inflame the gambling passion of the Rock Clan.

Therefore he was not surprised, when in the morning he sallied forth, to find the populace streaming out to see the race. Blue Feather thrilled at sight of the hosts of maidens, brightly clad, and in the gay mood that befitted the occasion. So far it had suited his purpose to remain aloof, impervious to the many shy advances they had ventured toward him. But this occasion might well be an auspicious one to begin his conquest of the maidens of the tribe.

Taneen and his chiefs and priests occupied seats at the top of the rock ledge. Below them and to each side extended the colorful throng, halfway round the oval field. Braves were tossing a ball to and fro.

Blue Feather stalked proudly before the double row of maidens. His heart swelled and for the time being he forgot the evil design he had upon this peaceful tribe. He reveled in the fluttering awe and admiration that he excited in them. His quick and roving eye soon picked out Ba-lee, one of the prettiest maidens of the clan, whose dusky glances toward him had not passed unnoticed.

He made her a gallant bow.

"There is no maiden to wear this for me," he said, touching the blue feather in his hair.

"Perhaps the Nopah runner has not asked," Ba-lee replied, her dark eyes alight. They told Blue Feather that he had not far to go to awaken fire in their slumbering depths.

"Blue Feather has not yet been so bold— but . . ." and he removed the long graceful ornament from its band.

Ba-lee gave a little gasp of expectant pleasure, while whispers and murmurs ran through the bevy of maidens with her.

At that moment Tith-lei, the Mole, rival runner to be paired with Blue Feather that day, came up escorted by many braves. He was little, and his mean, half-shut eyes no doubt had won him the sobriquet of "The Mole." His sight was keen, however, for he betrayed jealousy at the spectacle of Blue Feather before Ba-lee. The maiden reacted subtly to this encounter. Blue Feather's swift thought was that Tith-lei was deeply enamored of her, a passion which she did not return.

Blue Feather tendered his token to the maiden. "If Ba-lee will wear this the Nopah runner cannot lose the race."

She bent her glossy dark head while Blue

23

Feather stuck the feather in her hair, so that it stood up proudly. Tith-lei hissed like a snake. If he had not been Blue Feather's enemy before, he instantly became so now. Ba-lee threw back her dainty head and laughed with her maidens. But the swift half-veiled glance she shot Blue Feather told him of his conquest.

Then the runners were called to the starting point. Tith-lei stripped to his buckskin breechcloth. Blue Feather cast an inquisitive and critical gaze over his antagonist. Tith-lei's wide and deep chest, his narrow loins and his thin sinewy legs convinced Blue Feather that in a long race of endurance the Rock Clan racer would prove a rival to be feared. In a short race, however, he could not contend with the Nopah.

Poised, the racers toed the line. They were instructed to run around the stake at the far end of the field and back to the starting point. He who first touched the starter's hand would be declared the winner. A brave raised his drumstick. When the boom resounded the runners leaped into action.

Blue Feather kept pace with Tith-lei and watched him cunningly. The faster Tith-lei went the faster Blue Feather ran to keep up with him. Thus they reached and rounded the far stake. Then like an arrow from a bow Blue Feather shot ahead into his marvelous stride, that was twice as long and quick as Tith-lei's. He left the boasted racer of the Sheboyahs as if he had been rooted to the earth.

The yelling of the braves and the screaming of the maidens rang sweet in Blue Feather's ears. He had heard that blended roar before. If the Rock Clan loved a runner, let them see the greatest of the Nopahs in all his glory.

Taneen's tribe uncrowned a champion that eventful day. The chief came down from his seat to place a hand upon Blue Feather's heaving shoulder.

"The Nopah runs like the antelope," he said. "Taneen would be proud of such a son."

But the high priests glowered upon Blue Feather, and the panting Tith-lei cast malignant eyes of jealousy and hate upon him. Yet among the braves, even those who had lost their wagers to the Nopah, he became more popular than ever. And among the maidens, when he sought Ba-lee to retrieve his blue feather, he was a hero. Coyly Ba-lee held the feather behind her back, and besought him to give it to her to keep.

"Some day, perhaps, when the Nopah has won all—and you," replied Blue Feather boldly.

In the still, smoky days that followed, Blue Feather played and won at all the games of the Rock Clan except those which involved feats of strength. He held back here, letting the braves imagine that he was weak of arm and back. Then he taught them a Nopah game the tempo of which was very fast and furious. To win a player had to drive a ball with a crooked stick through a hole in the wall. Another game he taught them the braves liked even better. It was to knock a ball made of a kangaroo-rat skin into a hole at the top of a mound in the center of the court.

Blue Feather always won. At any game or contest or wager he was invariably the winner. But the fact that he seemed to shun feats of great strength left him vulnerable at one point. The braves taunted him with the one thing at which they believed he could be beaten.

One bright afternoon all the Rock Clan was again out upon the open field. The center of attraction appeared to be a round stone a little more than knee-high. Blue Feather asked of the maidens what the stone was for.

"That is the Man-Rock," replied Ba-lee, earnestly. "At a certain age every boy of the clan has to go out each day and tug at this stone and try to move it. When he can roll it he becomes a brave, and when he can lift it off the ground he is a man, and when he can carry it he becomes a chief.

"Blue Feather, you carry the Man-Rock," pleaded Ba-lee, her little brown hands clinging to him. "Ba-lee knows you can. Have you not lifted her as easily as though she were thistledown? . . . Show them and make Ba-lee rejoice. Tith-lei is jealous. He swears that you are weak. That he will kill you in battle. And, oh, my Nopah, if he does, Ba-lee will die and her soul will wander lost forever!"

Blue Feather joined the circle around the lifting stone. One young Indian after another tugged and heaved; others, more mature, budged and moved it. Tith-lei bent over it and the muscles of his back corded and strained. But loud cries from the watchers attested to the fact that he had lifted it off the ground. The medicine men proclaimed the feat to all. Tith-lei staggered erect, spent and purple of face, sweat pouring off his

27

shoulders. In triumph he confronted Blue Feather.

"No-pah!" he panted. "Winged foot—big talk—squaw hunter! . . . If you are—a man —lift the rock!"

Clodothie, the priest, gave vent to his long-damned up suspicion and hatred of this interloper from an unknown tribe.

"*Carry* the rock—if you would stay longer among the Sheboyahs!" he demanded.

"Little people, you would learn if the Nopahs are strong?" queried Blue Feather contemptuously, for once giving way to anger at these taunting enemies of his tribe. "Behold!"

Bending over the stone, he lifted it without apparent effort and carried it all the way back to the spot where it had rested when first the forefathers of the Rock Clan had instigated this man-building custom. The spectators exclaimed in wondrous awe at the feat. Blue Feather had carried the stone as far as had the combined efforts of hundreds of braves throughout the years. Then with wrath upon his brow he bounded up the ledge, and laying hold of a dead spruce tree he lifted with slow and tremendous might, getting it on his bowed shoulder. Staggering, with whistling breath, he carried it down to crash it at the feet of those who had been taunting him.

The high priest raised his arms as if in the presence of one imbued with godlike powers. Tith-lei's ghastly face betrayed the end of the bold plan that he must now abandon. Fear in the breasts of the braves overpowered their awe and admiration. But the squaws screeched their delight at Blue Feather's prowess, and the maidens gave him wild acclaim.

To these admirers, and to the few braves who pretended not to have been too deeply impressed by the dramatic revelation of Blue Feather's power, he gave an explanation of the reason that he always won. His grandmother had taught him a ceremony, through which, if successfully performed, the gods of chance would throw all in his favor; but if he failed in the least detail of this exceedingly difficulty legendary rite he would never win again at anything. Blue Feather told how he had dared. His ancient grandmother had bidden him take some corn pollen, and pollen from other plants, and lie down before the hole of a lizard, and place some of the pollen upon his hand, palm upward, and chant the four songs she taught him. He must wait until the lizard came out to eat the pollen, and the singer must not move while the lizard was out nor while he was singing, nor forget one single word of the songs.

"Teach us the songs," cried the ambitious braves. But Blue Feather shook his head.

Blue Feather had a great store of turquoise and jet, weapons of flint, bows and arrows, beaded buckskin moccasins and garments, sheaths and bags, necklaces of bone, skins and blankets, all of which he had won from the braves of the Rock Clan. They borrowed and begged and stole articles to pit against his acquired possessions, not that they dearly loved what they had lost, but because of their insatiable passion for gambling, which Blue Feather had encouraged.

This was what the crafty Nopah wanted. He refused to run more races or play more games, saying that it would be unfair to contest further with them in ways wherein he had established his superiority. But in gambling, which allowed them the same element of chance as himself, he would meet them halfway. So they fell to gambling, a practice which was forbidden by the medicine men. And as before, Blue Feather always won.

Now about this time Blue Feather imposed upon his victims a habit far more dangerous than gambling. He had brought in his large quiver a goodly supply of blue gum, which when chewed brought on a kind of intoxication. Blue Feather introduced this evil habit little by little, to one brave at a time. And the sweet and potent drug affected each so powerfully and ecstatically that he kept the use of it a secret. Blue Feather knew then that if he could brew the concoction in sufficient amounts it would not take long to corrupt the entire fighting force of the Rock Clan. This blue gum was made from the heart of a mescal plant boiled with a resinous pitch which exuded from some species of evergreen. Blue Feather knew how to make it if only he could find the ingredients.

His days then were consumed with gambling in secluded niches of the rocks or in abandoned kivas. His nights were devoted to exerting his powers of fascination upon the women.

One moonlight night Blue Feather waited for Ba-lee on a terrace at the lower end of the citadel. As he had arrived late at the rendezvous, he assumed that she had come and gone. He reflected wonderingly that Ba-lee seldom seemed to spend time with him late at night. The squaws were strict with their daughters; and upon Ba-lee especially there was a restraint that he could not understand.

Blue Feather gazed down into the black gulf of the chasms. He knew that his father, Nothis Toh, with his bravest warriors, was hidden in the green valley under the red walls, waiting for the spy to return and guide them to the massacre of the Rock Clan. But that hour had not yet come. Blue Feather's task was not yet accomplished.

On this night, as once before, there were spirits abroad on the cool wind; and their voices were unintelligible to the spy. They seemed not to bear messages from the gods of the Nopahs. Their presence around Blue Feather, as he waited for Ba-lee, weighed upon him and troubled him. Ruthless Nopah that he was, no remorse abided in his heart. But there was a mystery here that he could not fathom. And unknown terrible events to come seemed to bring warnings from the shadows.

Silence enfolded the scene, except for rustlings as of soft invisible wings on the air. It boded the death and loneliness and decay that hovered over this crag peopled with sleeping Sheboyahs. The silvered desert stretched away to the south, endless and desolate, untenanted by life or spirit.

Blue Feather shook off this nameless oppression and went his way. The next night when the moon was full he walked with Ba-lee along the western wall, and reproached her for her failure to meet the night before.

"Ba-lee was there," said the maiden. "But the hours are not all hers."

He faced her in the moonlight and drew her close with swift and rude hands.

"Blue Feather will kill that blinking, mole-eyed Tith-lei," he whispered passionately.

Like a bird in the coils of a snake Ba-lee quivered. "Ba-lee is true. She cannot help it that Tith-lei watches and plots."

"Then if Blue Feather kills him?"

"Ba-lee will not care. Her love is—here," whispered the maiden, her dusky eyes shining, and she laid her cheek upon his bare chest.

Blue Feather's jealousy seemed appeased, but he was not yet completely satisfied. Ba-lee loved him wildly, yet he did not believe that she would ever betray the secrets of the Rock Clan.

"Blue Feather soon must go back to his people."

"Ah! . . . He will forsake the Sheboyah girl. He has played with Ba-lee and her sisters. They, too, love him. And they are afraid. They do not trust the warrior from the north. Blue Feather is the lover of many."

"Does Ba-lee fear the Nopah?"

"Ba-lee does not know where love ends and fear begins," she replied mournfully.

"What do the old men say?"

"That the Nopah has weaned our braves from play and work to drunkenness and gambling . . . that he has cast a spell upon our maidens."

"Blue Feather wants to leave by night . . . not by the ladders . . . not to be seen. Tith-lei would shoot an arrow into his back . . . Will Ba-lee guide Blue Feather to the secret way down under the walls?"

The maiden shook in his arms. Her lips denied, but her eyes betrayed.

"Ha! So great is the love of Ba-lee for the Nopah! She will see him languish here."

"Not death for herself does Ba-lee fear . . . But for others as well—if she betrays."

Blue Feather was answered, and cold thrills coursed his frame. The maiden knew the secret passage. But more than honor sealed her lips. More than life itself! He was content to let that knowledge suffice for the time. But he would break her to his will. Then, sustained by the knowledge that his perilous enterprise was soon to be accomplished, he caressed the maiden until she lay spent and rapt upon his breast. For once she forgot the fleeting hours. When the white moon had soared high above, riding serene in the dark blue sky, Ba-lee seemed to awaken as from a trance. She uttered a dolorous little cry.

"Oh, the moon is high! It is late. Ba-lee must go," she whispered, trembling as she slipped from him.

"The squaws and old men are deep in slumber."

"No!" she cried, eluding his long arm.

"All are asleep, Ba-lee. Stay with Blue Feather."

"No!" she breathed, and fled.

Blue Feather watched her glide away and it struck him again that something vastly more vital than fear of her mother had possessed her. The dark eyes opening suddenly to the moon had expressed an emotion close to actual terror. Blue Feather had no faith in these Sheboyah maidens, but that might have derived from his contempt for an inferior race. Her people wanted her to become the wife of Tith-lei. She had probably been promised to the Mole. Whatever actuated her piqued anew Blue Feather's jealousy, and for the first time he followed her.

The moonlight divided the citadel into bars of silver and ebony. The hour was midnight. Ba-lee's gliding form melted into the shadow of a wall, reappeared to steal across a white lane into blackness again. Blue Feather quickened his step. Ba-lee had gone toward her dwelling, and then she had turned abruptly away from the center of the citadel. She was not going home. Blue Feather muttered a sibilant curse. He would surprise Ba-lee with Tith-lei and strangle them both.

Blue Feather lost trace of Ba-lee after she had stolen like a specter down the west terraces. The great arched crags loomed there, and in their shadow lay the granaries and cisterns. Blue Feather had been satisfied to ascertain that they were full and sealed. A shaft of moonlight came down from a ragged notch in the wall, to pierce the gloom. The keen-eyed spy saw Ba-lee cross it. To Blue Feather's amazement she appeared to be going on under the very arch of stone. Perhaps the cunning Tith-lei had arranged with her to meet him there.

At length Blue Feather passed out of the silver moonlight into the deep shadow. He was approaching the rough west side of the huge eminence upon which Taneen maintained his citadel. The crags rose high and they were utterly unscalable. A blank space appeared hollowed out under the rached cliff. It was a shallow cavern that by day Blue Feather had noticed was filled with firewood. Below it the ledges dropped down like steps to the gorge on the west.

Suddenly Blue Feather gave a quivering start, like that of a panther when it sights its prey. Moving forms were gliding out of the shadow into the moonlight. Slight forms to the number of three, one of which was clad all in white. Blue Feather thought he recognized Ba-lee, her stature and walk. Sheboyah girls bent on a midnight lark! Or did Ba-lee have friends who met their lovers in secret? The figures passed out of sight around the corner of the wall.

The spy ran with softly padding feet down to the point where the maidens had disappeared. Peeping around the corner, he stood transfixed and thrilled. The dark pool shone like burnished silver in the moonlight. Ba-lee and her accomplices in this mysterious midnight adventure were gliding through a fringe of willows. Blue Feather's grim mood lightened and he laughed noiselessly. The little devils meant to bathe in the crystal pool banned by the priests. Blue Feather resolved to surprise them in the act. Stealthily he descended, keeping in the dense shadows. Reaching the willows, he crawled very slowly and silently to a slight aperture in the foliage and peered out.

On the silver sand at the margin of the shimmering pool, scarcely three strides distant, stood the three maidens in a glory of moonlight that seemed to magnify the beauty of the place. Blue Feather remembered a dream of his mother's. Once in Blue Feather's life he was to meet something of transcendent beauty, from which, if he succumbed to it, must come certain ruin and death.

Ba-lee was binding up the shining black tresses of the maiden in the pale robe. She was taller than Ba-lee and her little head was borne on her slender neck with regal grace. Blue Feather could not see her face. The third girl was kneeling on the sand at her feet.

"O my mistress," Ba-lee was murmuring, in poignant contrition, "forgive Ba-lee! She was late again."

"Child, as you are beloved, so are you forgiven," replied a flutelike voice. "But Nashta cannot answer for the gods that hideous Clodothie prates about so continuously."

"Our Daughter of the Moon," said the kneeling maiden, "it is not long after midnight."

"My gentle slaves, you know that only the full moon at midnight must shine on Nashta when she is disrobed."

"Oh, dare we risk the anger of the gods?" cried Ba-lee fearfully. "They may tell Clodothie. He will see only evil befalling the Rock Clan."

"Nashta would risk more than that . . . just to have one brief adventure like Ba-lee's with the Nopah!"

"Ba-lee begs the gods forbid. She should keep her lips sealed."

"But Nashta is also a woman. Tell her more of him—the racer with the blue feather."

"Tonight Ba-lee went from Tith-lei to Blue Feather. And her heart is heavy. She is pledged to one. She loves the other. Blue Feather swears he will kill the Mole."

"Does Blue Feather love Ba-lee?"

"Oh, woe! He swears it with a laugh on

his lips. But he loves many. La-clos here will tell Nashta. *She* also loves the Nopah."

"La-clos, are you too such a fool?" queried the Daughter of the Moon as she slipped a dazzling white arm and shoulder from her robe.

"He is a master of women," mourned the maiden. "He is not of our race. He is beautiful—and terrible!"

"Ah! La-clos—Ba-lee, you fear this stranger?"

La-clos bowed her dark head. Ba-lee answered in shame, "Ba-lee's soul is not her own."

"Nashta has seen no man save her father and the priests. Then only by night. She would see this Nopah by day, though the sun strike her blind!"

"Hush, Nashta! . . . What is it that Ba-lee hears?"

They gazed around fearfully. Only the silence and moon-blanched water and silvery rocks were there; Nashta turned toward the willows, revealing a lovely face white as the white lily that blooms in the gorges. Her eyes were like two dark pools in the moonlight. Then Ba-lee stripped the robe from Nashta, and the white maiden stepped out of it, upon the moonlit sand.

Blue Feather felt something enter his heart that was like a piercing blade. The beauty and the warning of his mother's dream both had come true. In that instant he knew that though he was mortal what he now beheld was a spectacle reserved only for gods. But this Nashta, this maiden called Daughter of the Moon, was not a goddess. She moved, she emanated an exquisite fragrance upon the still night air, she shone white as the driven snow in the silver light. She embodied all the loveliness of all the dreams and the legends of the Nopahs.

Blue Feather hurled his transfixed body out upon the sand. Ba-lee fell to her knees with an agonized cry. La-clos became a statue of stone. Nashta neither started back nor uttered a sound. The wondering, enveloping flash of her great black eyes all but sent the bold intruder into precipitate flight. Nashta stood naked before him and unashamed. She seemed like a child who had never known any distinction between being naked and being clothed.

"Ba-lee, cover her," commanded Blue Feather.

Both maidens were galvanized into immediate action. In another moment Nashta stood

41

draped to her white face, out of which blazed her dark, proud, challenging eyes.

"Nashta, princess or maiden, you have your wish. It is the Nopah!"

"Oh, Ba-lee!" she faltered.

He no longer doubted that never before in this maiden's life had she gazed upon a young and ardent brave. When he enfolded her in his arms she let her lovely head fall upon his breast.

"Blue Feather," said the spy, his enraptured voice trembling with the great wonder that filled his heart.

II

Taneen commanded the presence of Blue Feather.

"Nopah, whence this wager with Tith-lei?"

"Chief, your braves have driven the Nopah mad with their gibes. And Tith-lei is first among them. Can Blue Feather withstand their taunts forever? The Nopahs are proud. My father would disown me did he know of the taunts I must endure."

The Sheboyah chieftain believed the young warrior's accusations to be only too true, and he was a fair and just man. Generation after generation the Rock Clan had been addicted to the vice of gambling. In times of drought, when there was no hunting, no visiting other clans, the braves had nothing to do but play and gamble. Taneen had been accustomed to look upon this weakness with a tolerant eye. But his priests had been harping upon these present vices as indicative of the decline of their race. Some strange form of intoxication seemed to attend their gambling of recent weeks.

"Taneen's wisdom judges Blue Feather as having been sent by the gods to test his people. If they have grown soft and weak then a time of trial should be welcome. What is this latest wager that has made Declis and Clodothie mouth like the brave with twisted mind—Dageel?"

"The Mole wants to drive the Nopah away. Ba-lee had looked upon the Nopah with favor. Tith-lei wagers that Blue Feather cannot descend from the walls unaided, kill an antelope and climb back with it before the sunset of the third day."

The chieftain made a gesture of impatience. "Tith-lei is not cunning. He is a fool. He taunts, he dares only in his own interest. He is unworthy of Taneen's clan!"

"Blue Feather accepted the Mole's wager," replied the Nopah loftily.

"It is death. No brave could scale these walls burdened with the carcass of an antelope. . . . Taneen will cancel the wager."

"No, Chief. Blue Feather's word is given."

Taneen laid aside his long staff. He had never been blessed with a son. His only child was Nashta, Daughter of the Moon, precious as the ruddy drops of Taneen's heart's blood.

But the sun was never to shine upon her beautiful face, and he could never stand before his clan proudly to acknowledge her. Now his sore and troubled breast received this Nopah, this alien, this blue-feathered young giant as he would receive a son. Taneen felt his love go out to him.

"What if the Nopah wins?" he asked.

"Tith-lei will meet him in mortal combat on the field."

"What if the Nopah loses?"

"Blue Feather returns all he has won and looks no more upon any maiden of the clan."

"Nopah, the antelope have gone from the valley," rejoined Taneen sternly.

"Blue Feather did not know. But he will track them."

Taneen took up his staff and motioned his attendants to leave the Nopah with him alone.

"Taneen's sun is setting. There is a step on his trail. His clan is spent. His days are numbered. Blue Feather can make the outcome of this test a happy one. Let him win this unfair wager. Let him kill Tith-lei!"

The Nopah gazed long into the dark inscrutable face of the chief. He could see that the old chieftain's simple words were sincere. They heaped more coals of fire upon Blue Feather's head. Already his conscience had been flayed by gentler, sweeter words, from the lovely lips of this great chief's hidden daughter.

Blue Feather had accepted Tith-lei's wager because it offered an excuse for him to leave the citadel. He must flee—from himself, from the carrying out of this ruthless and terrible plot that had ripened under his craft, flee from the loveliest and most loving maiden in all this world and that beyond.

"Taneen honors the Nopah. Not yet has he deserved honor. But if Blue Feather returns . . ."

He bowed himself out of the chief's presence. To utter still more falsehoods had become impossible. He had been stricken. He was no longer the infallible spy of the Nopahs.

Blue Feather took only time to fill his pouch with parched grain and dried meat, then snatching up his bow and quiver he ran out to leap down from the terraces, deaf to the plaudits of the braves, blind to the lament and the weeping of the maidens. Bounding along the ramparts like a mountain goat he chose a point on the south wall to descend. In that moment he could have bidden defiance to space itself. But his hands, his feet, clung like lichens to the rock, as down and down and down he went, swift and sure, to drop at last upon the slope at the base of the wall. Bobbing heads and flying hair and waving arms were silhouetted black against the sky line above. He waved in answer to the long shrill yells and bounded away over the rocks to the north, soon vanishing from sight.

That ragged slope was to Blue Feather as a multitude of enemies, every rock of which seemed a foe to spurn. He ran, he leaped. He set the avalanches rolling. He might have been pursued by the winged spirits of those who had died with twisted minds. That league-long slope of talus, ending in the red gorge, was as a short space of thin air to the Nopah. No feat of endurance in any game he had ever played, no race he had ever run to the plaudits of the clan, could compare to this descent alone, seen only by the spirits, driven as he was by his tortured conscience.

But at the mouth of the gorge, where Blue Feather halted, spent and hot and wet with perspiration, with the dust caked on his lips, he found that the demons he had fled from were beside him still. His labored heartbeats sounded in his ears like a muffled drum. Vain had been his pride, his vaunted boast, his blind conceit. He was no god. He was only a mortal Nopah. And death shuddered in his soul.

Far back up the endless slope, far above, he saw the gold-banded walls, the black-fringed line of the citadel of the Rock Clan. He had torn himself away from what was more precious than honor or glory or life itself.

The gorge below him was the gateway to the land of chasms. Down in there, in a green, watered valley, waited the Nopahs. Blue Feather spurred himself erect and strode on. He reached the bottom, where the dry stream bed wound, where the huge red rocks blocked the way, where the lizards basked in the sun. Gold faded off the rims of the walls; purple shadows fell like curtains; and the winding ribbon of blue sky above yielded to the deep blue of the night.

Blue Feather's violence had expended itself. He felt his way along in the pale gloom of the walls. His devils had lagged behind. He still heard them, threatening, whispering. But as he passed under the arch of stone there were silent voices that told him many things he had never dreamed before.

He had fled from Nashta and the love that had torn him asunder. All the hours of the many nights he had spent with her, under the dreaming walls, beside the shimmering pool, seemed to crowd upon him with their rapture. No maiden on earth or in heaven had ever been like Nashta. She was as lovely as the slender white blossom leaning to the wind from the side of the precipice. She was more innocent than any child. She was more loving than any woman. She knew but little. Fear did not abide in her, nor jealousy, nor temper, nor hate. The squaws who had taught her had left out knowledge of birth, death, battle, love, marriage—all the common things natural to a girl of the Rock Clan. The maidens who had attended her, after childhood, had only confused her with the legends, the games, the courtships of the tribe. Nashta had given to Blue Feather the wondrous worship of a strange and lovely creature born of the fatal and unquenchable love of a queen and chief whose clans were bitterly estranged. From the hour Blue Feather had clapsed her to his breast she had begun to live; and afterward every one of her endless queries, the sweet proofs that she lived only for the time she could be with him, the kisses at which first she laughed and then yearned for insatiably, seemed mute and tragic evidences that if she lost him she would die. Blue Feather had known this, but it was better that she die than live to be carried a naked captive to a Nopah cave. And on his side Blue Feather, too had been transformed, riven as if by the lightning blast, so that his ruthless purpose, his callous degrading of the braves, his gay conquest of the maidens, burned a living hell of remorse in his soul, and a torture of love that ended for him all hope and joy and beauty and labor and life, unless he could share them with Nashta.

In the long night hours those voices of the walls attended Blue Feather, and forced upon him that which he had not dreamed of before his flight.

Day had broken gray when Blue Feather smelled smoke and heard the barking of half-wild dogs. The gorge opened into a green valley enclosed by rounded walls of red, billowing upward to craggy heights.

The lean-jawed scouts who sighted him first heralded his return by whoops, which were answered in kind by the waiting hosts, so that a veritable thunder assailed the walls, and re-echoed from side to side, at last to rumble away along the distant cliffs.

Blue Feather had not before seen the

Nopah warriors through the vision now given him. A thousand strong were they, tall, gaunt, somber-eyed, hungry-jawed giants, eager to find, to slay, to take, to gorge. And his father, Nothis Toh, stern-visaged like a vulture, held war and blood in his commanding eye.

"Docleas," he said, with a kingly paternal pride in this great son, "the days were long. Nothis Toh gives welcome and rejoices. The Nopahs are hungry for corn and meat and squaws. What of the Little People?"

Blue Feather leaned on his bow. "Father, and chief, Docleas brings ill tidings. The Nopahs must hunt far across the red river, two moons away to the cedar plains of Shibeta. . . . Docleas found at last the Rock Clan of the Sheboyahs. Many little people, poor and sick in the midst of a famine. They live on a high cliff that Docleas could not climb without help. They have no meat, and the antelope have left their pastures. They have corn and water enough to last a siege, but for the Nopahs that siege would be folly. They have no treasure of turquoise, no skins, no blankets. The squaws are old and lean and shiftless. Their maidens have been mar-ried to a distant clan. . . . Docleas will try again, far to the west. But he must have many moons. Go home with your braves to our corn and meat and women. If Blue Feather does not return to his father before the green buds burst again—then he will never come."

"Docleas is a great son of a great chief," cried Nothis Toh, and gave order for his warriors to march to the north.

Before the sun descended that day Blue Feather stood upon a windy height, and with wet and gleaming eyes saw the Nopahs, like a slender column of marching ants, winding their way down a gorge toward the sullen river.

Both agony and joy stirred in his heart. He had failed his father, disowned his people, cast off forever the Nopah maiden who waited for him. He was lost to glory and wealth. He was a traitor to blood and creed.

With passion-shaken breath Blue Feather turned to the heights and swept a long arm upward.

"Docleas, the Nopah, is dead," he cried to the listening ears of the rocks. "Blue Feather will rise! He will have Nashta! He will save her people! He will bring the rains!"

His piercing cry pealed out over that lonely

land. From the cedared ridge beyond, a band of graceful animals trooped out in alarm or curiosity. They had gray bodies and white rumps. They were antelope! Blue Feather started at memory of his wager with Tithlei. Fixing an arrow to his bow, he let fly. The distance was too far and he missed. The antelope ran off and then stopped to gaze. Blue Feather sped another dart. Where was his vaunted skill, his uncanny power? The animals scampered off. The hunter trailed them over the gray ridges until at length he came upon one standing alone on a little rise of ground. At this distance there was little hope of killing the antelope, but Blue Feather thought of Nashta lying in the hollow of his arm, and he bent the bow prodigiously and held the notched arrow as steadily as if he had been turned to stone. Blue Feather did not see the flight of that arrow, but the antelope fell. He ran to find it pierced through the middle.

He rested that night on the far slope of the valley. Well Blue Feather knew the demand to be made upon his strength on the morrow. He ate and drank his fill. The darkness descended cool and restful to wrap him in slumber.

The wild dogs awakened him in the gray

dawn with their sharp and wailing barks that cut the frosty air. They smelled the fresh meat of the antelope Blue Feather had hung in a cedar.

This was the third day, and destined to be the most momentous Blue Feather had ever lived. He arose to meet it, calm in the realization that it would bring death or glory. When the wolves had fled, absolute silence pervaded the valley, gray with shadows lifting, tingeing to rose where the east brightened. There were no voices on the dead air, no steps on his trail. He was a man alone in the desert, dependent upon his own strength, his own wit. The gods of his people now would have abandoned him to his fate. He must win the allegiance of other gods. But that valley was not tenantless. For Blue Feather the rocks had a soul, the cedars were ripening their purple seeds to green the slope after they were old and gnarled hulks, the bleached grass had a spark in its roots, the solemn waiting air, with its sting and tang, was peopled with the invisible life of all that had gone before.

Blue Feather lifted his burden and strode down the slope, out of the cedars upon the frosted sage. Sharp and black against the reddening sky towered the rock of Taneen, the uneven turreted line of its citadel rising above the ragged ramparts.

The sage slope ended in the sandy waste and the dry meandering stream bed, upon the far bank of which spread the field of withered melon vines and seared corn. Beyond these began the rock slope that led up to the base of the wall. Blue Feather had been seen from afar. From rock to rock he stepped, zigzagging his way up slowly, conserving his strength. That the antelope seemed a light burden troubled Blue Feather. He did not trust this surging thing in his breast. Unless attended by superhuman power no man could hope to surmount this wall.

Sweat poured off Blue Feather's naked shoulders and breast, and like a bellows his broad chest heaved. The long jagged slope of weathered rocks at last lay beneath him, and the steep gray wall sheered upward. He laid down the antelope, and stripped bow and quiver from his back. Shrill cries reached him from above. Blue Feather craned his neck. Dark faces appeared along the rim. A maiden screamed his name. Blue Feather swept his gaze along the row of faces. Ba-lee! She alone was pale, with dark and staring eyes.

"Tith-lei relents," she called, wildly. "Go round to the ladders!"

"*No!*" he shouted upward. "Ba-lee, if Blue Feather falls . . ."

Other faces crowded into that line, to peer over the rim—the eagle face of Taneen, the distorted face of Clodothie, the weazened face of Declis, the pink face of the albino, Dageel. A ball of thong came unrolling down. Blue Feather tied the flapping end to his bow and quiver, and bade those above to haul them up. They complied. Again the buckskin thong came whipping down. A stentorian voice stilled the shrill babble. Blue Feather gazed upward in silence.

"Tie on the antelope," commanded the voice. It was that of the chief.

"*No!*"

"Taneen has no son!"

"The Sheboyah may have Blue Feather, when he is worthy," called the hunter, through his hands. Then he passed along the base of the wall to find the best place to attempt the ascent. All along the west side he hunted, and far around to the south. The place where he had descended sheered up at an unscalable slant. Therefore he passed back along the west side toward the north, only to be confronted by the perpendicular buttress

56

above which towered the arched wall and the crags. In all that half circle of the butte there was only one place that Blue Feather gave more than a single glance. It was a succession of bulging knobs, on a slight incline, one above the other, that led to a section where two walls met in a ragged right-angle corner. And at that instant a vision illumined Blue Feather's troubled mind. He saw himself carrying Nashta, and swift as a flash he ran back along the base of the wall. That which he prayed for swept over him, strong as the fire of the sun, unquenchable as life, as great as his love.

Blue Feather jerked the dangling thong from the wall, and bound the forefeet of the antelope, and then the hind feet. Next he drew the two pairs of feet toward each other, until they almost met, and made them fast. He carried the antelope to the point which he had chosen, and lowering it to the ground he filled his lungs to their uttermost depths, again and yet again. The clamor above fell upon his deaf ears. For a long moment he studied the steep ascent, marking his course to the rim. Then in his mind he was lifting Nashta instead of the antelope and slipping her bound arms over his head, and he was holding her with her body resting upon his breast. He made no more prayer to the unknown gods. Nashta was his goddess now. Then he began to ascend the wall.

His clawlike fingers clutched the rock; his moccasined toes clung to the all-too-scarce footholds. Up and up he climbed. He gazed only at the slanted wall before him. He held tenaciously with one hand and one foot while he reached out for some crevice or niche in the face of the rock. Up and up! It was nothing for Blue Feather, this climb, with the Daughter of the Moon on his breast.

The knobs on the cliff ended and so did the steep slant. He clung precariously at the base of the right-angled corner of two walls. They were farther apart than they had looked from below. He stretched a long leg across the void, and he was off balance when his toe touched the wall and froze there. Then, holding tight, he edged his body along inch by inch until he could brace his head and neck against the nearer wall. Quickly he shot his other foot across. Thus he formed a bridge with his body, his head higher than his feet, elbows and hands braced underneath, with the antelope (or was it Nashta?) upon his breast. He slid one foot upward and then the other. Then with tremendous muscular effort he shoved his back up a like distance.

Up! Up! The walls converged until he could brace himself with his knees, and the narrowing space permitted his broad back to fit tight against the stone. Up! The gray walls shortened and blurred against the bright blue of the sky where dark heads bobbed. Upward, faster now, he fought his painful way. Suddenly the deadening strain ceased. A multitude of hands dragged Blue Feather over the parapet where he fell with a swelling din in his ears.

When the darkness passed and he could see once more, Blue Feather was lying with his head upon Ba-lee's lap. Her warm tears were falling upon his face. A ring of maidens knelt around them. A ring of warriors whose dark visages registered eagerness and relief stood beyond the maidens. A babel rose about him. Blue Feather drew Ba-lee's head down to whisper in her ear. The maiden whispered back that Nashta had fallen like a stricken deer when she had learned of the wager— that she lay waiting for him or death—that if he came he must be generous enough to spare the jealous Tith-lei.

Blue Feather rose like a bent sapling that springs erect when the weight that holds it is removed. The faces of the braves were now the faces of brothers. But the hideous Dageel was foaming at the mouth; Benei, the star-gazer, seemed to be seeing something inimical in the sky; Declis swung his bags of sand and looked upon the stones; Clodothie wore a scowl like a black and forbidding storm. They had heard the poignant words of their chieftain. And he, Taneen, stood hard by, too proud to reveal his deep emotions, his stern accusing gaze upon Tith-lei. That brave knew full well that the reckoning was upon him. Sullen, yet awed by what he could not comprehend, he met no eye, nor looked up when Blue Feather confronted him to point at the dead antelope.

"Blue Feather is here and the sunset of the third day has not yet come."

"The Nopah is more than mortal man," returned Tith-lei, respect for his hated rival wrenched from his very soul.

Taneen came between them.

"Stand one hundred steps apart," he thundered. "Faces away. When Taneen calls, turn and fight!"

It was Ba-lee who fetched Blue Feather's bow and quiver.

"Nashta says spare the Mole. But Ba-lee says kill him," she whispered, her dusky, eloquent eyes bespeaking unselfish concern for this stranger who had won her love and her fear.

Silence enfolded the field. All of Taneen's Rock Clan, to the naked and wondering children, lined up on the walls and ledges. Blue Feather took his stand. Tith-lei stood far out, facing the multitude, desperate and shaken, sure now of his fate. The two rivals turned their backs upon one another. A brooding mantle of stillness fell upon the watchers. Then Dageel broke the spell with a series of low mournful sounds. The medicine men stood with uplifted arms as if to direct attention to the curse that had fallen upon them. The maidens wept under covered eyes. Then Taneen uttered a cry that held no note of sorrow.

Tith-lei turned quickly to dispatch an arrow that flashed into the sunlight. As Blue Feather turned, strangely cool and deliberate, Tith-lei's arrow struck him high in his shoulder and quivered in the flesh, while a red stream poured down his bare breast. Tith-lei let out a savage and triumphant yell, and swiftly strode toward his wounded rival, shooting as he approached an arrow that whizzed over Blue Feather's head.

A murmur went through the tense crowd

of watchers. Blue Feather astounded them with his deliberate action, as he fitted a long arrow to his great bow. Tith-lei came on, shooting again, a missile that grazed his foe's extended arm. But suddenly he halted, as if an invisible wall barred his progress. Blue Feather was bending his bow. It needed only one look to recognize in him the master archer. But the long arrow, slowly moving its bright flint head back toward the arching bow, was pointed far to one side. Blue Feather was not aiming at the Mole. To one side of Tith-lei and far beyond him, a sapling stood alone on the field. Blue Feather bent that prodigious bow until the tips almost met. He stood motionless as a stone image. *Twang!* That arrow might have been a winged spirit. No spectator saw it. But all saw the sapling shake and then bend its graceful green top. Suddenly drooping, it fell to the ground. Blue Feather's shaft gleamed halfway through the broken trunk.

Shrill and high rose the yells of the Rock Clan. They were acclaiming the marvelous skill of the bowman, but even more so the magnanimity of Tith-lei's rival.

"Begone!" thundered Taneen to the stunned and cowering Mole.

Then the chief approached the bleeding

Blue Feather, who stood quietly in the place where he had shot the arrow.

"May the enemies of Taneen find the Nopah upon his walls!"

Blue Feather waited in the shadows of the arch for Ba-lee. He feared the jealous maiden, knowing that both her dread and her love were beginning to wane. Would she betray to the chief his secret visits to the daughter of Taneen?

A half-moon shone past a gleaming silvered crag. The hour was late. Taneen's clan slept. A boding silence hovered over their dwellings. Blue Feather felt it, even though his rapt mind could think only of Nashta. What now menaced the Rock Clan? It was there in the cool gloom of the gorge.

Ba-lee came, slim in the moonlight, and stood before Blue Feather, with dusky unfathomable eyes. He importuned her about Nashta.

"She waits with La-clos. She bids you come. But Ba-lee tells you it is death to descend into the sacred kiva."

Ba-lee detained him with hand no longer timid. "Blue Feather spares Tith-lei, but kills the maiden." And she laid her hand over her heart. Dark doubt and yearning passion burned in her upturned gaze.

"You are Blue Feather's sister now," he whispered, taking her hands. "The Nopah is sorrowful that it cannot be more. He is changed. Nashta has visited upon him the sum of all that Blue Feather has made others suffer. He has spared the Mole. . . . Ba-lee, he has saved you, and Nashta, and La-clos and Taneen—all who are here on the great rock tonight."

The maiden turned her dark profile away. She did not want remorse in Blue Feather, or change, or generosity, or his strange new power to save. He felt a sinking of his heart.

Ba-lee gave a slight gesture for him to follow her. Keeping to the shadow of the arch, she stole silently far to the other side, beyond the corded stacks of wood and the domed granaries and cisterns, to the dark fissured wall. Here were the ceremonial houses, and farther on the place of the sacred kivas. Blue Feather trembled. No brave's foot had ever desecrated that spot. Ba-lee felt her way. A faint round patch of light shone on the black floor. It came from the open hole in the roof of a kiva. Ba-lee stepped down, whispering for him to follow. Blue Feather saw a ladder descending into this cavern in the rocks. Stepping carefully, he went down.

A little fire, blue-flamed and red-embered, dimly lighted a chamber so large that Blue Feather could not see the walls. He suspected that it was a subterranean cave utilized by Taneen for a sacred kiva. And herein must lie the secret of the underground passage which led down from the citadel to the open.

But Blue Feather had little interest in that or in the character of this kiva. Breathless and with bursting heart he strove to pierce the gloom. La-clos, beside the ladder, murmured a few words to him. She, as well as Ba-lee, was breaking the law of the tribe for Blue Feather, but she would be faithful.

"Nashta is here," said Ba-lee.

Blue Feather saw his goddess then, kneeling on pale robes of fur, with outstretched white arms like the opal marble in the chasms.

"Nashta lives again," she whispered, as swiftly he knelt to clasp her in his arms.

"Oh, Daughter of the Moon, my Nashta! Oh, joy and spirit—all that pierced the Nopah's blindness—he is here!" Blue Feather bent over the lovely face and felt that he held to his breast the link between his future and the voices down in the valley.

"Ba-lee, go above, and you, La-clos. Watch and listen. Blue Feather will be long here."

"Tith-lei hunts abroad at night like a bat," replied Ba-lee significantly, as she mounted the ladder.

Blue Feather placed Nashta's soft hand high up on his shoulder where a plaster of gum covered his wound. Nashta caressed the angry hot skin and placed her cool cheek upon it, and then her soft thrilling lips.

"Nashta was wrong. Never again will she beg Blue Feather to spare the Mole," she said, and it seemed that anger for the first time stirred in her.

"Ba-lee will tell Tith-lei and he will betray us."

"Taneen is my father. He would forgive."

"Yes, my princess. But Clodothie and Declis rule your tribe. They will throw me out to the wild dogs. Blue Feather must win your people to his side. He will bring the rains."

"Oh, my Nopah, Nashta believes that that of all things would overthrow Clodothie and his powers! You are a god to her, and her very breath, and beating blood."

"Nashta, it is little for the Nopahs to bring the rains. Blue Feather has learned. He has danced the rain dance many times. He knows the songs, and the drink of herbs that deadens the poison of the snakes."

"Snakes! The crawling things that rattle beside the pool? Ugh! The Daughter of the Moon has been taught to love everything. But her Nopah's kisses have made that teaching as if it were not. Nashta loves only Blue Feather. His smile, his voice, his touch are all of her world that matters now. She loves as her mother, the queen of the outcast Antelope Clan."

"Lonely maiden, do you know that sad history?"

"From Taneen himself. He, too, has broken the law of his tribe. He told me of my mother. Her love was great and true as the sun that has never shone upon Nashta. . . . Oh, my Nopah, consider. Nashta's fate will be like her mother's unless Blue Feather takes her away to his wigwam, to make her his bride, his people to be her people, his god her god."

"Nashta, never call him your Nopah again," replied Blue Feather. "He is no longer a Nopah. He has betrayed and disowned his people. He is an outcast. He has no name, no home, no treasure, nothing but his love for Nashta, for which he has lost all."

"Ah! What story is this? Let not Blue Feather bow his head! Nashta's love will recompense for loss of all."

"Listen. Blue Feather came first as a spy for the warrior tribe of Nothis Toh, his father. His work was to ply his cunning with the little people of the cliffs. He came, and the gods favored his work. The braves went crazy over the gambling games. They chewed the blue gum and found it sweet. The maidens fell into Blue Feather's power. Soon he would have gone forth in the night to lead the waiting warriors here to kill and destroy and capture and rape. But Blue Feather met Nashta, and his black soul went out into the darkness. He made excuse of Tith-lei's jealous wager, and accepting it he journeyed down into the chasm to find his father. Blue Feather lied. He told the greatest of all falsehoods. And he sent the Nopah warriors back across the red river to their far caves, and he returned to Nashta and her people forever."

Nashta's arms clung about his neck and she uttered a wail of fear that had birth in her then. She besought Blue Feather to use all his mastery to take her far away from the Sheboyahs, to be his slave, to live as other maidens, to see the marvelous sun, to feel the wind upon her face, to have them change her white blue-veined skin to the natural hue of her people.

Blue Feather held her to his throbbing heart and found no answer. He had asked only to see her, to hold her as now, to serve her and her people. But Nashta was not a goddess, nor a spirit, nor a speaking moonbeam. She was flesh and blood; she was life and love. All her years she had been cheated out of the things she longed for.

"Ba-lee has told Nashta what the squaws forbade her to know. Nashta laughed. She did not believe until Blue Feather's kisses were hard on her mouth. Nashta is a woman. She would be the outcast Nopah's bride, the proud mother of his children."

"Beloved," cried Blue Feather hoarsely. "Nashta breaks the outcast's heart. He is strong, he is swift, he is cunning. But he cannot change the law of your people."

"Blue Feather can carry the maiden down over the rocks. It is enough."

"Yes, in the dead of night he could lower Nashta, and follow. Will she have it so?" he whispered, weak in all his being.

"Nashta rejoices. The Nopah outcast and the Sheboyah princess will go. Blue Feather is a warrior. He knows what to do. Nashta has only beauty. She is not strong. The sun must shine on her only little by little."

"Blue Feather will plan," he replied ponderingly, the greatness of this plot weighing upon him. "Ba-lee . . . Tith-lei . . . Corn and meat and drink . . . A long rope . . ."

"Nashta is not entirely helpless. She knows the hidden passage out under the walls. It has many arms. Taneen comes through it when he visits Nashta here."

"Here!" cried Blue Feather, leaping erect with the maiden in his arms.

"Yes, Blue Feather. The hole is there in the darkness of the kiva. It is covered. Only Nashta knows."

Blue Feather tossed Nashta lightly up and lightly caught her as she fell into his arms with a little cry. He was the giant that he had dreamed of. The valley voices filled his ears like distant music. He called Nashta every beautiful and loving and tender name that he had learned in the language of the Rock Clan.

"More! More! All the Nopah words!" she breathed ecstatically. "Talk to Nashta always in Nopah. She learns. There are not enough

Sheboyah words to tell of her love, her happiness."

"Nashta must forget the Nopah language Blue Feather taught her."

"Taneen's daughter forgets nothing. Ah! She remembers all Ba-lee's gossip about Blue Feather. How he made Ba-lee's heart a fluttering captive bird. His laugh, his kiss! And her woe when he played with La-clos, and all the maidens . . ."

"Enough. Nashta may be the Daughter of the Moon, but she is as other maidens. Forgive Blue Feather. . . . Tomorrow night we flee!"

Blue Feather mounted the ladder, gazing through the round door in the roof of the kiva, beyond which he saw the half-moon riding in a strange sky. A corner of the black arch projected out into the pale light. He paused silently at the opening, his sense of peril returning to cloud the joy that had been his. He whispered for Ba-lee and La-clos. There was no answer except for the sound of a cold wind that wailed over the kiva! The maidens should have been there. Blue Feather put his head out to peer around him. The cavern under the arch was dark in the gloom; outside a pale moonlight brooded over the domed granaries. He called out, his voice low. Only the wind answered. The Nopah sensed then that the very air was oppressive with catastrophe. He stole away from the kiva, his eyes those of a fox at night, his ears attuned to the menace on the wind.

The tall granaries clustered thickly in the foreground, one casting a round shadow against the pale gleam of another. Blue Feather distrusted them, but he had to pass. Suddenly, out of their dark shadows, came a swift rush of padded feet. A swarm of braves seized Blue Feather from all sides. Blue Feather heaved them off and, whirling about, he flung them back, only to be seized from behind. He had not time to draw his weapon. With silent fury, like giants they surged over him and bore him to the ground. They bound him and dragged him forth into the moonlight.

Tith-lei, malevolent of face and swelling with triumphant hate, confronted the captive.

"Nopah dog! Now his blue crest droops! Where now is his boasted strength, his power to win, his gum that stole the wits of the Sheboyahs? Blue Feather gambled on Ba-lee and lost. He has betrayed Taneen's secret to the clan. He has bared the great Chief's dishonor to his people. The accursed Nopah will be split in the middle, torn apart and cast to the wild dogs!"

They dragged him by his bound feet and tumbled him into a dungeon, where he rolled and bumped down a flight of stone steps to lie bruised and bleeding on the dank floor. A network of black bars crossed the door of his prison. A dim beam of moonlight shone in on the wall, brooding there with the silver sheen that had been the ruin of the Nopah. At last the prophetic dream of his mother had come true. A cold and bitter breath of resignation flooded over Blue Feather's soul. He deserved his fate. He had held the Daughter of the Moon to his breast. Yet to have been beloved by Nashta made him a king on earth and would be enough recompense for the beyond. She would wilt like a flower in her kiva and surely her spirit would meet his far down under the rocks where the voices came from.

All night Blue Feather lay there upon his back, with the pain of his racked body slowly numbing his agony of mind. His grief was only for the loss of other hours with the lovely Nashta. In the cold gloom of dawn he fell into a sleep of exhaustion.

Rude and violent hands awakened Blue Feather. He was being dragged up the stone steps, out into the sunlight, upon the terraces of the citadel. All of the Rock Clan were abroad, joining in the procession. Blue Feather was looked upon as no more than one of the poison-fanged wild dogs of the desert. While his captors dragged him along, the lines of braves struck at him, the squaws spat upon him, the maidens cast looks of hatred upon his face, and the naked children struck him with sticks and stones. The citadel was in an uproar.

At last Blue Feather's captors halted with him in the great court before Taneen's dwelling. The thongs around his ankles were cut and he was jerked erect by brutal hands to be thrust forward through the crowd.

The booming of a drum and a sudden shrill cry silenced the multitude. Blue Feather faced his judges, standing free now, his head high, his falcon eyes blazing.

La-clos lay groveling on the stone floor of the court. A brave with a long leather lash stood over her. Ba-lee stood back to one side with Tith-lei. She seemed stunned by the enormity of what she had brought about. The Mole appeared to be treading on air, to expand beyond the bulk of his fellows. This

74

was his hour. Clodothie, Declis and Benei, with the other medicine men of the tribe, formed a line against the wall of Taneen's dwelling. All about, the roofs, the walls, the terraces were black with gleaming-eyed spectators. And at Blue Feather's back stood the dark-faced braves who had dragged him hither.

Taneen came forth from his dwelling, a stricken man, yet still with the bearing of a chief.

"Nopah," began Taneen, in stern and rolling voice, "Tith-lei bears testimony that you dared to enter the sacred kiva of the Daughter of the Moon."

"Blue Feather is loved by Nashta. For her he would dare wind and fire and death."

"The Nopah does not deny?"

"*No!*"

"He made Ba-lee and La-clos traitors to their sacred trust?"

"Taneen, the maidens are innocent. They feared the Nopah."

"Blue Feather speaks bold words of his entrance to the secret kiva of Taneen—of his violation of the law of the Sheboyahs—of an alien's passion for an outcast and sacred princess upon whom the sun never shone and eye of brave should never have rested!"

Blue Feather replied proudly to the chieftain. "The Nopah was dishonest till he saw Nashta. He was a Nopah spy, the son of Nothis Toh. And while the Nopah warriors with their great bows and long arrows waited down in the chasms Blue Feather worked his wiles upon the Rock Clan. Always he played, always he gambled, always he gave the sweet blue gum to the braves, always he won the love of the maidens. Always he waited for the time to go down and lead the Nopahs up to destroy Taneen's people. But one night by the moonlit pool he met Nashta. And the evil in him fled. Blue Feather went below, back to his father and the tall hungry-eyed warriors. And he lied to the great chief his father. The Sheboyahs, he told them, were poor. They lived amidst famine. They had no store of corn and meat. They had no treasure of turquoise and jet. Their squaws were old and lean and shiftless, their maidens given in marriage to another clan. And the Nopahs must return far across the red river to wait until Blue Feather found a richer clan! So he told them."

The listening priests smote the stones with their staffs and shouted: "Liar! Spy! Dog of a Nopah! The tall people with their great bows will come!"

Taneen stilled the tumult. "Does the Nopah speak truth?"

"Blue Feather ended with falsehood when he looked into the eyes of Nashta. He gave up his people. Now he is an outcast."

Taneen lifted his lean arms in tragic acceptance of a fate that he could not avert.

"Too late, Nopah!" he thundered, in a terrible denunciation of Blue Feather, of Nashta, of himself and the people who were abandoning him to the rule of the priests. "Taneen believes. He sees himself in the Nopah. He burns again in the love for which Blue Feather must die. But his power ends this day."

Taneen passed within his dwelling and suddenly the doorway darkened with moving figures.

"Death to the Nopah!" they cried.

Clodothie pounded a drum, and in the ensuing silence he harangued his fellows. At length the high priest turned to the Mole.

"Tith-lei, speak the death sentence of the Nopah spy."

The brave leaped up transfigured, knowing that in due time he would be made chief of the clan.

"Tie ropes to the Nopah's feet," he shrilled. "Spread them wide and split him asunder and throw the halves to the wild dogs."

"It is spoken. So the Nopah dies," solemnly stated Clodothie.

Then burst the pent-up fury of the populace, and around Blue Feather wheeled and screamed a mad circle of braves.

Tith-lei danced in a transport of joy before the proud rival whom he had doomed to a hideous death. Braves and maidens spread out before him in frantic evolutions. The Mole was as one possessed by devils of bliss. Wildly he ran across the court to leap upon the rampart of the outer wall. And there magnificently he spread his arms to the desert below, as if to acclaim his rise to rule nature and clan and god.

Suddenly the plumed spear in his right hand fell, to vanish into the depths below. An awful frenzied yell suddenly smote the ears of that watching, singing, dancing throng. Tith-lei's form drew back with terror. Then came a rustle as of a swift swallow's wings in flight—a slender gleam of light from below the wall—then a strange and solid thud.

From the center of Tith-lei's naked back protruded a dripping arrowhead. He screamed in mortal agony, and swung as if on a pivot to face the tribe he had been given to rule. A long feathered shaft of blue quivered in his breast. A dark crimson tide flowed down his convulsed body. His hands, like claws, clutched at the air. His distorted face told that in the instant of glory it had been transfixed with horror. His utterance strangled in a blood-choked throat.

Blue Feather pierced the air with a resounding cry.

"Behold! The long arrow of the Nopahs! Tith-lei dies!"

III

The savage Tith-lei swayed upon the wall of the citadel. And the stunned spectators, switching from wild exultance to sudden silence, gazed mutely upon the stricken brave, waiting for him to fall.

Backward he swayed until the shaft of the fatal arrow, plunged into his breast, pointed up at the sky. Then swiftly Tith-lei plummeted out of sight. From below the walls rose a prolonged and hideous shouting. The Sheboyahs had never before heard such a frightening sound.

Clodothie rushed at Blue Feather: "Who comes?"

"It is the war cry of the Nopahs," replied Blue Feather bitterly.

Braves raised aloft their stone-headed clubs to brain the Nopah captive.

"Hold!" commanded the high priest. "Save the cursed spy. He shall be torn limb from limb in the sight of his people."

They bound Blue Feather and left him

lying beside the beaten La-clos under the court wall.

Those of the Sheboyahs who had courage enough to peer over the parapet raised their hands above their heads in terror. The hour that had been presaged by the medicine men had struck at last. Clodothie shouted for their chief.

"Taneen! Taneen!"

The old Sheboyah came forth into the light. Clodothie and his followers confronted him.

"It has come!"

"Woe! Woe! The fate of the Antelope Clan is upon us."

"That Nopah dog of a spy lied to blind Taneen. The Nopah warriors are here. They shot Tith-lei off the wall. Their war cry is as the red river in flood!"

Taneen strode out to look over the parapet. The rough gray slope of weathered rocks, as familiar to Taneen as the terraces of his citadel, was not as he had known it all his life. It was like the slope of an ant hill, magnified by the gods, a moving colorful pageant frightful to behold. Taneen, too, as had his braves, threw aloft his arms in tragic awe.

Every rock held a giant with a great bow

and a long quiver of arrows. They stood tall and menacing, watching the walls. Like Blue Feather, they were lighter in color than the Sheboyahs. All wore feathers sticking from their headbands. Lines of warriors were ascending the tortuous trails up the slope. They climbed with burdens upon their shoulders of baskets and bags, and some had bundles with curious platforms on their heads. These were scaling ladders and shields to protect the tops of the ladders from missiles from above. Other warriors in smaller groups carried thin flattened poles with baskets at their tops. These, and other contrivances of war unknown to Taneen, proved the strength and cunning of a superior race.

Taneen's medicine men, cowards now that their doleful predictions had borne fruit, importuned the chief to save them and his tribe.

"Slink into your holes and pray!" cried the chief with a disdainful wave of his arm. Then he beat the drum to gather all the braves in to hear him.

"Taneen's people are besieged by an army of Blue Feathers!" he shouted. "It is the end of the Rock Clan of the Sheboyahs. . . . Fight! Let them find our bodies on the walls when they come."

Rows of boulders lay all along the inside

of the citadel walls, placed there for purposes of defense. When a thousand braves each lifted a rock to heave over the parapet the number of boulders in that long row appeared not to have decreased. Taneen joined his forces, giving command not to waste their precious ammunition. The archers of the clan stood ready with their small bows. When the chief's loud cry rang out all the defenders sprang up to throw rocks and shoot arrows.

This was the signal for a shining slant of arrows from below. Many found their mark in the chests, heads and arms of the brave Sheboyahs. Their rocks crashed harmlessly at the base of the wall, to clatter down the slope, and their arrows fell far short of their mark. Again that terrible war cry of the Nopahs sounded from below, only nearer now. The defenders had the advantage of position, but the besiegers were vastly more powerful and resourceful and numerous.

Taneen peered over again, sweat in his eyes and cold in his marrow. What he saw confirmed the foreboding in his heart. Here and there under the wall, lines of Nopahs to the number of ten in each band were advancing up the last slope with the long scaling ladders on their shoulders and the shieldlike platforms held forward to protect them from the rolling rocks. These ladders could be leaned and held against the wall, while the Nopahs swarmed up protected except for one last leap over the wall. Then Taneen ran to and fro along the parapet, driving his braves to stand and to shoot and throw while there was yet time to halt the storming warriors.

Like bees the defenders swarmed upon the walls, and the rocks rained down and their arrows were as wind-driven hail. It was then that the real battle began. The sight and smell of flowing blood, the shrieks of the wounded and the maledictions of the unscathed, the din of the avalanche of rolling rocks, the terrible flight of the long arrows upward and the war cry that accompanied them, the bravery of the squaws coming out to help, and lastly the knowledge that it was a matter of life or death now—these inflamed the Sheboyahs to a fury that surpassed fear, to a wildly inspired defense.

The Nopahs at last got their ladders against the wall, and climbed them as far up as the shields. Here the storm of arrows and deluge of rocks at close range held them.

Dageel, the idiot, the red-headed albino, appeared upon the wall. No brave could have told whence he came. His weapon was a long pole. With this he reached down to the platform of the nearest scaling ladder. Mightily he shoved, while the glancing arrows passed him. As he had no mind, so he had no fear. And he shoved that ladder away from the wall. It stood upright with its score of Nopahs, swayed for a moment, and then fell with a resounding crash. The yell of the Sheboyahs equaled that of the Nopahs. A hail of rocks accompanied the ladder's fall; those besiegers low down were maimed and broken by the stone missiles that fell from above.

The albino, his hair erect like a red mane, ran along the wall to the next scaling ladder. He seemed to bear a charmed life. The unerring aim of the Nopahs failed to stop him. Out from the wall he shoved the second ladder, his strength that of a Nopah. The fifty-foot ladder bore a man upon every rung. It stood upright an instant while many leaped off, like nuts falling from a tree. Then ponderously it fell with a crash, carrying death along with it.

Dageel ran on to the next ladder. The archers below had now concentrated upon his striking figure. A cloud of arrows sped upward. When he halted to shove at the third ladder his body seemed to give a sudden jerk. Then an arrow appeared sticking in his side. Another caught him in the leg. But Dageel did not hesitate. He sent the scalers on that ladder to their deaths. As he started on again, however, it was seen that he had been crippled. He hobbled. He fell. He dragged himself to the fourth ladder and, now on his knees, he savagely thrust it away from the wall. This one, also, went crashing down amidst the uproar of the fighting Sheboyahs. Suddenly Dageel lost his ferocity of action and his head drooped upon his breast. A long arrow had struck through his throat. From his kneeling posture he plunged off the wall.

Braves were eager to emulate the albino. Two fought for possession of the pole. But they did not bear Dageel's charmed life. A flight of arrows ended their struggle and dropped them with the long pole into the abyss.

Suddenly there came from below a tremendous twang, such as might have been made by a bow of the gods. Then a rock hurtled up to strike the rim of the wall with a resounding crack. Taneen gazed fearfully down at a new instrument of the war-skilled Nopahs. It appeared to be a kind of stationary sling. A thin flattened sapling seemed to project from behind a rock. It stood almost upright, with a basket on the end. A Nopah was in the act of placing a stone in the basket. Then other Nopahs below hauled on a rope and bent the sapling until their backs touched the ground. Then they let go their hold. With a loud twang the catapult hurled a heavy rock upward. It shot over the parapet, crushed a brave in passing, and smashed a section of the thick wall of a house above the terrace.

The long arrows, the scaling ladders, the slinging catapults were proofs of the Nopahs' greatness in battle. But they brought out in the Sheboyahs a heroism of the flesh which, while it lasted, made the two forces almost equal. If Taneen's manpower could hold out he might be able to drive off the besiegers. Nothis Toh reserved his scaling ladders while the catapults twanged incessantly. There were four of them, placed forty paces apart, and they hurled three rocks a minute. After the marksmen got the range few of these missiles struck the rim. They went over to maim and crush, to break the walls, to cave in the roofs. Dust rose in clouds and blood flowed in streams down the terraces.

The defenders behind the parapet grew

skilled at dodging the catapults' whistling rocks. They hurled many of them back at the enemy. The Nopahs were furnishing them with ammunition. Dust clouds along the walls handicapped the archers below, and favored those above. Then the squaws came with pots of scalding water and vessels of burning fagots, which the braves emptied over the wall, along the line of the besiegers. Thus again when it appeared that Nothis Toh's warriors were about to take the citadel, Taneen's braves were able to turn the tide of battle.

It waged hottest at the sunset hour. The huge missiles still came crashing over. All of the citadel along the north and east walls lay in ruins. Fire added to the terror of the besieged. The Nopahs were hurling over red-hot rocks, that broke through the walls and set aflame the interior of the dwellings. The enormous row of stones along the parapet was now half exhausted. Taneen, with broken arm and bleeding head, moved among his men and besought them to die on their feet.

Then at dusk the attack of the Nopahs ceased as suddenly as it had begun. The warriors of Nothis Toh withdrew to eat and drink, to look after their wounded and to rest. The stubborn resistance of the Rock Clan had surprised them. The Nopah chief took counsel with his priests. Were the stores and treasures of the citadel, of which they had received assurance despite the word of Docleas, worth further sacrifice?

Taneen had lost more than half his fighting force, and many of his squaws. The dust cloud lifted, the smoke cleared away, revealing ruin and agony and death. Clodothie lay in the court, dark-faced and still. Declis would paint no more sand pictures on the stone floor. Benei, the star-gazer, was dead. While the squaws prepared food and drink the crippled were cared for. When night fell, cold and clear, with the moon coming pitilessly over the crags, all of Taneen's force lay prone. Even the exhausted guards had succumbed to sleep.

Nashta lay wide-eyed in the silence and darkness of her kiva. The recollection of Blue Feather's kisses throbbed on her lips. Her blood raced in the transport of rapture that anticipation of her escape with him stirred within her. For long she had revolted against the mystery of her confinement, against the name Daughter of the Moon, the living maiden upon whom the sun must never shine. But, gentle and loving, she had accepted the decree of Taneen. Then worship of the Nopah had burned away all that had been taught her.

Her wondering mind had no conception of a future outside of that kiva, except the glory of freedom with Blue Feather. He would take her far away. She would see the earth and the sky by day, and the waters, the trees, the flowers, the birds, the tasseled corn and the golden melons—all that her maidens had told her of. The terrible sun would shine upon her face. That thought shook her heart.

Ba-lee and La-clos did not come back, a strange omission that Nashta noted, but did not consider in the enchantment of the hour. Sleep at last claimed her.

When Nashta awoke the round hole of her kiva let in a shaft of light that was gold instead of silver. It hurt her eyes. Nashta had never seen that before, or the door of her prison uncovered by day. She had slept late. Ba-lee and La-clos were not there. Suddenly Nashta sat up on her bed of furs. The habitual routine of her life had been broken.

She dressed in new garments of buckskin, a costume of long fashioning and a labor of love, over which she and the maidens had dreamily toiled, and for which the squaws had sent beads and bits of colored thong and buttons of turquoise. This gaudy garb, destined for the idle pleasure of the prisoner princess of the Rock Clan, must serve for the bride of an outcast Nopah. Would Blue Feather take pride in her? How good that her milk-white skin, through which the dark veins showed, would be hidden from his sight! She brushed and braided her black hair, whose long plaits hung down to her waist.

Still her attendants did not come. Nashta, unused to neglect, soon began to feel the pangs of hunger. She ate and drank of the remains of the cold meal of yesterday. Then she paced in the dim light of her kiva, vaguely conscious that all was not well.

A low, hollow roar suddenly floated down to her. It swelled, it rose and fell like thunder in the sky. She had never heard the like. But it bore a faint resemblance to the cheers of the Rock Clan on the singing days. Therefore it must come from men's voices. Nashta listened, slowly sinking down upon her knees. The disturbing sound died away, only to return, a concerted yell of many braves, with a discordant note that held no music. Taneen's people were not singing.

Nashta often had heard the songs, coming dimly to her from the terraces. She knelt there perplexed and troubled, realizing at last that there was some unusual reason for this strange uproar, and the absence of her maidens. Finally the tumult ceased.

Then the silence of her kiva seemed pierced by a single distant scream. Nashta had no memory of sound with which to compare it, yet her intuition connected it with things inimical to life—tragedy and pain and death.

That scream seemed to give birth to a veritable thunder of sound. But this was not the season of the rains. Had Blue Feather invoked the gods of the storm cloud? No— he would be concerned solely with Nashta.

Thunder indeed it seemed to be, but of a varying kind, rising and falling, now shrill, now low, a rumble as of rolling rocks, the trampling of many feet, the boom of drums and the chorus of yelling voices, and now and then a muffled crash.

"War!" gasped Nashta. "Taneen's enemies have come! The Antelope Clan—my mother's people! . . . Oh, woe to the Daughter of the Moon! The child of Taneen will be dragged into the sun!"

And Nashta fell upon her bed of furs, with the thunder in her ears and the prophecy of the priests whirling in her mind. They had foretold that she was to be the doom of the Rock Clan. She would be dragged into the great court, and stripped in the sunlight, so that all eyes could gaze upon her accursed white beauty, and she would be torn apart by the Antelope braves. A darkness filmed her sight and hitherto unknown anguish brought her close to oblivion. The hours passed.

"Nashta! Nashta!"

The kiva seemed to reverberate with the frantic call. Nashta started up. A canopy of twilight shaded the aperture above. In the glare of a torch La-clos appeared at the foot of the ladder. She moved as one crippled, and knelt to kindle the fagots on the floor. Nashta roused herself from her lethargy.

"La-clos! La-clos!"

"O mistress, forgive the maiden," came the mournful reply. "She could not come sooner."

"Ba-lee?"

"Last night she fought with La-clos. . . . She betrayed Blue Feather to Tith-lei. . . . The cunning Mole betrayed him to the priests. . . . They waited for him and seized him. La-clos was beaten. This morning Blue

Feather was brought before Taneen and his medicine men. The Nopah did not deny. He told how he had deceived his father, and the Nopah warriors, and set their faces away from the Sheboyahs. But the secret of the Daughter of the Moon dishonored Taneen before his clan. Tith-lei was given power. . . . To him was given to bespeak the manner of the Nopah spy's death. He proclaimed it. Blue Feather was to be torn apart and thrown to the wild dogs. Tith-lei leaped upon the wall to dance his joy. And suddenly as he gazed down from the wall a great arrowhead pierced his breast. Blue Feather cried out in a voice of the storm wind, 'Behold! the long arrow of the Nopahs!' "

Nashta sprang up vibrant with quickened, passionate life.

"Nopahs!—Blue Feather's warriors? . . . They make war on Taneen's citadel?"

"War! They are strong and terrible. They have great bows and long arrows and ladders with shields and things that throw rocks over the walls. But all day the Sheboyah braves held them below. Taneen's chiefs are dead, the medicine men are dead, half the braves and squaws are dead. Only Taneen lives to command. In another day he will live to drive the Nopahs off."

"Blue Feather?"

"They bound him and cast him under the court wall. La-clos lay beside him. When the battle is over the Sheboyahs that are left will make a holiday with the torture of the Nopah. They will drag Nashta into the sun and force her to see the rending of his beautiful body, the flowing blood, the broken bones, and the flesh thrown over the walls to the wild dogs."

"Never!" prayed Nashta, in a whisper to the gods of the outcasts.

"Listen. The battle ceases. Night comes. . . . Oh, Nashta, save the Nopah! Lose no time. When the sun rises again they will kill him."

"But how? Can La-clos lead Nashta to Blue Feather?"

"The maiden faints. . . . She is hurt unto death. . . . But that way for Nashta must not be. The Nopah lies on the court among the braves."

Nashta supported the tottering maiden. In the blaze of the fagots La-clos drooped with pale and dripping face.

"Nashta, my princess!" she whispered. "Ba-lee struck—a blade of flint—at La-clos' heart."

"La-clos! . . . Oh, to be without god or

friend or knowledge! What can this poor Nashta do? Princess—Ha! Nashta is the lowest—"

"Hush! . . . The Daughter of the Moon—will save the Nopah. It was—written. . . . La-clos can only—die!"

Nashta kept the fire alive while she paced her kiva like a caged lioness. She waited for the dead of night when the moon was waning in the sky. La-clos lay covered in the shadow.

At last she threw around her the white robe of deerskin and, taking up a torch of pine cones, she lighted her way into the secret passage under the rock. A branch led to the right, where in the darkness Nashta knew not. She crept along at a snail's pace, feeling the ragged wall. The passage opened wide and high. A cold wind blew in Nashta's face. She clung to the wall and moved around the chamber until she came to an abrupt descent. She who had neither strength nor skill climbed down with the same spirit that had enabled Blue Feather to surmount the face of the cliff. The torch went out. Suddenly the pitch blackness was split by a pale gleam. Nashta stole on. A narrow slit between sharp corners of rock let her out into the open. She faced the north. Night was Nashta's day and she knew the stars. Far across the valley, the dim moon was sinking behind the black horizon. She stood upon a ledge some distance above the slope. High behind her rose the north side of Taneen's rock, the precipitous side of crags. Far to the right Nashta saw the dying fires of the Nopahs. She climbed down to the base of the cliff, feeling no pain in her bleeding hands and feet. From below she could see the crack through which she had emerged. It was concealed in the gray obscurity of the rough stone face. She marked her position by a notch in the crags along the rim. Then she crept forward under the base of the wall.

Suddenly a giant sentry rose in her path. At the sight of the pale princess he dropped his weapons and fled. Soon Nashta encountered two tall Nopahs with drawn bows. Imperiously she raised her hand.

"Nashta, daughter of Taneen! She seeks Nothis Toh!"

Slowly the bows unbent, the glinting arrowheads descended. The Nopah guards appeared to be uncertain, muttering to each other. Another dark form loomed up, as if out of the ground. Piercing eyes, with the gleam of the moon in their black depths, peered from along the base of the wall. These sentinels obviously were terrified by the white apparition. They whispered among themselves. Then the leader cautiously extended his long bow, to touch Nashta's garment. She was real.

Nashta drew back her robe haughtily. "Touch not Taneen's Daughter of the Moon. She has come to save the Nopah spy."

"Docleas!" whispered the leader to his comrades, in tense excitement. Then he pointed the way for Nashta to go.

The girl stepped over bodies of the dead sprawling on the slope, past smoldering fires where Nopahs slept in rows, passing from rock to rock, to the camp of the chief. There fire burned. Warriors stood on guard. A murmur passed among them. Sleepers awakened to leap erect, to stare, to back away in fright.

"Nothis Toh," announced the leader of the three warriors who accompanied Nashta, "a maiden of the Sheboyahs dared alone to seek the chief."

Up from the blanketed ground rose the giant chieftain, his visage cruel like that of a vulture, his eyes of lightning flashing upon the maiden. With slow stride he confronted her, in the flickering light of the fire, while his warriors closed a weaponed circle around them.

"Squaw?" he rasped, haltingly.

"Nothis Toh speaks to a princess of the Sheboyahs."

He made a fierce gesture of impatience.

"Squaw, maiden, princess! All one to the Nopah. . . . Does the Sheboyah chief still live?"

"Yes, Taneen lives."

"Who dares seek Nothis Toh?"

"It is Nashta, daughter of Taneen."

"Ha! Does the chief send terms of surrender?"

"No. Taneen will fight. The Nopahs cannot scale the walls."

"What does the white maiden want of Nothis Toh?"

"She is the beloved of Blue Feather," cried Nashta proudly.

"Then Nothis Toh's son is there?" demanded the chief, his fierce gaze turning aloft.

"Yes."

"He is a spy no longer?"

"No."

"Docleas, the proud, the great! Swiftest of the Nopahs! Only son of Nothis Toh! He betrays his father—he disowns his people! . . . Would he had never been born!"

The chief's great breast labored and his dark face bowed in grief.

"What message sends he, no longer son of the Nopah?" he demanded presently.

"None. Blue Feather lies bound under the wall above. At sunrise he will be torn to pieces by the braves of Taneen."

"That is well. But why, since he failed the Nopahs?"

"Blue Feather dared to love the Daughter of the Moon, Taneen's child by an outcast queen. When he entered the sacred kiva of Nashta he brought ruin upon Taneen."

"Ah! Then what is it that the maiden with the white skin wishes?" asked Nothis Toh, his lean head shooting forward like a striking hawk.

"Nashta will betray her people for love of the Nopah."

The chief drew himself up sharply, striking his breast, his dark countenance strangely lighting. He gazed around the silent circle of priests and warriors who understood this message yet, as he, could not believe its import.

"Speak again, Sheboyah squaw! The Nopah is deaf!"

"Let the great chief gaze upon Nashta—into her eyes—her heart—to see the love and agony there," cried Nashta piteously. "She is an outcast princess upon whom the sun has never shown. But she would not lie. . . . Blue Feather betrayed his people for love of Nashta. She will betray her people for love of him."

The chieftain stroked his lean pointed chin, obviously convinced against his own will.

"Nothis Toh was not blind to love—long ago," he said, nodding solemnly. "Why could the Princess of the Moon betray Taneen?"

"She would save her lover."

"How will Nashta betray the great little people of the cliffs?"

"She will lead the Nopah warriors up through a secret passage under the wall."

A long silent column of tall dusky warriors moved along the base of the cliff. A slim white form led the way. The moon had gone down and the weird dark hour before the dawn had set in. Down in the valley the wild dogs were waiting. And out of the gulf of chasms came the faint roar of the sullen red river. Like a long shadow the column moved around the wall. Pale stars topped the rim above. A cold wind blew from across the wasteland. Low down in the east a pale gray softened the black. Dawn was not far off. A lonely nighthawk whirred above with melancholy cry.

The column moved, each member close upon the heels of the one before. Each carried a long bow, and a quiver of arrows slung on his back, and a stone-headed hatchet in his girdle.

Under the notched crag on the north wall the white-clad leader halted. Silently the long file of warriors came on, to mass at that point, to wait until all the column stood, dark faces raised upward, keen, like wolves on a scent.

A voice broke the silence, low but distinct, fearless yet respectful.

"One word, Nothis Toh?" asked a chief.

"Speak," came the stern reply.

"Is it well that Nopahs follow a squaw into the bowels of the rock?"

"Nothis Toh thinks it well."

"How does the great chief know that she is not sacrificing her life to draw the Nopahs into a trap?"

"He does not know."

"What then bids him follow?"

"Nothis Toh yields to that which made a traitor of a Nopah."

The white-clad leader above called, "Come, hand in hand. The way is short but dark."

Single file and linked together by hand clasps, the Nopahs entered the secret passage and wormed a tedious way up the steep ascent, through the cavern and the sacred kiva, up through the opening and under the shadow of the arches. They were still coming when the gray dawn broke over the sleeping citadel. And when the red light flushed in the east Nothis Toh and his warriors crouched grim and silent behind their coverts, ready to rush out to prevent the sunrise execution of their faithless spy.

The gray pall of night and the smoky mantle of war slowly lifted above the citadel. Soon along the bleak eastern horizon beyond the wasteland there appeared a red glow, sinister herald of a sunrise that would burst upon a day of blood. No birds sang. Only the vultures sailed in the paling sky, ever circling down and down. A cold stillness pervaded the morning atmosphere.

Suddenly this somber silence was rent by the wild yell of a Sheboyah brave. It rang clear with a triumphant note of joy, of deliverance. He had been the first to gaze down over the wall.

"The Nopahs are gone!" he screeched, awakening the guards who had slept on duty. They too started up, first in terror and then in glee, to overrun the terraces, shouting like madmen, "The Nopahs are gone! . . . They have abandoned their dead. . . . They have left their ladders. . . . The Rock Clan of the Sheboyahs has beaten the giants with the long bows."

All were awakened by these shrill cries of victory. The crippled lifted their weak voices to join in the rejoicing. Above the long rows of blanketed dead the squaws chanted, and the braves shouted their savage yells. The children screamed, though they did not understand what all the uproar was about. It had been the first siege laid against the Rock Clan, their first battle, their first victory; and it was a vindiction of their medicine men, of the sagacity of their chiefs, of the truth of the legends handed down to them.

A maiden with torn and blood-stained garments leaped high upon a wall, her black hair flying, her eyes like the hot bursts of jet in the lava below. She waved and screamed to silence the wild mob. It was Ba-lee.

"Blue Feather lives! The cursed Nopah spy lies unhurt! Kill him! Let the lover of the false Nashta die the death Tith-lei willed upon him!"

Her fury took hold in the breasts of braves, and they began to dance, breaking into the frenzy of a leaderless clan gone berserk.

"There under the wall—lies the Nopah!" shrieked the maddened Ba-lee as she tore her hair and her garments. But hate was stronger than grief. "Drag him forth—and Nashta—the moon-faced maiden who has disgraced the Sheboyahs!"

A knot of braves savagely split the jostling, screeching mob, and dragged into the center of the great court the prostrate form of the Nopah.

Taneen appeared in the doorway of his dwelling, tottering forth leaning upon his staff, a spent old man with death in his visage. He raised a shaking hand to still the tumult. Those who saw him quieted others, until the court became silent, standing in awe of the old man, and Blue Feather was left in the center. Taneen stood trembling, striving to gather the little strength that remained in his shrunken form. His people watched in respect for his courage, if not for his rank. In his weary eyes there was a last message to his clan. But though his lips moved, no utterance came forth, and he fell as the tree that is severed at the roots.

"Taneen dies!" screamed the wild Ba-lee upon the wall. No wail, no chant for the fallen! "This day the Rock Clan chooses a chief! A Brave who is young and fleet and bold shall lead the new Rock Clan! . . . He whose hate is greatest for the Nopah spy!"

From the open mouths and expanded lungs of all, as one single brave, there arose to the skies a magnificent, united yell. In that cry every brave proclaimed himself a chief. Silence fell. Who would lead the Rock Clan?

In that instant of shocked and waiting still-ness Ba-lee, the wily, projected once more her flaming jealous spirit.

"He who first drags forth Nashta, the false! . . . He who first strips her white beauty to the sun . . . who dashes her there, to be torn apart with her Nopah spy!"

Blue Feather raised his head from the stones of the court, and those who met the blaze of his eyes drew back.

"Sheboyah dogs! Fools!" he thundered, in a voice none of the Rock Clan had ever heard. "Little people of the cliffs! Little braves with little minds! The Nopahs do not run away. They have not fled. Nothis Toh is on the rock!"

Stricken dumb and appalled, his listeners stood like the gnarled cedars on the slopes.

Over their heads whizzed a level streak of blue, dark against the sky. Its flight, swifter than a swallow's, ended in quick death. The eyes of the braves turned in sudden terror. Then an awful scream smote their ears. Ba-lee staggered on the wall, falling backward, her little hands clutching at her breast, where gleamed the feathered shaft of a Nopah arrow. She fell. And the dumb watchers wheeled to hear the soft rushing sound of padded feet, to see the lanes, the roofs, the terraces glitter with a solid phalanx of giant archers, to face a swift and shining sheet of flying arrows.

The foremost line of Taneen's braves, appalled by the startling onslaught of the Nopahs, stood transfixed to receive that blue-streaked flight of arrows; and then they fell, as brittle reeds before the wind, with the broken shafts standing erect in their breasts.

Then the remaining Sheboyahs, massed in the courts and on the terraces and the roofs, sprang out of their tracks with wild shouts and screams that merged in the tragic wail of a doomed people. This sound was lost in the clarion warcry of the onrushing host. Once again the giant archers twanged their bows, and like hail before the blast the feathered arrows sped.

The Nopahs fell upon their victims, hatchets held high. Pandemonium reigned within the walled citadel of Taneen. The last of the Rock Clan made its last stand, in the courts, in the dwellings, on roofs and terraces. Surprised without weapons, many of them resorted to tooth and nail. Some charged to meet their foes, yelling defiance, swinging clubs or shooting with their little bows, soon to fall dead under the invaders' blows. Those frenzied by fright fled to the darkest holes, only to be dragged forth and slaughtered. Dust rose thick above the walls, and the terraces flowed with blood. The hoarse yells of combatants, the clash of flint, the dull blows on flesh and bone and the swift tread of many feet—these filled the morning air. It was a battle to the end.

Out on the playground retreated the last of the Rock Clan, and there before the empty stone seats, where often the chiefs, the squaws, the maidens had sat to award their heroes, they fought to the death. In the arena only puffs of dust rose from under warriors' feet. The brown bodies of the little men appeared dark against the lighter forms of the larger race. The eagle plumes of the Nopahs swept proudly, fiercely on.

Nothis Toh paced the court, amidst the dead and dying, awaiting his victorious warriors as they returned in companies, in smaller groups, in straggling twos and threes, and one by one. Among them were the bleeding and the crippled, but on the face of each gleamed the light of triumph. They had left on the stones many warriors upon whose dark faces no light would ever shine again.

Nothis Toh, majestic in mien, fierce of visage, terrible with the lust of battle still upon him, received the reports of his chiefs. The citadel had fallen. The Sheboyahs were destroyed. Weapons and garments, all the treasures of turquoise and jet and flints, the full granaries and the sealed cisterns—none of these had been lost or hidden, burned or emptied—a rich store for the hungry Nopahs.

But Nothis Toh glared like a baleful wolf who has been trapped with his whelps.

"Throw the Sheboyahs over the wall," he commanded. "The dead and the living! . . . This day Nothis Toh perpetuates for his tribe. Every year on this day the Nopahs will throw the little men over the cliffs, until all are gone!"

The dust and smoke lifted from the sacked and desolate citadel.

Nothis Toh stood before the dwelling of Taneen, facing the court, where all around the wide walls his warriors, ten deep, leaned upon their bows and awaited with glittering eyes their great chief's decree.

"Bring the Nopah warrior here," he ordered, his long, lean arm designating the empty center of the court.

With spears thrust out four giant warriors shoved Blue Feather into the open and left him standing there. The Nopah spy stood upright, his arms still bound behind his back. His scant garment was torn and caked with blood and dust, his leggings were ripped and hanging. Barefooted he stood, his splendid bared breast red with the blood of wounds. His once proud blue feather drooped defiled. But on his pale set face and in his grim eyes burned the spirit of the untamed.

A chief in revolt with his soul, Nothis Toh thundered at his son.

"Faithless son! Traitor to the Nopahs! . . . Speak!"

"Nothis Toh, the spring of Blue Feather's words is dry."

"Docleas will not beg for mercy?"

"No."

"What if he is thrown over the wall, to join the dead of the people he chose?"

"It is well."

Nothis Toh shook in his rage, and raised his long arms in despair, and dashed his stone mace to the floor.

"God of my forefathers—what has changed the blood of this boy!"

But only silence answered his passionate importuning. He bowed his vulture head to forces beyond the ken of his priests. He had sacked the citadel of Taneen, he had destroyed the Sheboyahs. Yet he was defeated. There was something here too great for Nothis Toh, and it expressed itself in his hate.

"Docleas failed his father?" he asked in loud and solemn voice.

"Yes," rang out Blue Feather's reply.

"The son of the Nopah does not bow his head?"

"No!"

"All for a squaw of the little people?" cried Nothis Toh, his face black with passion.

"All for Nashta, princess of the Sheboyahs, Daughter of the Moon, upon whom the sun has never shone!"

The chief made a fierce gesture to his guards. "Drag this wondrous squaw into the light!"

Blue Feather uttered a cry, and his form shook as a leaf on the bough.

"Father . . . then Nashta—"

"Does the traitor dare call Nothis Toh his father?"

A whisper ran through the waiting throng of warriors. Eager sloe-black eyes searched the terrace lane down toward the kivas. Silence as of the night before and as potent reigned over the ruined citadel. The white sun blazed piercingly down from the clear blue sky. Solemn and austere, the hour seemed to wait.

A white-robed maiden appeared, groping her way in front of guards no longer bold. They had to guide her steps. She sheltered her eyes under a mantle, and stumbled up the steps to the court. They placed her before the chief.

"Can the Sheboyah woman who betrayed her people see the Nopah?" asked the chief.

"She sees, Nothis, but not clearly. The sun burns and darkens her eyes."

"Blue Feather stands there, glad to be thrown over the wall to join the Sheboyah dead. . . . What would Nashta?"

"Throw the maiden, O great chief, but spare him!"

Nothis Toh turned to his attendant counselors, and spread wide his hands. They were mute. Was it the soul of this outcast princess that had possessed the great spy of the Nopahs? For Nothis Toh the bewilderment passed. It was what could be seen by the eye that had transformed his son, that vessel of flesh and blood which could be felt.

"Strip the maiden!" he commanded. "Let Nothis Toh see that which lost him a son!"

The warriors stared above dilating nostrils. These grim-lipped Nopahs, used to the hard fare of the trail, abstinent in all ways of the flesh, indifferent to their squaws, quivered under the new birth of a worship of beauty. They saw a slim form, white as driven snow, fragile, like the flower that leaned from the wall of the precipice.

Blue Feather wrenched mightily to burst the thongs that bound him. Snatching up the buckskin robe, he covered Nashta and held her close, while his stern face, like that of a god, mutely bade his father to visit upon them both the death they welcomed.

"It is enough!" cried the chief. "Nothis Toh forgives his son. He spares this outcast maiden, the last of the Sheboyahs, so that her blood may run in Nopah veins."

The Horse Thief

I

The lone horseman rode slowly up the slope, bending far down from his saddle in the posture customary for a range rider when studying hoof tracks. The intensity of his scrutiny indicated far more than the depth or direction of these imprints in the dust.

Presently the rider sat up and turned in his saddle to look back. While pondering the situation his eagle eyes swept the far country below. It was a scene like hundreds of others limned upon his memory—a vast and rugged section of the West, differing only in the elements of color, beauty, distance and grandeur that characterized the green Salmon River Valley, the gray rolling range beyond, the dead-white plain of alkali and the purple sawtoothed peaks piercing the sky in the far distance.

That the tracks of the stolen Watrous thoroughbreds would lead over the range into Montana had been the trailer's foregone conclusion. But that the mysterious horse thieves had so far taken little care to conceal their tracks seemed a proof of how brazen this gang had become. On the other hand Dale Brittenham reflected that he was a wild-horse hunter—that a trail invisible to most men would be like print to him.

He gazed back down the long slope into Idaho, pondering his task, slowly realizing that he had let himself in for a serious and perhaps deadly job.

It had taken Dale five hours to ride up to the point where he now straddled his horse, and the last from which he could see the valley. From here the stage road led north over the divide into the wild timbered range.

The time was about noon of an early summer day. The air at that height had a cool sweet tang, redolent of the green pines and the flowered mountain meadows. Dale strongly felt the beauty and allurement of the scene, and likewise a presentiment of trouble. The little mining town of Salmon, in the heyday of its biggest gold producing year—1886—nestled in a bend of the shining white-and-green river. Brittenham had many enemies down there and but few friends. The lonely life of a wild-horse hunter had not kept him from conflict with men. Whose toes might he not step upon if he tracked down these horse thieves? The country was infested with road agents, bandits, horse thieves; and the wildest era Idaho had ever known was in full swing.

"I've long had a hunch," Dale soliloquized broodingly. "There're men down there, maybe as rich and respectable as Watrous himself, who're in cahoots with these thieves. . . . Cause if there wasn't, this slick stealin' couldn't be done."

The valley shone green and gold and purple under the bright sun, a vast winding range of farms, ranches, pastures, leading up to the stark sawtooth mountains, out of which the river glistened like a silver thread. It wound down between grassy hills to meander into the valley. Dale's gaze fastened upon an irregular green spot and a white house surrounded by wide sweeping pastures. This was the Watrous ranch. Dale watched it, conscious of a pang in his heart. The only friendship for a man and love of a woman he had ever known had come to him there. Leale Hildrith, the partner of Jim Watrous in an extensive horse-breeding and trading business, had once been a friend in need to Brittenham. But for Hildrith, the wild-horse hunter would long before have taken the trail of the thieves who regularly several times a year plundered the ranches of the valley. Watrous had lost hundreds of horses.

"Dale, lay off," Hildrith had advised impatiently. "It's no mix of yours. It'll lead into more gunplay, and you've already got a bad name for that. Besides, there's no telling where such a trail might wind up."

Brittenham had been influenced by the friend to whom he owed his life. Yet despite his loyalty, he wondered at Hildrith's attitude. It must surely be that Hildrith again wanted to save him from harm, and Dale warmed to the thought. But when, on this morning, he had discovered that five of Edith Watrous's thoroughbreds, the favorite horses she loved so dearly, had been stolen, he said no word to anyone at the ranch and set out upon the trail.

At length Brittenham turned his back upon the valley and rode on up the slope toward the timber line, now close at hand. He reached the straggling firs at a point where two trails branched off the road. The right one led along the edge of the timber line and on it the sharp tracks of the shod horses showed plainly in the dust.

At this junction Dale dismounted to study the tracks. After a careful scrutiny he made the deduction that he was probably two hours behind the horse thieves, who were plainly lagging along. Dale found an empty whiskey bottle, which was still damp and strong with the fumes of liquor. This might in some measure account for the carelessness of the thieves.

Dale rode on, staying close to the fir trees, between them and the trail, while he kept a keen eye ahead. On the way up he had made a number of conjectures, which he now discarded. This branching off the road puzzled him. It meant probably that the horse thieves had a secret rendezvous somewhere off in this direction. After perhaps an hour of travel along the timber belt Dale entered a rocky region where progress was slow, and he came abruptly upon a wide, well-defined trail running at right angles to the one he was on. Hundreds of horses had passed along there, but none recently. Dale got off to reconnoiter. He had stumbled upon something that he had never heard the riders mention—a trail which wound up the mountain slope over an exceedingly rough route. Dale followed it until he had an appreciation of what a hard climb, partly on foot, riders must put themselves to, coming up from the valley. He realized that here was the outlet for horse thieves operating on the Salmon and Snake River ranges of Idaho. It did not take Dale long to discover that it was a one-way trail. No hoof tracks pointing down!

"Well, here's a dummy deal!" he ejaculated. And he remembered the horse traders who often drove bands of Montana horses down into Idaho and sold them all the way to Twin Falls and Boise. Those droves of horses came down the stage road. Suddenly Dale arrived at an exciting conclusion. "By thunder! Those Montana horses are stolen, too. By the same gang—a big gang of slick horse thieves. They steal way down on the Montana ranges—drive up over a hidden trail like this to some secret place where they meet part of their outfit who've been stealin' in Idaho. . . . Then they switch herds. . . . And they drive down, sellin' the Montana horses in Idaho and the Idaho horses in Montana. . . . Well! The head of that outfit has got brains. Too many to steal Jim Watrous's fine blooded stock! That must have been a slip. . . . But any rider would want to steal Edith Watrous's horses!"

Returning to his mount, Dale led him in among the firs and rocks, keeping to the line of the new trail but not directly upon it. A couple of slow miles brought him to the divide. Beyond that the land sloped gently, the rocks and ridges merged into a fine open forest. His view was unobstructed for several hundred yards. Bands of deer bounded away from in front of Dale to halt and watch with long ears erect. Dale had not hunted far over that range. He knew the Sawtooth Mountains in as far as Thunder Mountain. His wild-horse activities had been confined to the desert and low country toward the Snake River. Therefore he had no idea where this trail would lead him. Somewhere over this divide, on the eastern slope, lived a band of Palouse Indians. Dale knew some of them and had hunted wild horses with them. He had befriended one of their number, Nalook, to the extent of saving him from a jail sentence. From that time Nalook had been utterly devoted to Dale, and had rendered him every possible service.

By midafternoon Brittenham was far down on the forested tableland. He meant to stick to the trail as long as there was light enough to see. His saddlebag contained meat, biscuits, dried fruit and salt. His wild-horse hunts often kept him weeks on the trail, so his present pursuit presented no obstacles. Nevertheless, as he progressed he grew more and more wary. He expected to see a log cabin in some secluded spot. At length he came to a brook that ran down from a jumble of low bluffs and followed the trail. The water coursed in alternate eddies and swift runs. Beaver dams locked it up into little lakes. Dale found beaver cutting aspens in broad daylight, which attested to the wildness of the region. Far ahead he saw rocky crags and rough gray ridgetops. This level open forest would not last much farther.

Suddenly Brittenham's horse shot up his ears and halted in his tracks. A shrill neigh came faintly to the rider's ears. He peered ahead through the pines, his nerves tingling.

But Dale could not make out any color or movement, and the sound was not repeated. This fact somewhat allayed his fears. After a sharp survey of his surroundings Dale led his horse into a clump of small firs and haltered him there. Then, rifle in hand, he crept forward from tree to tree. This procedure was slow work, as he exercised great caution.

The sun sank behind the fringe of timber on the high ground and soon shadows appeared in thick parts of the forest. Suddenly the ring of an ax sent the blood back to Dale's heart. He crouched down behind a pine and rested a moment, his thoughts whirling. There were campers ahead, or a cabin; and Dale strongly inclined to the conviction that the horse thieves had halted for the night. If so, it meant they were either far from their rendezvous or taking their time waiting for comrades to join them. Dale pondered the situation. He must be decisive, quick, ruthless. But he could not determine what to do until he saw the outfit and the lay of the land.

Wherefore he got up, and after a long scrutiny ahead he slipped from behind the tree and stole on to another. He repeated this move. Brush and clumps of fir and big pines obstructed any considerable survey ahead. Finally he came to less thick covering on the ground. He smelled smoke. He heart faint indistinguishable sounds. Then a pinpoint of fire gleamed through the thicket in front of him. Without more ado Dale dropped on all fours and crawled straight for that light. When he got to the brush and peered through, his heart gave a great leap at the sight of Edith Watrous's horses staked out on a grassy spot.

Then he crouched on his knees, holding the Winchester tight, trying to determine a course of action. Various plans flashed through his mind. The one he decided to be the least risky was to wait until the thieves were asleep and quietly make away with the horses. These thoroughbreds knew him well. He could release them without undue excitement. With half a night's start he would be far on the way back to the ranch before the thieves discovered their loss. The weakness of this plan lay in the possibility of a new outfit joining this band. That, however, would not deter Dale from making the attempt to get the horses.

It occurred to him presently to steal up on the camp under cover of the darkness and if possible get close enough to see and hear the robbers. Dale lay debating this course and at last yielded to the temptation. Dusk settled down. The nighthawks wheeled and uttered their guttural cries overhead. He waited patiently. When it grew dark he crawled around the thicket and stood up. A bright campfire blazed in the distance. Dark forms moved to and fro across the light. Off to the left of Dale's position there appeared to be more cover. He sheered off that way, lost sight of the campfire, threaded a careful approach among trees and brush, and after a long detour came up behind the camp, scarcely a hundred yards distant. A big pine tree dominated an open space lighted by the campfire. Dale selected objects to use for cover and again sank to his hands and knees. Well he knew that the keenest of men were easier to crawl upon than wild horses at rest. He was like an Indian. He made no more noise than a snake. At intervals he peered above the grass and low brush. He heard voices and now and then the sputtering of the fire. He rested again. His next stop would be behind a windfall that now obscured the camp. Drawing a deep breath, he crawled on silently without looking up. The grass was wet with dew.

A log barred Dale's advance. He relaxed and lay quiet, straining his ears.

"I tell you, Ben, this hyar was a damn fool job," spoke up a husky-voiced individual. "Alec agrees with me."

"Wal, I shore do," corroborated another man. "We was drunk."

"Not me. I never was more clear-headed in my life," replied the third thief, called Ben. His reply ended with a hard chuckle.

"Wal, if you was, no one noticed it," returned Alec sourly. "I reckon you roped us into a mess."

"Aw hell! Big Bill will yelp with joy."

"Mebbe. Shore he's been growin' overbold these days. Makin' too much money. Stands too well in Halsey an' Bannock, an' Salmon. Cocksure no one will ever find our hole-up."

"Bah! Thet wouldn't faze Big Bill Mason. He'd bluff it through."

"Aha! Like Henry Plummer, eh? The coldest proposition of a robber thet ever turned a trick. Had a hundred men in his outfit. Stole damn near a million in gold. High respected citizen of Montana. Mayor of Alder Gulch . . . All the same he put his neck in the noose!"

"Alec is right, Ben," spoke up the third member in his husky voice. "Big Bill is growin' wild. Too careless. Spends too much time in town. Gambles. Drinks . . . Someday some foxy cowboy or hoss hunter will trail him. An' that'll be about due when Watrous finds his blooded horses gone."

"Wal, what worries me more is how Hildrith will take this deal of yours," said Alec. "Like as not he'll murder us."

Brittenham sustained a terrible shock. It was like a physical rip of his flesh. Hildrith! These horse thieves spoke familiarly of his beloved friend. Dale grew suddenly sick. Did not this explain Leale's impatient opposition to the trailing of horse thieves?

"Ben, you can gamble Hildrith will be wild," went on Alec. "He's got sense if

Big Bill hasn't. He's Watrous's partner, mind you. Why, Jim Watrous would hang him."

"We heerd talk this time thet Hild.ith was goin' to marry old Jim's lass. What a hell of a pickle Leale will be in!"

"Fellers, he'll be all the stronger if he does grab thet hoss-lovin' gurl. But I don't believe he'll be so lucky. I seen Edith Watrous in town with thet cowboy Les Crocker. She shore makes a feller draw his breath hard. She's younger an' she likes the cowboys."

"Wal, what of thet? If Jim wants her to marry his pardner, she'll have to."

"Mebbe she's a chip off the old block. Anyway, I've knowed a heap of women an' thet's my hunch. . . . Hildrith will be as sore as a bunged-up thumb. But what can he do? We got the hosses."

"So we have. Five white elephants! Ben, you've let *your* cravin' for fine hoss-flesh carry you away."

An interval of silence ensued, during which Dale raised himself to peer guardedly over the log. Two of the thieves sat with hard red faces in the glare of the blaze. The third had his back to Dale.

"What ails *me,* now I got 'em, is can I

keep 'em," this man replied. "Thet black is the finest hoss I ever seen."

"They're all grand hosses. An' thet's all the good it'll do you," retorted the leaner of the other two.

"Ben, them thoroughbreds air known from Deadwood to Walla Walla. They can't be sold or rid. An' shore as Gawd made little apples, the stealin' of them will bust Big Bill's gang."

"Aw, you're a couple of yellow pups," rejoined Ben contemptuously. "If I'd known you was goin' to show like this I'd split with you an' done the job myself."

"Uhuh! I recollect now thet *you* did the watchin' while Steve an' me stole the horses. An' I sort of recollect dim-like thet you talked big about money while you was feedin' us red likker."

"Yep, I did—an' I had to get you drunk. Haw! Haw!"

"On purpose? Made us trick the outfit an' switch to your job, huh?"

"Yes, on purpose."

"So! . . . How you like this on purpose, Ben?" hissed Alec, and swift as a flash he whipped out a gun. Ben's hoarse yell of protest died in his throat with the bang of the big Colt.

The bullet went clear through the man to strike the log uncomfortably near Dale. He ducked instinctively, then sank down again, tense and cold.

"My Gawd! Alec, you bored him," burst out the man Steve.

"I shore did. The damn bullhead! . . . An' thet's our out with Hildrith. We're gonna need one. I reckon Big Bill won't hold it hard agin us."

Dale found himself divided between conflicting courses—one, to shoot these horse thieves in their tracks, and a stronger one, to stick to his first plan and avoid unnecessary hazard. Wherewith he noiselessly turned and began to crawl away from the log. He had to worm under spreading branches. Despite his care, a dead limb, invisible until too late, caught on his long spur, which gave forth a ringing metallic peal. At the sudden sound, Dale sank prone, his blood congealing in his veins.

"Alec! You hear thet?" called Steve, his husky voice vibrantly sharp.

"By Gawd I did! . . . Ring of a spur! I know thet sound."

"Behind the log!"

The thud of quick footsteps urged Dale

out of his frozen inaction. He began to crawl for the brush.

"There Steve! I hear someone crawlin'. Smoke up thet black patch!"

Gunshots boomed. Bullets thudded all around Dale. Then one tore through his sombrero, leaving a hot sensation in his scalp. A gust of passion intercepted Dale's desire to escape. He whirled to his knees. Both men were outlined distinctly in the firelight. The foremost stood just behind the log, his gun spouting red. The other crouched peering into the darkness. Dale shot them both. The leader fell hard over the log, and lodged there, his boots beating a rustling tattoo on the ground. The other flung his gun high and dropped as if his legs had been chopped from under him.

Brittenham leaped erect, working the lever of his rifle, his nerves strung like wires. But the engagement had ended as quickly as it had begun. He strode into the campfire circle of light. The thief Ben lay on his back, arms wide, his dark visage distorted and ghastly. Dale's impulse was to search these men, but resisting it he hurriedly made for the horses. The cold sick grip on his vitals eased with hurried action, and likewise the fury.

Presently he reached the grassy plot where the horses were staked out. They snorted and thumped the ground.

"Prince," he called, and whistled.

The great stallion whinnied recognition. Dale made his way to the horse. Prince was blacker than the night. Dale laid gentle hands on him and talked to him. The other horses quieted down.

"Jim. . . Jade. . . Ringspot. . . Blue-grass," called Dale, and repeated the names as he passed among the horses. They were all pets except Jade, and she was temperamental. She had to be now. Presently Dale untied her long stake rope, and after that the ropes of the other horses. He felt sure Prince and Jim would follow him anywhere, but he did not want to risk it then.

He led the five horses back, as nearly as he could, on the course by which he had approached the camp. In the darkness the task was not easy. He chose to avoid the trail, which ran somewhere to his left. A tree and a thicket here and there he recognized. But he was off his direction when his own horse nickered to put him right again.

"No more of that, Hoofs," he said, when he found his animal. Cinching his saddle, he gathered up the five halters and mounted. "Back trail yourself, old boy!"

The Watrous horses were eager to follow, but the five of them abreast on uneven and obstructed ground held Dale to a slow and watchful progress. Meanwhile, as he picked his way, he began figuring the situation. It was imperative that he travel all night. There seemed hardly a doubt that the three thieves would be joined by others of their gang. Anyone save a novice could track six horses through a forest. Dale meant to be a long way on his back trail before dawn. The night was dark. He must keep close to the path of the horse thieves so that he would not get lost in this forest. Once out on the stage road he could make up for slow travel.

Trusting to Hoofs, the rider advanced, peering keenly into the gloom. He experienced no difficulty in leading the thoroughbreds; indeed they often slacked their halters and trampled almost at his heels. They knew they were homeward bound, in the charge of a friend. Dale hoped all was well, yet could not rid himself of a contrary presentiment. The reference of one of the horse thieves to Ben's double-crossing their comrades seemed to Dale to signify that the remaining outfit might be down in the Salmon River Valley.

At intervals Dale swerved to the left far enough to see the trail in the gloom. When he could hear the babble of the brook he knew he was going right. In due time he worked out of the open forest and struck the grade, and eventually got into the rocks. Here he had to follow the path, but he endeavored to keep his tracks out of it. And in this way he found himself at length in a shallow, narrow gulch, the sides of which appeared unscalable. If it were short, all would be well; on the other hand he distrusted a long defile, where it would be perilous if he happened to encounter any riders. They would scarcely be honest riders.

The gulch was long. Moreover it narrowed and was dark as pitch except under the low walls. Dale did not like Hoofs's halting. His trusty mount had the nose and the ears of the wild horses he had hunted for years.

"What ails you, hoss?" queried Dale.

Finally Hoofs stopped. Dale, feeling for his ears, found them erect and stiff. Hoofs smelled or heard something. It might be a bear or a cougar, both of which the horse disliked exceedingly. It might be more horse thieves, too. Dale listened and thought hard.

Of all things, he did not want to retrace his steps. While he had time then, and before he knew what menaced further progress, he dismounted and led the horses as far under the dark wall as he could get them. Then he drew their heads up close to him and called low, "Steady, Prince . . . Jade, keep still . . . Blue, hold now. . . ."

Hoofs stood at his elbow. It was Dale's voice and hand that governed the intelligent animals. Then as a low trampling roar swept down the gully they stood stiff. Dale tingled. Horses coming at a forced trot! They were being driven when they were tired. The sound swelled, and soon it was pierced by the sharp calls of riders.

"By thunder!" muttered Dale, aghast at the volume of sounds. "My hunch was right! . . . Big Bill Mason has raised the valley. . . . Must be over a hundred head in that drove."

The thudding, padded roar, occasionally emphasized by an ironshod hoof ringing on stone, or a rider's call, swept down the gully. It was upon Dale before he realized the drove was so close. He could see a moving, obscure mass coming. He smelled dust. "Git in thar!" shouted a weary voice. Then followed a soft thudding of hoofs on sand.

Dale's situation was precarious, for if one of his horses betrayed his whereabouts, there would be riders sheering out for strays. He held the halters with his left hand, and pulled his rifle from its saddle sheath. If any of these raiders bore down on him, he would be forced to shoot and take to flight. But his thoroughbreds, all except Jade, stood like statues. She champed her bit restlessly. Then she snorted. Dale hissed at her. The moment was one to make him taut. He peered through the gloom, expecting riders to loom up, and he had the grim thought that it would be death for them. Then followed a long moment of sustained suspense, charged with incalculable chance.

"Go along there, you lazy hawses," called a voice.

The soft thumping of many hoofs passed. Voices trailed back. Dale relaxed in immeasurable relief. The driving thieves had gone by. He thought then for the first time what a thrilling thing it was going to be to return these thoroughbreds to Edith Watrous.

Hard upon that came the thought of Leale Hildrith—his friend. It was agony to think that Leale was involved with these horse thieves. On the instant Dale was shot through with the memory of his debt to Hildrith—of that terrible day when Hildrith had found him out on the range, crippled, half starved and frozen, and had, at the risk of his own life, carried Dale through the blizzard to the safety of a distant shelter. A friendship had sprung up between the two men, generous and careless on Hildrith's part, even at times protective. In Dale had been engendered a passionate loyalty and gratitude, almost a hero worship for the golden-bearded Hildrith.

What would come of it all? No solution presented itself to Dale at the moment. He must meet situations as they arose, and seek in every way to protect his friend.

Toward sunset the following day Dale Brittenham rode across the clattering old bridge, leading the Watrous thoroughbreds into the one and only street of Salmon. The dusty horses, five abreast, trotting at the end of long halters, would have excited interest in any Western town. But for some reason that puzzled Dale, he might have been leading a circus or a band of painted Indians.

Before he had proceeded far, however, he grasped that something unusual accounted for the atmosphere of the thronged street.

Seldom did Salmon, except on a Saturday night, show so much activity. Knots of men, evidently in earnest colloquy, turned dark faces in Dale's direction; gaudily dressed dance-hall girls, black-frocked gamblers, and dusty-booted, bearded miners crowded out in the street to see Dale approach; cowboys threw up their sombreros and let out their cracking whoops; and a throng of excited youngsters fell in behind Dale, to follow him.

Dale began to regret having chosen to ride through town, instead of fording the river below and circling to the Watrous ranch. He did not like the intense curiosity manifested by a good many spectators. Their gestures and words, as he rode by, he interpreted as more speculative and wondering than glad at his return with the five finest horses in Idaho.

When Dale was about halfway down the wide street, a good friend of his detached himself from a group and stepped out.

"Say, Wesley, what'n hell's all this hubbub about?" queried Brittenham as he stopped.

"Howdy, Dale," returned the other, offering his hand. His keen eyes flashed like sunlight on blue metal and a huge smile wrinkled his bronzed visage. "Well, if I ain't glad to see you I'll eat my shirt. . . . Just like you, Dale, to burst into town with thet bunch of hosses!"

"Sure, I reckoned I'd like it. But I'm gettin' leary. What's up?"

"Hoss thieves raided the river ranches yesterday," replied the other swiftly. "Two hundred head gone! . . . Chamberlain, Trash, Miller—all lost heavy. An' Jim Watrous got cleaned out. You know, lately Jim's gone in for cattle buyin', an' his riders were away somewhere. Jim lost over a hundred head. He's ory-eyed. An' they say Miss Edith was heartbroke to lose hers. Dale, you sure got the best of her other beaux with this job."

"Stuff!" ejaculated Dale, feeling the hot blood in his cheeks, and he sat up stiffly. "Wes, damn you—"

"Dale, I've had you figgered as a shy hombre with girls. Every fellow in this valley, except you, has cocked his eyes at Edith Watrous. She's a flirt, we all know. . . . Listen. I been achin' to tell you my sister Sue is a friend of Edith an' she says Edith likes you pretty well. Hildrith only has the inside track cause of her father. I'm tellin' you, Dale."

"Shut up, Wes. You always hated Hildrith, an' you're wrong about Edith."

"Aw, hell! You're scared of her an' you

overrate what Hildrith did for you once. Thet's all. This was the time for me to give you a hunch. I won't shoot off my chin again."

"An' the town's all het-up over the horse-thief raid?"

"You bet it is. Common talk runs thet there's some slick hombre here who's in with the hoss thieves. This Salmon Valley has lost nigh on to a thousand head in three years. An' everyone of the big raids come at a time when the thieves had to be tipped off."

"All big horse-thief gangs work that way," replied Dale, ponderingly. Wesley was trying to tell him that suspicion had fallen upon his head. He dropped his eyes as he inquired about his friend Leale Hildrith.

"Humph! In town yesterday, roarin' louder than anybody about the raid. Swore this stealin' had to be stopped. Talked of offerin' ten thousand dollars reward—that he'd set an outfit of riders after the thieves. You know how Leale raves. He's in town this mornin', too."

"So long, Wes," said Dale soberly, and was about to ride on when a commotion broke the ring of bystanders to admit Leale Hildrith himself.

Dale was not surprised to see the golden-bearded, booted-and-spurred partner of Watrous, but he did feel a surprise at a fleeting and vanishing look in Hildrith's steel-blue eyes. It was a flash of hot murderous amazement at Dale there with Edith Watrous's thoroughbreds. Dale understood it perfectly, but betrayed no sign.

"Dale! You son-of-a-gun!" burst out Hildrith in boisterous gladness, as he leaped to seize Dale's hand and pumped it violently. His apparent warmth left Dale cold, and bitterly sad for his friend. "Fetched Edith's favorites back! How on earth did you do it, Dale? She'll sure reward you handsomely. And Jim will throw a fit. . . . Where and how did you get back these horses?"

"They were stolen out of the pasture yesterday mornin' about daylight," replied Dale curtly. "I trailed the thieves. Found their camp last night. Three men, callin' themselves Ben, Alec an' Steve. They were fightin' among themselves. Ben tricked them, the other two said. An' one of them shot him. . . . They caught me listenin'—an' forced me to kill them."

"You killed them!" queried Hildrith hoarsely, his face turning pale. His eyes held a peculiar oscillating question.

"Yes. An' I didn't feel over-bad about

142

it, Leale," rejoined Dale with sarcasm. "Then I wrangled the horses an' rode down."

"Where—was this?"

"Up on the mountain, over in Montana somewhere. After nightfall I sure got lost. But I hit the stage road. . . . I'll be movin' along, Leale."

"I'll come right out to the ranch," replied Hildrith, and hurried through the crowd.

"Open up there," called Dale to the staring crowd. "Let me through."

As he parted the circle and left it behind, a taunting voice cut the silence. "Cute of you, Dale, fetchin' the high-steppers back. Haw! Haw!"

Dale rode on as if he had not heard, though he could have shot the owner of that mocking voice. He had been implicated in this horse stealing. Salmon was full of shifty-eyed, hard-lipped men who would have had trouble in proving honest occupations. Dale had clashed with some of them, and he was hated and feared. He rode on through town and out into the country. He put the horses to a brisk trot, as he wanted to reach the Watrous ranch ahead of Hildrith.

Dale stood appalled at the dual character of the man to whom he considered himself so deeply indebted, whom he had looked on as a friend and loved so much. It was almost impossible to believe. Almost every man in the valley liked Leale Hildrith and called him friend. The women loved him, and Dale felt sure, despite Wesley's blunt talk, that Edith Watrous was one of them. And if she did love him, she was on the way to disgrace and misery. Leale, the gay handsome blade, not yet thirty, so good-natured and kindly, bighearted and openhanded, was secretly nothing but a low-down horse thief. Dale had hoped against hope that when he saw Hildrith the disclosures of the three horse thieves would somehow be disproved. But that had not happened. Hildrith's eyes, in only a flash, had betrayed him. Dale suffered the degradation of his own disillusion. Yet the thought of Edith's unhappiness hurt him even more.

He had not gotten anywhere in his perplexed and bewildered state of mind when the bronze-and-gold hills of the Watrous ranch loomed before him. From the day he had ridden up to it, Dale had loved this great ranch, with its big old weatherbeaten house nestling among the trees up from the river, its smooth shining hills bare to the gray rocks and timber line, its huge fields of corn and alfalfa green as emerald, its level range spreading away from the river gateway to the mountains. From that very day, too, Dale had loved the lithe, free-stepping, roguish-eyed daughter of Jim Watrous—a melancholy and disturbing fact that he strove to banish from his consciousness. Her teasing and tormenting, her fits of cold indifference and her resentment that she could not make him bend to her like her other admirers, her flirting before his eyes plainly to make him jealous—all these weaknesses of Edith's did not equal in sum her kindness to him, and the strange inexplicable fact that when she was in trouble she always came to him.

As Dale rode around the grove into the green square where the gray ranch house stood on its slope, he was glad to see that Hildrith had not arrived. Three saddled horses standing bridles down told Dale that Watrous had callers. They were on the porch and they had sighted him. Crowding to the high steps, they could be heard exclaiming. Then gray-haired Jim Watrous, stalwart of build and ruddy of face, descended down a step to call lustily, "Edith! Rustle out there. Quick!"

Dale halted on the green below the porch. It was going to be a hard moment. Watrous and his visitors could not disturb him.

But Edith! . . . Dale heard the swift patter of light feet—then a little scream, sweet, high-pitched, that raised a turbulent commotion in his breast.

"Oh Dad! . . . My horses!" she cried in ecstasy, and she clasped her hands.

"They sure are, lass," replied Watrous gruffly.

"Ha! Queer Brittenham should fetch them," added a man back of Watrous.

In two leaps Edith came down the high steps, supple as a cat, and bounded at Dale, her bright hair flying, her dark eyes shining.

"Dale! Dale!" she cried rapturously, and ran to clasp both hands around his arm. "You old wild-horse hunter! You darling!"

"Well, I'll stand for the first," said Dale, smiling down at her.

"You'll stand for that—and hugs—kisses when I get you alone, Dale Brittenham. . . . You've brought back my horses! My heart was broken. I was crazy. I couldn't eat or sleep. . . . Oh, it's too good to be true! Oh, Dale, I can never thank you enough."

She left him to throw her arms around Prince's dusty neck and to cry over him. Watrous came slowly down the steps, followed by his three visitors, two of whom

Dale knew by sight. He bent the eyes of a hawk upon Dale.

"Howdy, Brittenham. What have you got to say for yourself?"

"Horses talk, Mr. Watrous, same as money," replied Dale coolly. He sensed the old horse trader's doubt and dismay.

"They sure do, young man. There's ten thousand dollars' worth of horseflesh. To Edith they're priceless. What's your story?"

Dale told it briefly, omitting the description of the horse-thief trail and the meeting upon it with the raided stock from the valley. He chose to save these details until he had had more time to ponder over them.

"Brittenham, can you prove those three horse thieves are dead—an' that you made away with two of them?" queried Watrous tensely.

"Prove!" ejaculated Dale, sorely nettled. "I could prove it—certainly, sir, unless their pards came along to pack them away. . . . But my word should be proof enough, Mr. Watrous."

"I reckon it would be, for me, Brittenham," returned the rancher hastily. "But this whole deal has a queer look. . . . This gang of horse thieves has an accomplice—maybe more than one—right here in Salmon."

"Mr. Watrous, I had the same thought," said Dale shortly.

"Last night, Brittenham, your name was whispered around in this connection."

"That doesn't surprise me. Salmon is full of crooked men. I've clashed with some. I've only a few friends an'—"

Edith whirled to confront her father with pale face and blazing eyes.

"Dad! Did I hear aright? What did you say?"

"I'm sorry, lass. I told Brittenham he was suspected of bein' the go-between for this horse-thief gang."

"For shame, father! It's a lie. Dale Brittenham would not steal, let alone be a cowardly informer."

"Edith, I didn't say I believed it," rejoined Watrous, plainly upset. "But it's bein' said about town. It'll fly over the range. An' I thought Brittenham should know."

"You're right, Mr. Watrous," said Dale. "Thank you for tellin' me."

The girl turned to Dale, evidently striving for composure.

"Come, Dale. Let us take the horses out."

She led them across the green toward the lane. Dale had no choice but to follow, though he desperately wanted to flee. Before the men were out of range of his acute hearing, one of them exclaimed to Watrous, "Jim, he didn't deny it!"

"Huh! Did you see his eyes?" returned the rancher shortly. "I'd not want to be in the boots of the man who accuses him to his face."

"Here comes Hildrith, drivin' as if the devil was after him."

Dale heard the clattering buckboard, but he did not look. Neither did Edith. She walked with her head down, deep in thought. Dale dared to watch her, conscious of inexplicable feelings.

The stable boy, Joe, ran out to meet them, with a face that was a study in inexpressible wonder and delight. Edith did not relinquish the halters until she had led the horses up the incline into the wide barn.

"Joe, water them first," she said. "Then wash and rub them down. Take a look at their hoofs. Feed them grain and a little alfalfa. And watch them every minute till the boys get back."

"Yes, Miss Edith, I shore will," he replied eagerly. "We done had words they'll be hyar by dark."

Dale dismounted and removed saddle and bridle from his tired horse.

"Let Joe watch your horse, Dale. I want to talk to you."

Dale leaned against some bales of hay, not wholly from weariness. He had often been alone with Edith Watrous, but never like this.

"Reckon I ought to—to clean up," he stammered, removing his sombrero. "I—I must look a mess."

"You're grimy and worn, yes. But you look pretty proven and good to me, Dale Brittenham. . . . What's that hole in your hat?"

"By thunder! I forgot about that. It's a bullet hole."

"Oh—so close . . . Who shot it there, Dale?"

"One of the horse thieves."

"It was self-defense, then?"

"You just bet it was."

"I've hated your shooting scrapes, Dale," she rejoined earnestly. "But here I see I'm squeamish—and unreasonable. . . . Only the reputation you have—your readiness to shoot —that's all I never liked about it."

"I'm sorry. But I can't help that," replied Dale, turning his sombrero round and round with restless hands.

"You needn't be sorry this time. . . . Dale, look me straight in the eye."

Thus so earnestly urged, Dale had to comply. Edith appeared pale of face and laboring under suppressed emotion. Her dark eyes had held many expressions for him, mostly roguish and coquettish, and sometimes blazing, but at this moment they were beautiful with a light, a depth he had never seen in them before. And it challenged him with a truth he had always driven from his consciousness—that he loved this bright-haired girl.

"Dale, I was ashamed of Dad," she said. "I detest that John Stafford. He is the one who brought the gossip from town—that you were implicated in this raid. I don't believe it."

"Thanks, Edith. It's good of you."

"Why didn't you say something?" she asked spiritedly. "You should have cussed Dad roundly."

"I was sort of flabbergasted."

"Dale, if this whole range believed you were a horse thief, I wouldn't. Even if your faithful Nalook believed it—though he never would."

"No. I reckon that Indian wouldn't believe bad of me."

"Nalook thinks heaps of you, Dale—and—and that's one reason why I do—too."

"Heaps?"

"Yes, heaps."

"I'd never have suspected it."

"Evidently you never did. But it's true. And despite your—your rudeness—your avoidance of me, now is the time to tell it."

Dale dropped his eyes again, sorely perturbed and fearful that he might betray himself. Edith was not bent on conquest now. She appeared roused to championship of him, and there was something strange and soft about her that was new and bewildering.

"I never was rude," he denied stoutly.

"We won't argue about that now," she went on hurriedly. "Never mind about me and my petty vanity. . . . I'm worried about this gossip. It's serious, Dale. You'll get into trouble and go gunning for somebody—unless I keep you from it. I'm going to try. . . . Will you take a job riding for me—taking care of my horses?"

"Edith! . . . I'm sure obliged to you, for that offer. But Watrous wouldn't see it."

"I'll make him see it."

"Hildrith? . . . He wouldn't like that idea—now."

"Leale will like anything I want him to."

"Not this time."

"Dale, *will* you ride for me?" she queried impatiently.

"I'd like to—if—if . . . .Well, I'll consider it."

"If you would that'd stop this gossip more than anything I can think of. . . . I'd like it very much, Dale. I'll never feel safe about my horses again. Not until these thieves are rounded up. If you worked for me I could keep you here—out of that rotten Salmon. And you wouldn't be going on those long wild-horse hunts."

"Edith, you're most amazin' kind an'—an' thoughtful all of a sudden." Dale could not quite keep a little bitter surprise out of his voice.

She blushed vividly. "I might have been all that long ago—if you had let me," she responded.

"Who am I to aspire to your kindness?" he said almost coldly. "But even if I wasn't a poor wild-horse hunter I'd never run after you like these—these—"

"Maybe that's one reason why . . . well, never mind," she interrupted, with a hint of her old roguishness. "Dale, I'm terribly grateful to you for bringing back my horses. I know you won't take money. I'm afraid

153

you'll refuse the job I offered. . . . So, Mister Wild-Horse Hunter, I'm going to pay you as I said I would—back at the house."

"No!" he cried, suddenly weak. "Edith, you wouldn't be so silly—so—Aw, it's just the devil in you."

"I'm going to, Dale."

Her voice drew him as well as her intent; and forced to look up, he was paralyzed to see her bending to him, her face aglow, her eyes alight. Her hands flashed upon his shoulders—slipped back—and suddenly pressed like bands of steel. Dale somehow recovered strength to stand up and break her hold.

"Edith, you're out of—your head," he said huskily.

"I don't care if I am. I always wanted to, Dale Brittenham. This was a good excuse. . . . And I'll never get another."

The girl's face was scarlet as she drew back from Dale, but it paled before she concluded her strange speech.

"You're playin' with me—you darned flirt," he blurted out.

"Not this time, Dale," she replied soberly, and then Dale grasped that something deeper and hitherto unguessed had followed hard on her real desire to reward him for his service.

"It'll be now or never, Dale. . . . For this morning at breakfast I gave in at last to Dad's nagging—and consented to marry Leale Hildrith."

"Then it'll be never, my strange girl," replied Dale hoarsely, shot through with anguish for Edith and his treacherous friend. "I—I reckoned this was the case. . . . You love Leale?"

"I think—I do," replied Edith, somewhat hesitantly. "He's handsome and gay. Everybody loves Leale. You do. All the girls are mad about him. I—I love him, I guess. . . . But it's mostly Dad. He hasn't given me any peace for a year. He's set on Hildrith. Then he thinks I ought to settle down—that I flirt—that I have all his riders at odds with each other on my account. . . . Oh, it made me furious."

"Edith, I hope you will be happy."

"A lot *you* care, Dale Brittenham."

"I cared too much. That was the trouble."

"*Dale!* . . . So that was why you avoided me?"

"Yes, that was why, Edith."

"But you are as good as any man."

"You're a rich rancher's daughter. I'm a poor wild-horse hunter."

"Oh! As if that made any difference between friends."

"Edith, it does," he replied sadly. "An' now they're accusin' me of bein' a horse thief. . . . I'll have to kill again."

"No! You mustn't fight," she cried wildly. "You might be shot. . . . Dale, promise me you'll not go gunning for anyone."

"That's easy, Edith. I promise."

"Thanks, Dale . . . Oh, I don't know what's come over me." She dropped her head on his shoulder. "I'm glad you told me. It hurts—but it helps somehow. I—I must think."

"You should think that you must not be seen—like this," he said gently.

"I don't care," she flashed, suddenly aroused. Edith's propensity to change was one of her bewildering charms. Dale realized he had said the wrong thing and he shook in her tightening grasp. "You've cheated me, Dale, of a real friendship. And I'm going to punish you. I'm going to keep my word, no matter what comes of it. . . . Oh, you'll believe me a flirt—like Dad and all of these old fools that think I've kissed these beaux of mine. But I haven't—well, not since I was a kid. Not even Leale! . . . Dale, you might have kissed me if you'd had any sense."

"Edith, have *you* lost all sense—of—of—" he choked out.

"Of modesty? . . . I'm not in the least ashamed." But her face flamed as she tightened her arms around him and pressed sweet cool lips to his cheek. Dale was almost unable to resist crushing her in his arms. He tried, weakly, to put her back. But she was strong, and evidently in the grip of some emotion she had not calculated upon. For her lips sought his and their coolness turned to sweet fire. Her eyelids fell heavily. Dale awoke to spend his hunger for love and his renunciation in passionate response.

That broke the spell which had moved Edith.

"Oh Dale!" she whispered, as she wrenched her lips free. "I shouldn't have. . . . Forgive me. . . . I was beside myself."

Her arms were sliding from his neck when quick footfalls and the ring of spurs sounded in the doorway. Dale looked up to see Hildrith, livid under his golden beard, with eyes flaring, halting at the threshold.

"What the hell!" he burst out incredulously.

Dale's first sensation was one of blank dismay, and as Edith, with arms dropping, drew back, crimson of face, he sank against the pile of bales like a guilty man caught in some unexplainable act.

"Edith! What did I see?" demanded Hildrith in jealous wrath.

"Not very much! You were too late. Why do you slip up on people like that?" the girl returned with a tantalizing laugh. She faced him, her blush and confusion vanishing. His strident voice no doubt roused her imperious spirit.

"You had your arms around Dale?"

"I'm afraid I had."

"You kissed him?"

"Once . . . No, twice, counting a little one," returned this amazing creature. Dale suffered some kind of torture only part of which was shame.

"Well, by heaven!" shouted Hildrith furiously. "I'll beat him half to death for that."

Edith intercepted him and got between him and Dale. She pushed him back with no little force. "Don't be a fool, Leale. It'd be dangerous to strike Dale. Listen . . ."

"I'll call him out," shouted her lover.

"And get shot for your pains. Dale has killed half a dozen men. . . . Let me explain."

"You can't explain a thing like this."

"Yes, I can. I admit it looks bad, but it really isn't. . . . When Dale brought my horses back, I was so crazy with joy that I wanted to hug and kiss him. I told him so. But I couldn't before Dad and all those men. When we came out here I—I tried to, but Dale repulsed me—"

"Edith! Do you expect me to believe that?" interposed Hildrith.

"Yes. It's true. . . . But the second time I succeeded—and you almost caught me in the act."

"You damned little flirt!"

"Leale, I wasn't flirting. I wanted to kiss Dale; I was in rapture about my horses. And before that Dad and those men hinted Dale was hand and glove with these horse thieves. I hated that. It excited me. Perhaps I was out of my head. Dale said I was. But you shall not blame him. It was my fault."

"Oh hell!" fumed Hildrith in despair. "Do you deny the poor beggar is in love with you?"

"I certainly do deny that," she retorted, and her gold-tan cheeks flamed red.

"Well, he is. Anybody could see that."

"I didn't. And if it's true he never told me."

Hildrith began to pace the barn. "Good God! Engaged to marry me for half a day, and you do a brazen thing like that. . . . Watrous is sure right. You need to be tied down. Playing fast and loose with every rider on the range! Coaxing your Dad to set our marriage day three months off! . . . Oh, you drive me mad, I'll tell you, young woman, when you *are* my wife . . ."

"Don't insult me, Mr. Hildrith," interrupted Edith coldly. "I'm not your wife yet. . . . I was honest with you, because I felt sure you'd understand. I'm sorry I told you the truth and I don't care whether you believe me or not."

With her bright head erect, she walked past Hildrith, avoiding him as he reached for her, and she was deaf to his entreaties.

"Edith, I'll take it all back," he cried after her. But so far as Dale could see or hear she made no response. Hildrith turned away from the door, wringing his hands. It was plain that he worshiped the girl, that he did not trust her, that he was inordinately suspicious, that for an accepted lover he appeared the most wretched of men. Dale watched him, seeing him more clearly in the revelation of his dual nature. Just how far Hildrith had gone with this horse-stealing gang, Dale did not want to know. Dale did see that his friend's redemption was possible—that if he could marry this girl, and if he could be terribly frightened with possible exposure, he might be weaned from whatever association he had with Mason, and go honest and make Edith happy. It was not a stable conviction, but it gripped Dale. He had his debt to pay to Hildrith and a glimmering of a possible way to do it formed in his mind. Even at that moment, though, he felt the ax of disillusion and reality at the roots of his love for this man. Hildrith was not what he had believed him. But that would not deter Dale from paying his debt a thousandfold. Lastly, if Edith Watrous loved this man, Dale felt that he must save him.

Hildrith whirled upon Dale. "So this is how you appreciate what I've done for you, Dale. You made love to my girl. You damned handsome ragamuffin—you worked on Edith's sympathy! You've got me into a hell of a fix."

"Leale, you sure are in a hell of a fix," replied Dale with dark significance.

"What do you mean?" queried Hildrith sharply, with a quick uplift of head.

"You're one of Big Bill Mason's gang," rejoined Dale deliberately.

Hildrith gave a spasmodic start, as if a blade had pierced his side. His jaw dropped and his face blanched to an ashen hue under his blond beard. He tried to speak, but no words came.

"I sneaked up on the camp of those three horse thieves. I listened. Those low-down thieves—Ben, Alec, Steve—spoke familiarly of you. Alec an' Steve were concerned over what you'd do about the theft of the Watrous horses. Ben made light of it. He didn't care. They talked about Big Bill. An' that talk betrayed you to me. . . . Leale, you're the range scout for Mason. You're the man who sets the time for these big horse raids."

"You know! . . . Oh, my God!" cried Hildrith abjectly.

"Yes, I know that an' more. I know the trail to Mason's secret rendezvous. I was on that trail an' saw this last big drove of stolen horses pass by. I figured out how Mason's gang operates. Pretty foxy. I'll say. But it was too good, too easy, too profitable. It couldn't last."

"For God's sake, Dale, don't squeal on me!" besought Hildrith, bending over Dale with haggard, clammy face. "I've money. I'll pay you well—anything. . . ."

"Shut up! Don't try to buy me off, or I'll

despise you for a yellow cur. . . . I didn't say I'd squeal on you. But I do say you're a madman to think you can work long at such a low-down game."

"Dale, I swear to God this was my last deal. Mason forced me to one more, a big raid which was to be his last in this valley. He had a hold on me. We were partners in a cattle business over in Montana. He roped me into a rustling deal before I knew what it actually was. That was three years ago, over in Kalispel. Then he found a hiding place—a box canyon known only to the Indians—and that gave him the idea of raiding both Montana and Idaho ranges at the same time—driving to the canyon and there changing outfits and stolen horses. While a raid was on over there, Mason made sure to be in Bannock or Kalispel, and he roared louder than anyone at the horse thieves. He had the confidence of all the ranchers over there. My job was the same here in the Salmon Valley. But I fell in love with Edith and have been trying to break away."

"Leale, you say you swear to God this was your last deal with Mason?"

"Yes, I swear it. I have been scared to death. I got to thinking it was too good to last. I'd be found out. Then I'd lose Edith."

"Man, you'd not only lose her. But you'd be shot—or worse, you'd be hanged. These ranchers are roused. Watrous is ory-eyed, so Wesley told me. They'll organize an' send a bunch of Wyomin' cowboys out on Mason's trail. I'll bet that's exactly what Watrous is talkin' over now with these visitors."

"Then it's too late. They'll find me out. God! Why didn't I have some sense?"

"They won't find you out if you quit. Absolutely quit! I'm the only man outside the Mason gang who knows. If some of them are captured an' try to implicate you, it wouldn't be believed. I'll not give you away."

"Dale, by heaven, that's good of you," said Hildrith hoarsely. "I did you an injustice. Forgive me. . . . Dale, tell me what to do. I'm in your hands. I'll do anything. Only save me. I wasn't cut out for a horse thief. It's galled me. I've been sick after every raid. I haven't the guts. I've learned an awful lesson."

"Have you any idea how Edith would despise you, if she knew?"

"That's what makes me sweat blood. I worship the very ground she walks on."

"Does she love you?"

"Oh, Lord, I don't know now. I thought so. She said she did. But she wouldn't. . . .

164

She promised to marry me. Watrous wants her settled. If she will marry me, I know I can make her love me."

"Never if you continued to be a two-faced, dirty, lousy, yellow dog of a horse thief," cried Dale forcefully. "You've got to perform a miracle. You've got to change. That's the price of my silence."

"Dale, I'm torn apart. . . . What use to swear? You know I'll quit—and go straight all my life. For Edith! What man wouldn't? You would if she gave herself . . . any man would. Don't you see that?"

"Yes, I see that, an' I believe you," replied Dale, convinced of the truth in Hildrith's agony. "I'll keep your secret, an' find a way to save you if any unforeseen thing crops up. . . . An' that squares me with you, Leale Hildrith."

Swift light footsteps that scattered the gravel cut short Hildrith's impassioned gratitude. Edith startled Dale by appearing before them, her hand at her breast, her face white as a sheet, her eyes blazing.

Hildrith met her on the incline, exclaiming, "Why, Edith! Running back like that! What's wrong?"

She paid no heed to him, but ran to Dale, out of breath and visibly shaking.

165

"Oh—Dale—" she panted. "Stafford sent —for the sheriff! . . . They're going to— arrest you."

"Stafford? Who's he? That man in the black coat?"

"Yes. He's lately—got in with Dad. . . . Cattle. It's his outfit—of cowboys coming. . . . He's hard as nails."

"Are they here?"

"Will be—directly. I tore loose from Dad—and ran all the way. . . . Oh, Dale what will you do?" She was unconscious of her emotion—and she put an appealing hand upon Dale's arm. Dale had never seen her like that, nor had Hildrith. They were deeply struck, each according to his reception of her white-faced, earnest demeanor.

"Edith, you can bet I won't run," declared Dale grimly. "Thank you, girl, all the same. . . . Don't take this so—so strangely. Why, you're all upset. They can't arrest me."

Hildrith drew back from the wide door. He appeared no less alarmed and excited than Edith. "They're coming, Dale," he said thickly. "Bayne and Stafford in the lead . . . That sheriff has it in for you, Dale. Only last night I heard him swear he'd jail you if you came back. . . . It's ticklish business. What'll you do?"

"I'm sure I don't know," returned Dale with a laugh.

Edith besought him, "Oh, Dale, don't kill Bayne! . . . For my sake!"

"If you brace up, I reckon maybe I can avoid that."

Dale led his horse out of the barn, down the runway into the open. Then he stepped aside to face the advancing men, now nearly across the wide court. The dark-garbed Stafford was talking and gesticulating vehemently to a stalwart booted man. This was the one officer that Salmon supported, and it had been said of him that he knew which side of the law to be on. Watrous and three other men brought up the rear. They made no bones about sheering off to the side. Stafford, however, a swarthy and pompous man, evidently accustomed to authority, remained beside Bayne.

"Hey, you," called out Dale, far from civilly. "If you want to talk with me—that's close enough."

Hildrith, to Dale's surprise, came down the incline, and took up a stand beside Dale.

"What you mean by this turkey-strutting?" he demanded, and his simulation of resentment would have deceived anyone but Dale.

"Hildrith, we got business with Brittenham," declared Bayne harshly.

"Well, he's my friend, and that concerns me."

"Thanks, Leale," interposed Dale. "But let me handle this. Bayne, are you looking for me?"

"I sure am."

"At whose instigation?"

"Mr. Stafford, here. He sent for me, an' he orders you arrested."

Watrous broke in to say nervously, "Brittenham, I advised against this. I have nothing to do with it. I don't approve of resorting to law on the strength of gossip. If you'll deny any association with horse thieves, that will do for me. If your word is good to Edith, it ought to be for me."

"Jim Watrous, you're a fool," rasped out Stafford. "Your daughter is apparently infatuated with this—this . . ."

"Careful!" cut in Dale. "You might say the wrong thing. An' leave Miss Edith's name out of this deal. . . . Stafford, what's your charge against me?"

"I think you're one of this horse-raiding gang," declared Stafford stoutly, though he turned pale.

"On what grounds?"

"I wasn't influenced by gossip, sir. I base my suspicion on your fetching back those thoroughbred horses. They must have been driven off by mistake. Any horse thief would know they couldn't be ridden or sold in Montana or Idaho. They'd be recognized. So you fetched them back because it was good business. Besides, it'd put you in better with Watrous, and especially his—"

"Shut up! If you speak of that girl again I'll shoot your leg off," interrupted Dale. "An' you can gamble on this, Stafford. If I don't shoot you anyhow it'll be the only peg on which you can hang a doubt of my honesty."

"You insolent ruffian!" ejaculated Stafford, enraged and intimidated. "Arrest him, sheriff."

"Brittenham, you'll have to come with me," spoke up Bayne with an uneasy cough. "You appear to be a talker. You'll get a chance to talk in court at Twin Falls."

"You're tryin' to go through with it?" asked Dale derisively.

"I say you're under arrest."

"What's *your* charge?"

"Same as Mr. Stafford's."

"But that's ridiculous, Bayne. You can't arrest a man for bringing back stolen horses.

There's not the slightest case against me. Stafford has heard gossip in town—where half the population is crooked. How do *I* know an' how do *you* know that Stafford himself is not the big hand in those horse-stealin' gang? There's some big respectable rancher on this range who stands in with the thieves. Why do you pick on a poor wild-horse hunter? A ragamuffin, as he has called me. Look at my boots! Look at my saddle! If I was the go-between, wouldn't I have better equipment? You're not very bright, Bayne."

"Aw, thet's all bluff. Part of your game. An' you've sure pulled it clever around here for three years."

While Dale had prolonged this argument, his mind had been conceiving and fixing upon a part he wanted to play. It would have been far easier but for Edith's inexplicable importunity. She had awakened to something strange and hitherto unrevealed. It must have been pity, and real sincerity and regret come too late. Then the girl had always been fair in judging something between others. If Dale had had an inkling it was anything else, he never could have made the sacrifice, not even to save Hildrith. But she loved Hildrith; she would become his wife, and that surely meant his salvation. Dale felt that ignominy, a bad name thrust upon him, and acknowledged by his actions, could not make much difference to him. He was only a wild-horse hunter. He could ride away to Arizona and never be heard of again. Still he hated the thing he felt driven to do.

Then Edith stepped into the foreground, no longer the distraught girl who had arrived there a few moments ago to warn Dale. Had she read his mind? That suspicion affected him more stirringly than anything yet that had happened.

"Sheriff Bayne, you must not try to arrest Dale without proof," she said earnestly.

"I'm sorry, lady. It's my duty. He'll get a fair trial."

"Fair!" exclaimed the girl scornfully. "When this arrest is so unfair! Bayne, there's something wrong—something dishonest here —and it's not in Dale."

"Edith, don't say more," interposed her father. "You're overwrought."

Hildrith strode to her side, hurried in manner, dark and strained of face.

"Leale, why don't you speak up for Dale?" she queried, and her eyes blazed upon him with a marvelously penetrating and strange look.

"Bayne, let Dale off," Hildrith said huskily. "Don't make a mistake here. You've no proof—and you can't arrest him."

"Can't! Why the hell can't I?" rejoined the sheriff.

"Because he won't let you. Good God, man, haven't you any mind?"

"Humph! I've got mind enough to see there's somethin' damn funny here. But it ain't in me. . . . Brittenham, you're under arrest. Come on, now, no bucklin'."

As he made a step forward Dale's gun gleamed blue and menacing.

"Look out, Bayne! If you move a hand I'll kill you," he warned.

He backed cautiously down the court, leading his horse to one side.

"I see what I'm up against here, an' I'm slopin'," went on Dale. "Stafford, you had it figured. Watrous, I engineered thet raid. . . . Edith, I fetched your horses back because I was in love with you." A strange laugh followed his words.

Dale backed across the square to the lane, where he leaped into his saddle and spurred swiftly out of sight.

II

Dale's campfire that night was on a bend of the brook near where he had surprised the three horse thieves, and had recovered the Watrous thoroughbreds.

Upon riding away from the Watrous ranch he had halted in Salmon long enough to buy supplies, then he had proceeded down the river to a lonely place where he had rested his horse and slept. By dawn he was climbing the mountain into Montana and by sundown that night he was far down the horse-thief trail.

Notwithstanding the fact that Dale had branded himself by shouldering Hildrith's guilt, he had determined to find Big Bill Mason's rendezvous and evolve a plan to break up the horse-thief band. Born of his passion at riding away from the Watrous Ranch a fugitive, leaving Edith to regret her faith in him, this plan seemed to loom as gigantic and impossible after the long hours of riding and thinking. But he would not abandon it.

"Stafford and Bayne will send a big outfit after me," he muttered as he sat before his little campfire. "An' I'll lead them to Mason's hiding place. Failin' thet, I'll go down on the range below Bannock an' get the ranchers there to raise a big posse of cowboys. One way or another I'm goin' to break up Mason's gang."

Dale had not thought of that in the hour of his sacrifice for Hildrith and Edith. He had meant to take his friend's ignominy and ride away from Idaho forever. But two things had operated against this—first, the astounding and disturbing fact that Edith Watrous, in her stress of feeling, had betrayed not only faith in him but more real friendship than she had ever shown; and secondly, his riding away in disgrace would leave the Mason gang intact, free to carry on their nefarious trade. He was the man for the job. If he broke up the gang, it would remove the stain from his name. Not that he would ever want to or dare to go back to the Watrous Ranch! But there was a tremendous force in the thought that he might stand clean and fine again in Edith Watrous's sight. How strangely she had reacted to that situation when her father and the others had confronted him! What could she have meant when she said there was something wrong, something dishonest there in that climax? Could she have had a glimmering of the truth? This thought was so disturbing that it made Dale catch his breath. Edith was a resourceful, strong-minded girl, once she became aroused. On reflection, however, he eased away that doubt, and also the humanly weak joy at a possible indestructible faith in him. No! He felt sure Hildrith would be safe. Once the Mason outfit was broken up, with the principals killed and the others run out of the country, Hildrith would be safe, and Edith's happiness would be assured.

In hours past, Dale had, in the excitement of his flight, believed that he could kill his love for Edith Watrous and forget her. This proved to be an illusion, the recognition of which came to him beside his lonely campfire. He would love her more, because his act had been something big and for her sake, and in his secret heart he would know that if she could be told the truth, she would see her faith justified, and whatever feeling she had for him would be intensified.

He saw her dark proud eyes and her white face in the opal glow of his fire. And having succumbed to that he could not help but remember her boldness to reward him, her arms and her kiss and, most poignant of all, the way she had been betrayed by her impulse, how that kiss had trapped her into emotion she had not intended. Was it possible that he had had this chance for Edith Watrous and had never divined it? The thought was torture, and he put it from him, assuring himself that the girl's actions had been the result of her gratitude and joy at the return of her beloved horses.

The fire died down to ruddy coals; the night wind began to seep through the grass and brush; four-footed prowlers commenced their questing. Standing erect, Dale listened. He heard his horse cropping the grass. A brooding solitude lay upon the forest.

He made his bed close under the side of a fallen pine, using his saddle for a pillow. So many nights of his life he had lain down to look up at the open dark sky with its trains of stars. But this night the stars appeared closer and they seemed to talk to him. He was conscious that his stern task, and the circumstances which had brought it about, had heightened all his faculties to a superlative degree. He seemed vastly different man, and he conceived that it might develop that he would revel in what fate had set him to do.

At last he fell asleep. During the night he awoke several times, and the last time, which was near dawn and nippingly cold, he got up and kindled a fire. All about him rose dark gray forest wall, except in the east, where a pale brightening betokened dawn.

It was Dale's custom to cook and eat a hearty breakfast, so that he could go long on this meal if he had to. His last task before saddling was to obliterate signs of his camp. Then, with light enough to see clearly, he mounted and was off on his perilous quest.

All the way Dale had kept off the main trail. It would take an Indian or a wild-horse hunter to track him. He traveled some few paces off the horse-thief trail, but kept it in sight. And every mile or so he would halt, dismount, and walk a few steps away from his horse to listen. In that silent forest he could have heard a sound at a considerable distance.

By sunrise he was down out of the heavy timber belt and riding out upon a big country of scaly rock and immense thickets of evergreen and cedar, with only an occasional large pine. The brook disappeared—probably dried up, or sunk into the earth. The trail led on straight as a beeline, for a while.

The sun rose high, and grew hot. With the morning half spent, he figured that he had traveled fifteen miles from his last camp. Occasionally he had glimpses of the lower range, gray and vast and dim below. The trail turned west, into more rugged plateaus and away from the descent. But presently, beyond a long fringe of evergreen thicket, he saw the peculiar emptiness that proclaimed the presence of a void.

Dale knew before he reached it that he had come upon the hole in the ground where Big Bill Mason had his hideout. Leaving the proximity of the trail, Dale rode to a little higher ground, where a gray stone eminence, less thickly overgrown, seemed to offer easy access to the place. Here he dismounted and pushed his way through the evergreens. At once he emerged upon a point, suddenly to stand rooted to the spot.

"What a wonderful place!" he exclaimed, as he grasped the fact that his sight commanded. He stood upon the rim of a deep gorge a mile long and half as wide. On all sides, the walls sheered down a thousand feet, gray and craggy, broken and caverned, lined by green benches, and apparently unscalable. Of course trails led in and out of this hole, but Dale could not see where. The whole vast level bottomland was as green as an emerald. At each end, where the gorge narrowed, glistened a lake. All around the rims stood up a thick border of evergreens, which screened the gorge from every side. Hunters and riders could pass near there without ever guessing the presence of such a concealed pocket in the mountain plateau.

"Ahuh. No wonder Mason can steal horses wholesale," soliloquized Dale. "All he had to do was to hide his tracks just after he made a raid."

Dale reflected that the thieves had succeeded in this up to the present time. However, any good tracker could sooner or later find this rendezvous for resting and shifting droves of horses. Dale was convinced that Stafford and Watrous would send out a large outfit of riders as soon as they were available.

It struck Dale singularly that he could not see an animal or a cabin in the gorge below. But undoubtedly there were points not visible to him from this particular location. Returning to his horse, he decided to ride around the gorge to look for another trail.

He found, after riding for a while, that although the gorge was hardly more than three or four miles in circumference, to circle it on horseback or even on foot, a man would have to travel three times that far. There were canyon offshoots from the main valley and these had to be headed.

At the west side Dale found one almost as long as the gorge itself. But it was narrow. Here he discovered the first sign of a trail since he had left the main one. And this was small, and had never been traveled by a drove of horses. It led off to the south toward Bannock. Dale deliberated a moment. If he were to risk going down to investigate, this trail, about halfway between the lakes at each end, should be the one for him to take. Certainly it did not show much usage. At length he rode down, impelled by a force that seemed to hold less of reason than of presagement.

It grew steep in the notch and shady, following a precipitous water course. He had to get off and lead his horse. Soon trees and brush obstructed his view. The trail was so steep that he could not proceed slowly, and before he surmised that he was halfway down, he emerged into the open to see a beautiful narrow valley, richly green, enclosed by timbered slopes. A new cabin of peeled logs stood in the lea of the north side. He saw cattle, horses and finally a man engaged in building a fence. If Dale had encountered an individual laboring this way in any other locality he would have thought him a homesteader. It was indeed the most desirable place to homestead and ranch on a small scale that Dale had ever seen in his hunting trips.

The man saw Dale just about as quickly as Dale had seen him. Riding by the cabin, where a buxom woman and some children peeped out fearfully, Dale approached the man. He appeared to be a sturdy thickset farmer, bearded and sharp-eyed. He walked forward a few steps and stopped significantly near a shiny rifle leaning against the fence. When Dale got close enough, he recognized him.

"Well, Rogers, you son-of-a-gun! What're you doin' down here?"

"Brittenham! By all thet's strange. I might ask you the same," was the hearty reply, as he offered a horny hand. Two years before Dale had made the acquaintance of Rogers back in the Sawtooth range.

"When'd you leave Camus Creek?" he asked.

"This spring. Fine place, thet, but too cold. I was snowed in all winter. Sold out to a Mormon."

"How'd you happen to locate in here?"

"Just accident. I went to Bannock, an' from there to Halsey. Liked thet range country. But I wanted to be high, where I could hunt an' trap as well as homestead. One day I hit the trail leadin' in here. An' you bet I located pronto."

"Before ridin' out in the big valley?"

"Yes. But I saw it. What a range! This was big enough for me. If I'm not run out I'll get rich here in five years."

"Then you located before you found out you had neighbors?"

"What do you know about them?" queried Rogers, giving Dale a speculative glance.

"I know enough."

"Brittenham, I hope to heaven you're not in thet outfit."

"No. An' I hope the same of you. Have you got wise yet to Mason's way of operatin'?"

"Mason! You don't mean the rancher an' horse trader Bill Mason?"

"Same hombre. Big Bill—the biggest horse thief in this country."

"So help me—! If thet's true, who can a man trust?"

"It's true, Rogers, as you can find out for yourself by watchin'. Mason runs a big outfit. They split. One operates in Idaho, the other in Montana. They drive the stolen horses up here an' switch men an' herds. They sell the Montana stock over in Idaho an' the Idaho stock over on the Montana ranges."

"Hell you say! Big idee an' sure a bold one. I savvy now why these men politely told me to pull up stakes an' leave. But I had my cabin up an' my family here before they found out I'd located. Then I refused to budge. Reed, the boss of the outfit, rode down again last week. Offered to buy me out. I thought thet strange. But he didn't offer much, so I refused to sell. He said his boss didn't want any homesteaders in here."

"Rogers, they'll drive you out or kill you," said Dale.

"I don't believe it. They're bluffin'. If they murdered me it'd bring attention to this place. Nobody knows of it. I haven't told about it yet. My wife would, though, if they harmed me."

"This gang wouldn't hesitate to put you

all out of the way. They just don't take you seriously yet. Think they can scare you out."

"Not me! Brittenham, how'd you come to know about this horse stealin' an' to find this hole?"

Dale told him about the theft of the Watrous thoroughbreds, how he had trailed the robbers up the mountain, what happened there, and lastly about the big raid that followed hard the same day.

"I'll tell you, Rogers. I got blamed for bein' the scout member of Mason's outfit. It made me sore. I left Salmon in a hurry, believe me. My aim in findin' this hole is to organize a big posse of cowboys an' break up Mason's gang."

"Humph! You ain't aimin' to do much, atall."

"It'll be a job. There's no tellin' how many outfits Mason runs. It's a good bet thet his ranch outfit is honest an' don't suspect he's a horse thief. I'll bet he steals his own horses. If I can raise a hard-fightin' bunch an' corral Mason's gang all here in this hole . . . To catch them here—thet's the trick. I'd reckon they'll be stragglin' in soon. It doesn't take long to sell a bunch of good horses. Then they'd hide here, gamblin' an' livin' fat until time for another raid. . . . Rogers, breakin'

184

up this outfit is important to you. How'd you like to help me?"

"What could I do? Remember I'm handicapped with a wife an' two kids."

"No fightin' an' no risk for you. I'd plan for you to watch the valley, and have some kind of signs I could see from the rim to tell me when the gang is here."

"Get down an' come in," replied the homesteader soberly. "We'll talk it over."

"I'll stop a little while. But I mustn't lose time."

"Come set on the porch. Meet the wife an' have a bit to eat. . . . Brittenham, I think I'll agree to help you. As for signs . . . Do you see thet bare point of rock up on the rim? . . . There. It's the only place on the rim from which you can see my valley an' cabin. I've a big white cowhide thet I could throw over the fence. You could see it much farther than thet. If you did see it, you'd know the gang was here."

"Just the trick, Rogers. An' no risk to you," replied Dale with satisfaction. He unsaddled Hoofs and let him free on the rich grass. Then he accompanied Rogers to the cabin, where he spent a restful hour. When he left, Rogers walked with him to the trail. They understood one another and were in accord on the plan to break up Mason's band. Dale climbed on foot to the rim, his horse following, and then rode east to the point designated by the homesteader. Rogers watched for him and waved.

Across the canyon Dale located a curve in the wall which partly enclosed a large area black with horses. He saw cattle, too, and extensive gardens, and far up among the trees yellow cabins amidst the green. He rode back to Rogers' trail and headed for Bannock, keen and grim over his project.

The trail zigzagged gradually down toward lower country. Dale was always vigilant. No moving object escaped him. But there was a singular dearth of life along this scantily timbered eastern mountain slope. Toward late afternoon he found himself in broken country again, where the trail wound between foothills. It was dark when he rode into Bannock.

This town, like Salmon, was in the heyday of its productivity. And it was considerably larger. Gold and silver mining were its main assets, but there was some cattle trade, and extensive business in horses, and the providing of supplies for the many camps in the hills. Gambling halls of the period, with all their manifest and hidden evils, flourished flagrantly.

A miner directed Dale to a stable where he left his horse. Here he inquired about his Indian friend, Naloo. Then he went uptown to find a restaurant. He did not expect to meet anyone who knew him unless it was the Indian. Later that contingency would have to be reckoned with. Dale soon found a place to eat. Next to him at the lunch counter sat a red-faced cowboy who answered his greeting civilly.

"How's the hash here?" asked Dale.

"Fair to middlin' . . . Stranger hereabouts, eh?"

"Yep. I hail from the Snake River country."

"I see you're a range rider, but no cowman."

"You're a good guesser. My job is horses."

"Bronco buster, I'll bet."

"Nope. But I can an' do break wild horses."

"Reckon you're on your way to Halsey. There's a big sale of Idaho stock there tomorrow."

"Idaho horses. You don't say?" ejaculated Dale, pretending surprise. "I hadn't heard of it."

"Wal, I reckon it wasn't advertised over your way," replied the cowboy with a short laugh. "An' when you buy fine horses at half their value, you don't ask questions."

"Cowboy, you said a lot. I'm goin' to have a look at thet bunch. How far to Halsey?"

"Two hours for you, if you stretch leather. It takes a buckboard four."

Dale then attended to the business of eating, but that did not keep his mind from functioning actively. It staggered him to think that it was possible Mason had the brazen nerve to sell stolen Idaho horses not a hundred miles across the line.

"How about buckin' the tiger?" asked Dale's acquaintance as they went out into the street.

"No gamblin' for me, cowboy. I like to look on, though, when there's some big bettin'."

"I seen a game today. Poker. Big Bill Mason won ten thousand at Steen's. You should have heard him roar. 'Thet pays up for the bunch of hosses stole from me the other day!'"

"Who's Big Bill Mason?" asked Dale innocently.

"Wal, he's about the whole cheese down

Halsey way. Got his hand in most everythin'. I rode for him a spell."

"Does he deal much in horses?"

"Not so much as with cattle. But he always runs four or five hundred haid on his ranch."

Presently Dale parted from the cowboy and strolled along the dimly lighted street, peering into the noisy saloons, halting near groups of men, and listening. He spent a couple of hours that way, here and there picking up bits of talk. No mention of the big steal of Idaho horses came to Dale's ears. Still, with a daily stagecoach between the towns it was hardly conceivable that some news had not sifted through to Bannock.

Before leaving town, Dale bought a new shirt and a scarf. He slept that night in the barn where he had his horse put up. A pile of hay made a better bed than Dale usually had. But for a disturbing dream about Edith Watrous, in which she visited him in jail, he slept well. Next morning he shaved, and donned his new garments, after which he went into the town for breakfast. He was wary this morning. Early though the hour, the street was dotted with vehicles, and a motley string of pedestrians passed to and fro on the sidewalks.

Dale had a leisurely and ample breakfast, after which he strolled down the street to the largest store and entered, trying to remember what it was that he had wanted to purchase.

"*Dale!*" A voice transfixed him. He looked up to be confronted by Edith Watrous.

A red-cheeked, comely young woman accompanied Edith, and looked at Dale with bright, curious eyes.

He stammered confusedly in answer to Edith's greeting.

"Susan, this is my friend Dale Brittenham." Edith introduced him hurriedly. "Dale—Miss Bradford . . . I came over here to visit Susan."

"Glad to meet you, Miss," returned Dale, doffing his sombrero awkwardly.

"I've heard about you," said the girl, smiling at Dale. But evidently she saw something was amiss for she turned to Edith and said, "You'll want to talk. I'll run do my buying."

"Yes, I want to talk to my friend Dale Brittenham," agreed Edith seriously. Her desire to emphasize the word "friend" could not be mistaken. She drew him away from the entrance of the store to a more secluded space. Then: "Dale!" Her voice was low and full of suppressed emotion. Pale, and with eyes dark with scorn and sorrow, she faced him.

"How'd you come over here?" he queried, regaining his coolness.

"Nalook drove me in the buckboard. He returned to the ranch after you left. We got here last night."

"I'm sorry you had the bad luck to run into me."

"Not bad luck, Dale. I followed you. I was certain you'd come here. There's no other town to go to."

"Followed me? Edith, what for?"

"Oh, I don't know—yet. . . . After you left I had a quarrel with Leale and Dad. I upbraided them for not standing by you. I swore you couldn't be a horse thief. I declared you were furious—that in your bitterness you just helped them to think badly of you."

"How could they help that when I admitted my—my guilt?"

"They couldn't—but *I* could. . . . Dale, I know you. If you had been a real thief, you'd never—never have told me you—you loved me that last terrible moment. You couldn't. You wanted me to know. You looked bitter—hard—wretched. There was nothing low-down or treacherous about you."

"Edith, there you're wrong," returned Dale hoarsely. "For there is."

"Dale! Don't kill my faith in you. . . . Don't kill something I'm—I'm afraid . . ."

"It's true—to my shame an' regret."

"Oh! . . . So that's why you never made love to me like the other boys? You were man enough for that, at least. I'm indebted to you. But I'll tell you what I've found out. If you had been the splendid fellow I thought you—and if you'd had sense enough to tell me sooner that you loved me—well—there was no one I liked better, Dale Brittenham."

"My God!—Edith, don't—I beg you—don't say thet now," implored Dale, in passionate sadness.

"I care a great deal for Leale Hildrith. But it was Dad's match. I told Leale so. I would probably have come to it of my own accord in time. Yesterday we had a quarrel. He made an awful fuss about my leaving home, so I slipped away unseen. But I'll bet he's on the way here right now."

"I hope he comes after you," said Dale, bewildered and wrenched by this disclosure.

"He'd better not. . . . Never mind him, Dale. You've hurt me. Perhaps I deserved it. For I have been selfish and vain with my friends. To find out you're a—a thief—Oh, I hate you for making me believe it! It's just sickening. But you can't—you simply can't have become callous. You always had queer notions about range horses being free. There are no fences in parts of Idaho—Oh, see how I make excuses for you! Dale, promise me you will never help to steal another horse so long as you live."

Dale longed to fall upon his knees to her and tell her the truth. She was betraying more than she knew. He had seen her audacious and winning innumerable times, and often angry, and once eloquent, but never so tragic and beautiful as now. It almost broke down his will. He had to pull his hand from hers—to force a hateful stand utterly foreign to his nature.

"Edith, I won't lie to you—"

"I'm not so sure of that," she retorted, her eyes piercing him. They had an intense transparency through which her thought, her doubt, shone like a gleam.

"Nope. I can't promise. My old wild-horse business is about played out. I've got to live."

"Dale, I'll give—lend you money, so you can go away far and begin all over again. Please, Dale?"

"Thanks, lady," he returned, trying to be laconic. "Sure I couldn't think of thet."

"You're so strange—so different. You didn't use to be like this. . . . Dale, is it my fault you went to the bad?"

"Nonsense!" he exclaimed in sudden heat. "Reckon it was just in me."

"Swear you're not lying to me."

"All right, I swear."

"If I believed I was to blame, I'd follow you and *make* you honest. I ought to do it anyhow."

"Edith, I'm sure glad you needn't go to such extremes. You can't save a bad egg."

"Oh—Dale . . ." She was about to yield further to her poignant mood when her friend returned.

"Edie, I'd have stayed away longer," said Susan, her eyes upon them. "Only if we're going to Halsey we must rustle pronto."

"Edith, are you drivin' over there?" asked Dale quickly.

"Yes. Susan's brother is coming. There's a big horse sale on. I'm curious to see if there will be any of Dad's horses there."

"I'm curious about that, too," admitted Dale soberly. "Good-by, Edith. . . . Miss Bradford, glad to meet you, an' good-by."

Dale strode swiftly out of the store, though

Edith's call acted upon him like a magnet. Once outside, with restraint gone, he fell in a torment. He could not think coherently, let alone reason. That madcap girl, fully aroused, might be capable of anything. Dale suffered anguish as he rushed down the street and to the outskirts of town, where he saddled his horse and rode away down the slope to the east. There were both horsemen and vehicles going in the same direction, which he surmised was toward Halsey. Dale urged his mount ahead of them and then settled down to a steady sharp gait. He made no note of time, or the passing country. Long before noon he rode into Halsey.

The town appeared to be deserted, except for clerks in stores, bartenders at the doors of saloons, and a few loungers. Only two vehicles showed down the length of the long street. Dale did not need to ask why, but he did ask to be directed to the horse fair. He was not surprised to find a couple of hundred people, mostly men, congregated at the edge of town, where in an open green field several score of horses, guarded by mounted riders, grazed and bunched in front of the spectators. Almost the first horse he looked at twice proved to be one wearing the Watrous brand.

Then Dale had a keen eye for that drove of horses and especially the horsemen. In a country where all men packed guns, their being armed did not mean anything to casual observers. Nevertheless to Dale it was significant. They looked to him to be a seasoned outfit of hard riders. He hid Hoofs in the background and sauntered over toward the center of activities.

"Where's this stock from?" he asked one of a group of three men, evidently ranchers, who were bystanders like himself.

"Idaho. Snake River range."

"Sure some fine saddle hosses," went on Dale. "What they sellin' for?"

"None under a hundred dollars. An' goin' like hot cakes."

"Who's the hoss dealer?"

"Ed Reed. Hails from Twin Falls."

"Ahuh. Gentlemen, I'm a stranger in these parts," said Dale deliberately. "I hear there's no end of hoss business goin' on—hoss sellin', hoss buyin', hoss tradin'—an' *hoss stealin'*."

"Wal, this is a hoss country," spoke up another of the trio dryly, as he looked Dale up and down. Dale's cool speech had struck them significantly.

"You all got the earmarks of range men," Dale continued curtly. "I'd like to ask, without 'pearin' too inquisitive, if any one of you has lost stock lately?"

There followed a moment of silence, in which the three exchanged glances and instinctively edged close together.

"Wal, stranger, I reckon thet's a fair question," replied the eldest, a gray-haired, keen-eyed Westerner. "Some of us ranchers down in the range have been hit hard lately."

"By what? Fire, flood, blizzard, drought—or hoss thieves?"

"I reckon thet last, stranger. But don't forget you said it."

"Fine free country, this, where a range man can't talk right out," rejoined Dale caustically. "I'll tell you why. You don't know who the hoss thieves are. An' particular, their chief. He might be one of your respectable rancher neighbors."

"Stranger, you got as sharp a tongue as eye," returned the third member of the group. "What's your name an' what's your game?"

"Brittenham. I'm a wild-horse hunter from the Snake River Basin. My game is to get three or four tough cowboy outfits together."

"Wal, thet oughtn't be hard to do in this country, if you had reason," returned the rancher, his eyes narrowing. Dale knew he did not need to tell these men that the drove of horses before them had been stolen.

"I'll look you up after the sale," he concluded.

"My name's Strickland. We'll sure be on the lookout for you."

The three moved on toward the little crowd near the horses at that moment under inspection. "Jim, if we're goin' to buy some stock we've got to hustle," remarked one.

Dale sauntered away to get a good look at the main drove of horses. When he recognized Dusty Dan, a superb bay that he had actually straddled himself, a bursting gush of hot blood burned through his veins. Deliberately he stepped closer, until he was halted by one of the mounted guards.

"Whar you goin', cowboy?" demanded this individual, a powerful rider of matured years, clad in greasy leather chaps and dusty blouse. He had a bearded visage and deep-set eyes, gleaming under a black sombrero pulled well down.

"I'm lookin' for my hoss," replied Dale mildly.

The guard gave a slight start, barely perceptible.

"Wal, do you see him?" he queried insolently.

"Not yet."

"What kind of hoss, cowboy?"

"He's a black with white face. Wearin' a W brand like that bay there. He'd stand out in thet bunch like a silver dollar in a fog."

"Wal, he ain't hyar, an' you can mosey back."

"Hell you say," retorted Dale, changing his demeanor in a flash. "These horses are on inspection. . . . An' see here, Mr. Leather Pants, don't tell *me* to mosey anywhere."

Another guard, a lean, sallow-faced man, rode up to query, "Who's this guy, Jim?"

"Took him for a smart-alec cowboy."

"You took me wrong, you Montana buckaroos," interposed Dale, cool and caustic. "I'll mosey around an' see if I can pick out a big black hoss with the W brand."

Dale strode on, but he heard the guard called Jim mutter to his companion, "Tip Reed off." Presently Dale turned in time to see the rider bend from his saddle to speak in the ear of a tall dark man. Thus Dale identified Ed Reed, and without making his action marked, he retraced his steps. On his way he distinguished more W brands and recognized more Watrous horses.

Joining the group of buyers, Dale looked on from behind. After one survey of Big

Bill Mason's right-hand man Dale estimated him to be a keen, suave villain whose job was to talk, but who would shoot on the slightest provocation.

"Well, gentlemen, we won't haggle over a few dollars," Reed was saying blandly as he waved a hairy brown hand. "Step up and make your offers. These horses have got to go."

Then buying took on a brisk impetus. During the next quarter of an hour a dozen and more horses were bought and led away, among them Dusty Dan. That left only seven animals, one of which was the white-faced black Dale had spoken about to the guard, but had not actually seen.

"Gentlemen, here's the pick of the bunch," spoke up Reed. "Eight years old. Sound as a rock. His sire was blooded stock. I forget the name. What'll you offer?"

"Two hundred fifty," replied a young man eagerly.

"That's a start. Bid up, gentlemen. This black is gentle, fast, wonderful gait. A single-footer. You see how he stacks up."

"Three hundred," called Dale, who meant to outbid any other buyers, take the horse and refuse to pay.

"Come on. Don't you Montana men know horseflesh when . . ."

Reed halted with a violent start and the flare of his eyes indicated newcomers. Dale wheeled with a guess that he verified in the sight of Edith Watrous and Leale Hildrith, with another couple behind them. He also saw Nalook, the Indian, at the driver's seat of the buckboard. Hildrith's face betrayed excessive emotion under control. He tried to hold Edith back. But, resolute and pale, she repelled him and came on. Dale turned swiftly so as not to escape Reed's reaction to this no doubt astounding and dangerous interruption. Dale was treated to an extraordinary expression of fury and jealousy. It passed from Reed's dark glance and dark face as swiftly as it had come.

Dale disliked the situation that he saw imminent. There were ten in Reed's gang— somber, dark-browed men, whom it was only necessary for Dale to scrutinize once to gauge their status. On the other hand the majority of spectators and buyers were not armed. Dale realized that he had to change his mind, now that Edith was there. To start a fight would be foolhardy and precarious.

The girl had fire in her eyes as she addressed the little group.

"Who's boss here?" she asked.

"I am, Miss. . . . Ed Reed, at your service." Removing his sombrero he made her a gallant bow. His face strong and not unhandsome in a bold way. Certainly his gaze was one of unconcealed admiration.

"Mr. Reed, that black horse with the white face belongs to me," declared Edith imperiously.

"Indeed?" replied Reed, exhibiting apparently genuine surprise. "And who're you, may I ask?"

"Edith Watrous. Jim Watrous is my father."

"Pleased to meet you. . . . You'll excuse me, Miss Watrous, if I ask for proof that this black is yours."

Edith came around so that the horse could see her, and she spoke to him. "Dick, old boy, don't you know me?"

The black pounded the ground, and with a snort jerked the halter from the man who held him. Whinnying, he came to Edith, his fine eyes soft, and he pressed his nose into her hands.

"There! . . . Isn't that sufficient?" asked Edith.

Reed had looked on with feigned amusement. Dale gauged him as deep and resourceful.

"Sam, fetch my hoss. I'm tired standing and I reckon this lady has queered us for other buyers."

"Mr. Reed, I'm taking my horse whether you like it or not," declared Edith forcefully.

"But, Miss Watrous, you can't do that. You haven't proved to me he belongs to you. I've seen many fine horses that'd come to a woman."

"Where did you get Dick?"

"I bought him along with the other W-brand horses."

"From whom?" queried Edith derisively.

"John Williams. He's a big breeder in horses. His ranch is on the Snake River. I daresay your father knows him."

Dale stepped out in front. "Reed, there's no horse breeder on the Snake River," he said.

The horse thief coolly mounted a superb bay that had been led up, and then gazed sardonically from Edith to Dale.

"Where do you come in?"

"My name is Brittenham. I'm a wild-horse hunter. I know every foot of range in the Snake between the falls an' the foothills."

"Williams' ranch is way up in the foothills," rejoined Reed easily. He had not exactly made a perceptible sign to his men, but they had closed in, and two of them slipped out of their saddles. Dale could not watch them and Reed at the same time. He grew uneasy. These thieves, with their crafty and bold leader, were masters of the situation.

"Lady, I hate to be rude, but you must let go that halter," said Reed, with an edge on his voice.

"I won't."

"Then I'll have to be rude. Sam, take that rope away from her."

"Leale, say something, can't you? What kind of a man are you, anyway?" cried Edith, turning in angry amazement to her fiancé.

"What can I say?" asked Hildrith, spreading wide his hands, as if helpless. His visage at the moment was not prepossessing.

"What! Why tell him you know this is my horse?"

Reed let out a laugh that had bitter satisfaction as well as irony in it. Dale had to admit that the predicament for Hildrith looked extremely serious.

"Reed, if Miss Watrous says it's her horse, you can rely on her word," replied the pallid Hildrith.

"I'd take no woman's word," returned the leader.

"Dale, you know it's my horse. You've ridden him. If you're not a liar, Mr. Reed knows you as well as you know me."

"Excuse me, lady," interposed Reed. "I never saw your wild-horse-hunter champion in my life. If he claims to know me, he is a liar."

"*Dale!*" Edith transfixed him with soul-searching eyes.

"I reckon you forget, Reed. Or you just won't own up to knowin' me. Thet's no matter. . . . But the horse belongs to Miss Watrous. I've ridden him. I've seen him at the Watrous Ranch every day or so for years."

"Brittenham. Is that what you call yourself? I'd lie for her, too. She's one grand girl. But she can't rob me of this horse."

"Rob! That's funny, Mr. Reed," exclaimed Edith hotly. "You're the robber! I'll bet Dick against two bits that *you're* the leader of this horse-thief gang."

"Well, I can't shoot a girl, much less such a pretty and tantalizing one as you. But don't say that again. I might forget my manners."

"You brazen fellow!" cried Edith, probably as much incensed by his undisguised and bold gaze as by his threat. "I not only think you're a horse thief, but I call you one!"

"All right. You can't be bluffed, Edith," he returned grimly. "You've sure got nerve. But you'll be sorry, if it's the last trick I pull on this range."

"Edith, get away from here," ordered Hildrith huskily, and he plucked at her with shaking hands. "Let go that halter."

"No!" cried Edith, fight in every line of her face and form, and as she backed away from Hildrith, she inadvertently drew nearer to Reed.

"But you don't realize who—what this man—"

"Do you?" she flashed piercingly.

Dale groaned in spirit. This was the end of Leale Hildrith. The girl was as keen as a whip and bristling with suspicion. The unfortunate man almost cringed before her. Then Reed rasped out, *"Rustle there!"*

At the instant that Reed's ally Sam jerked the halter out of Edith's hand, Dale felt the hard prod of a gun against his back. "Put 'em up, Britty," called a surly voice. Dale lost no time getting his hands above his head and he cursed under his breath for his haste and impetuosity. He was relieved of his gun. Then the pressure on his back ceased.

Reed reached down to lay a powerful left hand on Edith's arm.

"Let go!" the girl burst out angrily, and she struggled to free herself. "Oh—you hurt me! Stop, you ruffian."

"Stand still, girl," ordered Reed, trying to hold her and the spirited horse. "He'll step on you—crush your foot."

"Ah-h!" screamed Edith, in agony, and she ceased her violent exertion to stand limp, holding up one foot. The red receded from her face.

"Take your hand off her," shouted Hildrith, reaching for a gun that was not there.

"Is that your stand, Hildrith?" queried Reed, cold and hard.

"What do you—mean?"

"It's a showdown. This jig is up. Show yellow—or come out with the truth before these men. Don't leave it to me."

"Are you drunk—or crazy?" screamed Hildrith, beside himself. He did not grasp Reed's deadly intent, whatever his scheme was. He thought his one hope was to play his accustomed part. Yet he suspected a move that made him frantic. "Let her go! . . . Damn your black hide—let her go!"

"Black, but not yellow, you traitor!" wrung out Reed as he leveled a gun at Hildrith. "We'll see what the boss says to this. . . . Rustle, or I'll kill you. I'd like to do it. But you're not my man. . . . Get over there quick. Put him on a horse, men, and get going. . . . Sam, up with her!"

Before Dale could have moved, even if he had been able to accomplish anything, unarmed as he was, the man seized Edith and threw her up on Reed's horse, where despite her struggles and cries he jammed her down in the saddle in front of Reed.

As Reed wheeled away, looking back with menacing gun, the spectators burst into a loud roar. Sam dragged the black far enough to be able to leap astride his own horse and spur away, pulling his captive into his stride. The other men, ahead of Reed, drove the unsaddled horses out in front. The swiftness and precision of the whole gang left the crowd stunned. They raced out across the open range, headed for the foothills. Edith's pealing cry came floating back.

III

Dale was the first to recover from the swift raw shock of the situation. All around him milled an excited crowd. Most of them did not grasp the significance of the sudden exodus of the horse dealers until they were out of sight. Dale, nearly frantic, lost no time in finding Strickland.

"Reckon I needn't waste time now convincin' you there are some horse thieves in this neck of the woods?" he spat out sarcastically.

"Brittenham, I'm plumb beat," replied the rancher, and he looked it. "In my ten years on this range I never saw the like of that. . . . My Gawd! What an impudent rascal! To grab the Watrous girl right under our noses! Not a shot fired!"

"Don't rub it in," growled Dale. "I had to watch Reed. His man got the drop on me. A lot of slick hombres. An' thet's not sayin' half."

"We'll hang every damn one of them," shouted Strickland harshly.

"Yes. After we save the girl . . . Step aside here with me. Fetch those men you had. . . . Come, both of you. . . . Now, Strickland, this is stern business. We've not a minute to waste. I want a bunch of hard-ridin' cowboys here *pronto*. Figure quick now, while I get my horse, an' find thet Indian."

Dale ran into the lithe, dark, buckskin-clad Nalook as he raced for his horse. This Indian had no equal as a tracker in Idaho.

"Boss, you go me," Nalook said in his low voice, with a jerk of his thumb toward the foothills. Apparently the Indian had witnessed the whole action.

"Rustle, Nalook. Borrow a horse an' guns. I've got grub."

Dale hurried back, leading Hoofs. Reaching Strickland and his friends, he halted with them and waited, meanwhile taking his extra guns out of his pack.

"I can have a posse right here in thirty minutes," declared the rancher.

"Good. But I won't wait. The Indian here will go with me. We'll leave a trail they can follow on the run. Tracks an' broken brush."

"I can get thirty or more cowboys here in six hours."

"Better. Tell them the same."

Nalook appeared at his elbow. "Boss, me no find hoss."

"Strickland, borrow a horse for this Indian. I'll need him."

"Joe, go with the Indian," said Strickland. "Get him horse and outfit if you have to buy it."

"You men listen and hold your breath," whispered Dale. "This Reed outfit is only one of several. Their boss is Big Bill Mason."

The ranchers were beyond surprise or shock. Strickland snapped his fingers.

"That accounts. Dale, I'll tell you something. Mason got back to Halsey last night from Bannock, he said. He was not himself. This morning he sold his ranch—gave it away, almost—to Jeff Wheaton. He told Wheaton he was leaving Montana."

"Where is he now?"

"Must have left early. You can bet something was up for him to miss a horse sale."

"When did Reed's outfit arrive?"

"Just before noon."

"Here's what has happened," Dale calculated audibly. "Mason must have heard thet Stafford an' Watrous was sendin' a big posse out on the trail of Mason's Idaho outfit."

"Brittenham, if this Ed Reed didn't call Hildrith to show his hand for or against that outfit, then I'm plumb daft."

"It looked like it," admitted Dale gloomily.

"I thought he was going to kill Hildrith."

"So did I. There's bad blood between them."

"Hildrith has had dealings of some kind with Reed. Remember how Reed spit out, 'We'll see what the boss says about this. . . . I'd like to kill you'? . . . Brittenham, I'd say Hildrith has fooled Watrous and his daughter, and this Mason outfit also."

Dale was saved from a reply by the approach of Nalook, mounted on a daughty mustang. He carried a carbine and wore a brass-studded belt with two guns.

"We're off, Strickland," cried Dale, kicking his stirrup straight and mounting. "Hurry your posse an' outfits. Pack light, an' rustle's the word."

Once out of the circle of curious onlookers, Dale told Nalook to take the horse thieves' trail and travel. The Indian pointed toward the foothills.

"Me know trail. Big hole. Indian live there long time. Nalook's people know hoss thieves."

"I've been there, Nalook. Did you know Bill Mason was chief of thet outfit?"

"No sure. See him sometime. Like beaver. Hard see."

"We'd better not short-cut. Sure Reed will make for the hideout hole. But he'll camp on the way."

"No far. Be there sundown."

"Is it that close from this side? . . . All the better. Lead on, Nalook. When we hit the brush we want to be close on Reed's heels."

The Indian followed Reed's tracks at a lope. They led off the grassy lowland toward the hills. Ten miles or more down on the range to the east Dale spied a ranch, which Nalook said was Mason's. At that distance it did not look pretentious. A flat-topped ranch house, a few sheds and corrals, and a few cattle dotting the grassy range inclined Dale to the conviction that this place of Mason's had served as a blind to his real activities.

Soon Nalook led off the rangeland into the foothills. Reed's trail could have been followed in the dark. It wound through ravines and hollows between hills that soon grew high and wooded on top. The dry wash gave place to pools of water here and there, and at last a running brook, lined by grass and willows growing green and luxuriant.

At length a mountain slope confronted the trackers. Here the trail left the watercourse and took a slant up the long incline. Dale sighted no old hoofmarks and concluded that Reed was making a short cut to the rendezvous. At intervals Dale broke branches on the willows and brush he passed, and let them hang down, plainly visible to a keen eye. Rocks and brush, cactus and scrub oak grew increasingly manifest, and led to the cedars, which in turn yielded to the evergreens.

It was about midafternoon when they surmounted the first bench of the mountain. With a posse from Halsey possibly only a half hour behind, Dale slowed up the Indian. Reed's tracks were fresh in the red bare ground. Far across the plateau the belt of pines showed black, and the gray rock ridges stood up. Somewhere in that big rough country hid the thieves' stronghold.

"Foller more no good," said Nalook, and left Reed's tracks for the first time.

Dale made no comment. But he fell to hard pondering. Reed, bold outlaw that he was, would this time expect pursuit and fight, if he stayed in the country. His abducting the girl had been a desperate unconsidered impulse, prompted by her beauty, or by desire for revenge on Hildrith, or possibly to hold her for ransom, or all of these together. No doubt he knew this easy game was up for Mason. He had said as much to Hildrith. It was not conceivable to Dale that Reed would stay in the country if Mason was leaving. They had made their big stake.

Nalook waited for Dale on the summit of a ridge. "Ugh!" he said, and pointed.

They had emerged near the head of a valley that bisected the foothills and opened out upon the range, dim and hazy below. Dale heard running water. He saw the white flags of deer in the green brush. It was a wild and quiet scene.

"Mason trail come here," said the Indian, with an expressive gesture downward.

Then he led on, keeping to the height of slope; and once over that, entered rough and thicketed land that impeded their progress. In many places the soft red and yellow earth gave way to stone, worn to every conceivable shape. There were hollows and up-standing grotesque slabs and cones, and long flat stretches, worn uneven by erosion. Evergreens and sage and dwarf cedars found lodgment in holes. When they crossed this area to climb higher and reach a plateau, the sun was setting gold over the black mountain heights. Dale recognized the same conformation of earth and rock that he had found on the south side of the robbers' gorge. Nalook's slow progress and caution brought the tight cold stretch to Dale's skin. They were nearing their objective.

At length the Indian got off his horse and tied it behind a clump of evergreens. Dale followed suit. They drew their rifles.

"We look—see. Mebbe come back," whispered Nalook. He glided on without the slightest sound or movement of foliage, Dale endeavoring to follow his example. After traversing half a mile in a circuitous route, he halted and put a finger to his nose. "Smell smoke. Tobac."

But Dale could not catch the scent. Not long afterward, however, he made out the peculiar emptiness behind a line of evergreens and this marked the void they were seeking. They kept on at a snail's pace.

Suddenly Nalook halted and put a hand back to stop Dale. He could not crouch much lower. Warily he pointed over the fringe of low evergreens to a pile of gray rocks. On the summit sat a man with his back to the trackers. He was gazing intently in the opposite direction. This surely was a guard stationed there to spy any pursuers, presumably approaching on the trail.

"Me shoot him," whispered Nalook.

"I don't know," whispered Dale in reply, perplexed. "How far to their camp?"

"No hear gun."

"But there might be another man on watch."

"Me see."

The Indian glided away like a snake. How invaluable he was in a perilous enterprise like this! Dale sat down to watch and wait. The sun sank and shadows gathered under the evergreens. The scout on duty seemed not very vigilant. He never turned once to look back. But suddenly he stood up guardedly, and thrust his rifle forward. He took aim and appeared about to fire. Then he stiffened strangely, and jerked up as if powerfully propelled. Immediately there followed the crack of a rifle. Then the guard swayed and fell backward out of sight. Dale heard a low crash and a rattle of rocks. Then all was still. He waited. After what seemed a long anxious time, the thud of hoofs broke the silence. He sank down, clutching his rifle. But it was Nalook coming with the horses.

"We go quick. Soon night," said the

Indian, and led the way toward the jumble of rocks. Presently Dale saw a trail as wide as a road. It led down. Next he got a glimpse of the gorge. From this end it was more wonderful to gaze down into, a magnificent hole, with sunset gilding the opposite wall, and purple shadows mantling the caverns, and the lake shining black.

Viewed from this angle Mason's rendezvous presented a different and more striking spectacle. This north end where Dale stood was a great deal lower than the south end, or at least the walls were lower and the whole zigzag oval of rims sloped toward him, so that he was looking up at the southern escarpments. Yet the floor of the gorge appeared level. From this vantage point the caverns and cracks in the walls stood out darkly and mysteriously, suggesting hidden places and perhaps unseen exits from this magnificent burrow. The deep indentation of the eastern side, where Mason had his camp, was not visible from any other point. At that sunset hour a mantle of gold and purple hung over the chasm. All about it seemed silent and secretive, a wild niche of nature, hollowed out for the protection of men as wild as the place. It brooded under the gathering twilight. The walls gleamed dark with a forbidding menace.

Nalook started down, leading his mustang. Then Dale noted that he had a gun belt and long silver spurs hung over the pommel of his saddle. He had taken time to remove these from the guard he had shot. This trail was open and from its zigzag corners Dale caught glimpses of the gorge, and of droves of horses. Suddenly he remembered that he had forgotten to break brush and otherwise mark their path after they had sheered off Reed's tracks.

"Hist!" he whispered. The Indian waited. "It's gettin' dark. Strickland's posse can't trail us."

"Ugh. They foller Reed. Big moon. All same day."

Thus reassured, Dale followed on, grimly fortifying himself to some issue near at hand.

When they came out into the open valley below, dusk had fallen. Nalook had been in that hole before, Dale made certain. He led away from the lake along a brook, and let his horse drink. Then he drank himself, and motioned Dale to do likewise. He went on then in among scrub-oak trees to a grassy open spot where he halted.

"Mebbe long fight," he whispered. "I rope

hoss." Dale removed saddle and bridle from Hoofs and tied him on a long halter.

"What do?" asked Nalook.

"Sneak up on them."

By this time it was dark down in the canyon, though still light above. Nalook led out of the trees and, skirting them, kept to the north wall. Presently he turned and motioned Dale to lift his feet, one after the other, to remove his spurs. The Indian hung them in the crotch of a bush. Scattered trees of larger size began to loom up on this higher ground. The great black wall stood up rimmed with white stars. Dim lights glimmered through the foliage and gradually grew brighter. Nalook might have been a shadow for all the sound he made. Intensely keen and vigilant as Dale was, he could not keep from swishing the grass or making an occasional rustle in the brush. Evidently the Indian did not want to lose time, but he kept cautioning Dale with an expressive backward gesture.

Nalook left the line of timber under the wall and took out into the grove. He now advanced more cautiously than ever. Dale thought his guide must have the eyes of a nighthawk. They passed a dark shack which was open in front and had a projecting roof.

Two campfires were blazing a hundred yards farther on. And a lamp shone through what must have been a window of a cabin.

Presently the Indian halted. He pointed. Then Dale saw horses and men, and he heard gruff voices and the sound of flopping saddles. Some outfit had just arrived. Dale wondered if it was Reed's. If so, he had tarried some little time after getting down into the gorge.

"We go look—see," whispered Nalook in Dale's ear. The Indian seemed devoid of fear. He seemed actuated by more than friendship for Dale and gratitude to Edith Watrous. He hated someone in that horse-thief gang.

Dale followed him, growing stern and hard. He could form no idea of what to do except get the lay of the land, ascertain if possible what Reed was up to, and then go back to the head of the trail and wait for the posse. But he well realized the precarious nature of spying on these desperate men. He feared, too, that Edith Watrous was in vastly more danger of harm than of being held for ransom.

The campfires lighted up two separate circles, both in front of the open-faced shacks. Around the farther one, men were cooking a meal. Dale smelled ham and coffee. The second fire had just been kindled and its bright blaze showed riders moving about still with chaps on, unsaddling and unpacking. Dale pierced the gloom for sight of Edith but failed to locate her.

The Indian sheered away to the right so that a cabin hid the campfires. This structure was a real log cabin of some pretensions. Again a lamp shone through a square window. Faint streaks of light, too, came from chinks between the logs. Dale tried to see through the window, but Nalook led him at a wrong angle. Soon they reached the cabin. Dale felt the rough peeled logs. Nalook had an ear against the log wall. No sound within! Then the Indian, moving with extreme stealth, slipped very slowly along the wall until he came to one of the open chinks. Dale suppressed his eagerness. He must absolutely move without a sound. But that was easy. Thick grass grew beside the cabin. In another tense moment Dale came up with Nalook, who clutched his arm and pulled him down.

There was an aperture between the logs where the mud filling had fallen out. Dale applied his eyes to the small crack. His blood leaped at sight of a big man sitting at a table. Black-browed, scant-bearded, leonine Bill Mason! A lamp with a white globe shed a bright light. Dale saw a gun on the corner of the table, some buckskin sacks, probably containing gold, in front of Mason, and some stacks of greenbacks. An open canvas pack sat on the floor beside the table. Another pack, half full, and surrounded by articles of clothing, added to Dale's conviction that the horse-thief leader was preparing to leave this rendezvous. The dark frown on Mason's brow appeared to cast its shadow over his strong visage.

A woman's voice, high-pitched and sweet, coming through the open door of the cabin, rang stingingly on Dale's ears.

". . . I told you. . . . Keep your horsy hands off me. I can walk."

Mason started up in surprise. "A woman! Now what in hell—?"

Then Edith Watrous, pale and worn, her hair disheveled and her dress so ripped that she had to hold it together, entered the cabin to fix dark and angry eyes upon the dual-sided rancher. Behind her, cool and sardonic, master of the situation, appeared Reed, blocking the door as if to keep anyone else out.

"Mr. Mason, I am Edith—Watrous," panted the girl.

"You needn't tell me that. I know you. . . . What in the world are you doing here?" rejoined Mason slowly, as he arose to his commanding height. He exhibited dismay, but he was courteous.

"I've been—treated to an—outrage. I was in Halsey—visiting friends. There was a horse sale. . . . I went out. I found my horse Dick—and saw other Watrous horses in the bunch. . . . I promptly told this man Reed—it was my horse. He argued with me. . . . Then Hildrith came up—and that precipitated trouble. Reed put something up to Hildrith—I didn't get just what. But it looks bad. I thought he was going to kill Hildrith. But he didn't. He cursed Hildrith and said he'd see what the boss would do about it. . . . They threw me on Reed's horse—made me straddle his saddle in front—and I had to endure a long ride—with my dress up to my head—my legs exposed to brush—and what was more to—to the eyes of Reed and his louts. . . . It was terrible. . . . I'm so perfectly furious that—that—"

She choked in her impassioned utterance.

"Miss Watrous, I don't blame you," said

Mason. "Please understand this is not my doing." Then he fastened his black angry eyes upon his subordinate. "Fool! What's your game?"

"Boss, I didn't have any," returned Reed coolly. "I just saw red. It popped into my head to make off with this stuck-up Watrous woman. And here we are."

"Reed, you're lying. You've got some deep game. . . . Jim Watrous was a friend of mine. I can't stand for such an outrage to his daughter."

"You'll have to stand it, Mason. You and I split, you know, over this last deal. It's just as I gambled would happen. You've ruined us. We're through."

"Ha! I can tell you as much."

"There was a wild-horse hunter down at Halsey—Dale Brittenham. I know about him. He's the man who trailed Ben, Alec and Steve—killed them. He's onto us. I saw that. He'll have a hundred gunners on our trail by sunup."

"Ed, that's not half we're up against," replied the chief gloomily. "This homesteader Rogers, with his trail to Bannock—that settled our hash. Stafford and Watrous have a big outfit after us. I heard it at Bannock.

That's why I sold out. I'm leaving here as soon as I can pack."

"Fine. That's like you. Engineered all the jobs and let us do the stealing while you hobnobbed with the ranchers you robbed. Now you'll leave us to fight. . . . Mason, I'm getting out too—and I'm taking the girl."

"Good God! Ed, it's bad enough to be a horse thief. But to steal a beautiful and well-connected girl like this . . . Why man, it's madness! What for, I ask you?"

"That's my business."

"You want to make Watrous pay to get her back. He'd do it, of course. But he'd tear Montana to pieces, and hang you."

"I might take his money—later. But I confess to a weakness for the young lady. . . . And I'll get even with Hildrith."

"Revenge, eh? You always hated Leale. But what's he got to do with your game?"

"He's crazy in love with her. Engaged to marry her."

"He *was* engaged to me, Mr. Mason," interposed Edith scornfully. "I thought I cared for him. But I really didn't. I despise him now. I wouldn't marry him if he was the last man on earth."

"Reed, does she know?" asked Mason significantly.

"Well, she's not dumb, and I reckon she's got a hunch."

"I'll be _____" Whatever Mason's profanity was he did not give it utterance. "Hildrith! But we had plans to pull stakes and leave this country. Did he intend to marry Miss Watrous and bring her with us? . . . That's not conceivable."

"Boss, he cheated you. He never meant to leave."

Mason made a passionate gesture, as if to strike deep and hard, and his big eyes rolled in a fierce glare. It was plain now to the watching Dale why Reed had wanted Hildrith to face his chief.

"Where's Hildrith?" growled Mason.

"Out by the fire under guard."

"Call him in," Reed went out.

Then Edith turned wonderingly and fearfully to Mason.

"Hildrith is *your* man!" she affirmed rather than queried.

"Yes, Miss Watrous, he was."

"Then *he* is the spy, the scout—the traitor who acted as go-between for you."

"Miss Watrous, he certainly has been my right-hand man for eight years. . . . And I'm afraid Reed and you are right about his being a traitor."

At that juncture Hildrith lunged into the cabin as if propelled viciously from behind. He was ashen-hued under his beard. Reed stamped in after him, forceful and malignant, sure of the issue. But just as Mason, after a steady hard look at his lieutenant, was about to address him, Edith flung herself in front of Hildrith.

"It's all told, Leale Hildrith," she cried, with a fury of passion. "Reed gave you away. Mason corroborated him. . . . *You* are the tool of these men. *You* were the snake in the grass. *You*, the liar who ingratiated himself into my father's confidence. Made love to me! Nagged me until I was beside myself! . . . But your wrong to me—your betrayal of Dad—these fall before your treachery to Dale Brittenham. . . . You let *him* take on your guilt. . . . Oh, I see it all now. It's ghastly. That man loved you. . . . You despicable—despicable—"

Edith broke off, unable to find further words. With tears running down her colorless cheeks, her eyes magnificent with piercing fire, she manifestly enthralled Reed with her beauty and passion. She profoundly impressed Mason and she struck deep into what manhood the stricken Hildrith had left.

"All true, Bill, I'm sorry to confess," he

said, his voice steady. "I'm offering no excuse. But look at her, man . . . look at her! And then you'll understand."

"What's that, Miss, about Dale Brittenham?" queried Mason.

"Brittenham is a wild-horse hunter," answered Edith, catching her breath. "Hildrith befriended him once. Dale loved Hildrith. . . . When Stafford came to see Dad—after the last raid—he accused Dale of being the spy who kept your gang posted. The go-between. He had the sheriff come to arrest Dale. . . . Oh, I see it all now. Dale *knew* Hildrith was the traitor. He sacrificed himself for Hildrith—to pay his debt—or because he thought I loved the man. For us both! . . . He drew a gun on Bayne—said Stafford was right—that *he* was the horse-thief spy . . . then he rode away."

It was a poignant moment. No man could have been unaffected by the girl's tragic story. Mason paced to and fro, then halted behind the table.

"Boss, that's not all," interposed Reed triumphantly. "Down at Halsey, Hildrith showed his color—and what meant most to him. Brittenham was there, as I've told you. And *he* was onto us. I saw the jig was up. I told Hildrith. I put it up to him. To de-

229

clare himself. Every man there had waked up to the fact that we were horse thieves. I asked Hildrith to make his stand—for or against us. He failed us, boss."

"Reed, that was a queer thing for you to insist on," declared Mason, in stern doubt. "Hildrith's cue was the same as mine. Respectability. Could you expect him to betray himself there—before all Halsey and his sweetheart, too?"

"I knew he wouldn't. But I meant it."

"You wanted to show him up, before them all, especially her?"

"I certainly did."

"Well, you're low-down yourself, Reed, when it comes to one you hate."

"All's fair in love and war," replied the other with a flippant laugh.

The chief turned to Hildrith. "I'm not concerned with the bad blood between you and Reed. But—is he lying?"

"No. But down at Halsey I didn't understand he meant me to give myself away," replied Hildrith, with the calmness of bitter resignation. He had played a great game, for a great stake, and he had lost. Friendship, loyalty, treachery, were nothing compared to his love for this girl.

"Would you have done so if you had understood Reed?"

"No. Why should I? There was no disloyalty in that. If I'd guessed that, I'd have shot him."

"You didn't think quick and right. That'd have been your game. Too late, Hildrith. I've a hunch it's too late for all of us. . . . You meant to marry Miss Watrous if she'd have you?"

"Why ask that?"

"Well, it was unnecessary. . . . And you really let this Brittenham sacrifice himself for you?"

"Yes, I'd have sacrificed anyone—my own brother!"

"I see. That was dirty, Leale. . . . But after all these things, don't . . . You've been a faithful pard for many years. God knows a woman . . ."

"Boss, he betrayed *you*," interrupted Reed stridently. "All the rest doesn't count. He split with you. He absolutely was not going to leave the country with you."

"I get that—hard as it is to believe," rasped Mason, and he took up the big gun from the table and deliberately cocked it.

Edith cried out low and falteringly. "Oh— don't kill him! If it was for me—spare him!"

Reed let out that sardonic laugh. "Bah! He'll deny—he'll lie with his last breath."

"That wouldn't save you, Leale—but—" Mason halted, the dark embodiment of honor among thieves.

"Hell! I deny nothing," rang out Hildrith, with something grand in his defiance. "It's all true. I broke over the girl. I was through with you, Mason—you and your raids, you and your lousy sneak here—you and your low-down . . ."

The leveled gun boomed to cut short Hildrith's wild denunciation. Shot through the heart, he swayed a second, his distorted visage fixing, and then, with a single explosion of gasping breath, he fell backward through the door.

IV

A heavy cloud of smoke obscured Dale's sight of the center of the cabin. As he leaned there near the window, strung like a quivering wire, he heard the thump of Mason's gun on the table. It made the gold coins jingle in their sacks. The thud of boots and hoarse shouts arose on the far side of the cabin. Then the smoke drifted away to expose Mason hunched back against the table, peering through the door into the blackness. Reed knelt on the floor where Edith had sunk in a faint.

Other members of the gang arrived outside the cabin. "Hyar! It's Hildrith. Reckon the boss croaked him."

"Mebbe Reed did it. He sure was hankerin' to."

"How air you, chief?" called a third man, presenting a swarthy face in the lamplight.

"I'm—all right," replied Mason huskily. "Hildrith betrayed us. I bored him. . . .

Drag him away. . . . You can divide what you find on him."

"Hey, I'm in on that," called Reed, as the swarthy man backed away from the door. "Lay hold, fellers."

Slow, labored footfalls died away. Mason opened his gun to eject the discharged shell and to replace it with one from his belt.

"She keeled over," said Reed as he lifted the girl's head.

"So I see. . . . Sudden and raw for a tenderfoot. I'm damn glad she hated him. . . . Did you see him feeling for his gun?"

"No. It's just as well I took that away from him on the way up. Nothing yellow about Hildrith at the finish."

"Queer what a woman can do to a man! Reed, haven't you lost your head over this one?"

"Hell yes!" exploded the other.

"Better turn her loose. She'll handicap you. This hole will be swarming with posses tomorrow."

"You're sloping tonight?"

"I am. . . . How many horses did you sell?"

"Eighty odd. None under a hundred dollars. And we drove back the best."

"Keep it. Pay your outfit. We're square.

My advise is let this Watrous girl go, and make tracks away from here."

"Thanks . . . But I won't leave my tracks," returned Reed constrainedly. "She's coming too."

"Pack her out of here. . . . Reed, I wouldn't be in your boots for a million."

"And just why, boss?"

"Women always were your weakness. Your only one. You'll hang on to the Watrous girl."

"You bet your life I will."

"Don't bet my life on it. You're gambling your own. And you'll lose it."

Reed picked up the reviving Edith and took her through the door, turning sidewise to keep from striking her head. Dale's last glimpse of his gloating expression, as he gazed down into her face, nerved him to instant and reckless action. Reed had turned to the left outside the door, which gave Dale the impression that he did not intend to carry the girl toward the campfires.

Nalook touched Dale and silently indicated that he would go around his end of the cabin. Dale turned to the left. At the corner he waited to peer out. He saw a dark form cross the campfire light. Reed! He was turning away from his comrades, now engaged in a heated hubbub, no doubt over money and valuables they had found on Hildrith.

Dale had to fight his overwhelming eagerness. He stole out to follow Reed. The man made directly for the shack that Dale and Nalook had passed on their stalk to the cabin. Dale did not stop to see if the Indian followed, though he expected him to do so. Dale held himself to an absolutely noiseless stealth. The deep grass made that possible.

Edith let out a faint cry, scarcely audible. It seemed to loose springs of fire in Dale's muscles. He glided on, gaining upon the outlaw with his burden. They drew away from the vicinity of the campfires. Soon Dale grew sufficiently accustomed to the starlight to keep track of Reed. The girl was speaking incoherently. Dale would rather have had her still unconscious. She might scream and draw Reed's comrades in that direction.

Under the trees, between the bunches of scrub oak, Reed hurried. His panting breath grew quite audible. Edith was no slight burden, especially as she had begun to struggle in his arms.

"Where? . . . Who? Let me down," she cried, but weakly.

"Shut up, or I'll bat you one," he panted.

The low shack loomed up blacker than the shadows. A horse, tethered in the gloom, snorted at Reed's approach. Dale, now only a few paces behind the outlaw, gathered all his forces for a spring.

"Let me go. . . . Let me go. . . . I'll scream—"

"Shut up, I tell you. If you scream I'll choke you. If you fight, I'll beat you."

"But, Reed—for God's sake! . . . You're not drunk. You must be mad—if you mean . . ."

"Girl, I didn't know what—I meant—when I grabbed you down there," he panted, passionately. "But I know now. . . . I'm taking you away—Edith Watrous—out of Montana. . . . But tonight, by heaven! . . ."

Dale closed in swiftly and silently. With relentless strength he crushed a strangling hold around Reed's neck. The man snorted as his head went back. The girl dropped with a sudden gasp. Then Dale, the fingers of his left hand buried in Reed's throat, released his right hand to grasp his gun. He did not dare to shoot, but he swung the weapon to try to stun Reed. He succeeded in landing only a glancing blow.

"Aggh!" gasped Reed, and for an instant his body appeared to sink.

Dale tried to strike again. Because of Reed's sudden grip on his arm he could not exert enough power. The gun stuck. Dale felt it catch in the man's coat. Reed let out a strangled yell, which Dale succeeded in choking off again.

Suddenly the outlaw let go Dale's right hand and reached for his gun. He got to it, but could not draw, due to Dale's constricting arm. Dale pressed with all his might. They staggered, swayed, bound together as with bands of steel. Dale saw that if his hold loosened on either Reed's throat or gun hand, the issue would be terribly perilous. Reed was the larger and more powerful, though now at a disadvantage. Dale hung on like the grim death he meant to mete out to this man.

Suddenly, with a tremendous surge Reed broke Dale's hold and bent him back. Then Dale saw he would be forced to shoot. But even as he struggled with the gun, Reed, quick as a cat, intercepted it, and with irresistible strength turned the weapon away while he drew his own. Dale was swift to grasp that with his left hand. A terrific struggle ensued, during which the grim and silent combatants both lost hold of their guns.

Reed succeeded in drawing a knife, which

he swung aloft. Dale caught his wrist and jerked down on it with such tremendous force that he caused the outlaw to stab himself in the side. Then Dale grappled him round the waist, pinning both arms to Reed's sides, so that he was unable to withdraw the knife. Not only that, but soon Dale's inexorable pressure sank the blade in to the hilt. A horrible panting sound escaped Reed's lips.

Any moment Nalook might come to end this desperate struggle. The knife stuck in Reed's side, clear to the hilt. Dale had the thought that he must hold on until Reed collapsed. Then he would have to run with Edith and try to get up the trail. He could not hope to find the horses in that gloomy shadow.

Reed grew stronger in his frenzy. He whirled so irresistibly that he partly broke Dale's hold. They plunged down, with Dale on the top and Reed under him. Dale had his wind almost shut off. Another moment . . . But Reed rolled like a bear. Dale, now underneath, wound his left arm around Reed. Over and over they rolled, against the cabin, back against a tree, and then over a bank. The shock broke both Dale's holds. Reed essayed to yell, but only a hoarse sound came forth. Suddenly he had weakened. Dale beat at him with his right fist. Then he reached for the knife in Reed's side, found the haft, and wrenched so terrificly that he cracked Reed's ribs. The man suddenly relaxed. Dale tore the knife out and buried it in Reed's breast.

That ended the fight. Reed sank shudderingly into a limp state. Dale slowly got up, drawing the knife with him. He had sustained no injury that he could ascertain at the moment. He was wet with sweat or blood, probably both. He slipped the knife in his belt, and untied his scarf to wipe his hands and face. Then he climbed up the bank, expecting to see Edith's white blouse in the darkness.

But he did not see it. Nor was Nalook there. He called low. No answer! He began to search around on the ground. He found his gun. Then he went into the shack. Edith was gone and Nalook had not come. Possibly he might have come while the fight was going on down over the bank and, seeing the chance to save Edith, had made off with her to the horses.

Dale listened. The crickets were in loud voice. He could see the campfires, and heard nothing except the thud of hoofs. They seemed fairly close. He retraced his steps back to the shack. Reed's horse was gone. Dale strove for control over his whirling thoughts. He feared that Edith, in her terror, had run off at random, to be captured again by some of the outlaws. After a moment's consideration, he dismissed that as untenable. She had fled, unquestionably, but without a cry, which augured well. Dale searched the black rim for the notch that marked the trail. Then he set off.

Reaching the belt of brush under the rim he followed it until he came to an opening he thought he recognized. A stamp of hoofs electrified him. He hurried toward it and presently emerged into a glade less gloomy. First his keen sight distinguished Edith's white blouse. She was either sitting or lying on the ground. Then he saw the horses. As he hurried forward, Nalook met him.

"Nalook! Is she all right?" he whispered eagerly.

"All same okay. No hurt."

"What'd you do?"

"Me foller. See girl run. Me ketch."

"Go back to that shack and search Reed. He must have a lot of money on him. . . . We rolled over a bank."

"Ugh!" The Indian glided away.

Dale went on to find Edith sitting propped against a stone. He could not distinguish her features but her posture was eloquent of spent force.

"Edith," he called gently.

"Oh—Dale! . . . Are you—?"

"I'm all right," he replied hastily.

"You—you killed him?"

"Of course. I had to. Are you hurt?"

"Only bruised. That ride! . . . Then he handled me—Oh, the brute! I'm glad you killed . . . I saw you bend him back—hit him. I knew you. But it was awful. . . . And seeing Leale murdered—so suddenly—right before my eyes—that was worse."

"Put all that out of your mind. . . . Let me help you up. We can't stay here long. Your hands are like ice," he whispered as he got her up.

"I'm freezing—to death," she replied. "This thin waist. I left my coat in the buckboard."

"Here. Slip into mine." Dale helped her into his coat, and then began to rub her cold hands between his.

"Dale, I wasn't afraid of Reed—at first. I scorned him. I saw how his men liked that. I kept telling him that you would kill him for this outrage to me. That if *you* didn't

Dad would hang him. But there in Mason's cabin—there I realized my danger. . . . You must have been close."

"Yes. Nalook and I watched between the logs. I saw it all. But I tell you to forget it."

"Oh, will I ever? . . . Dale, you saved me from God only knows what," she whispered, and putting her arms around his neck, she leaned upon his breast, and looked up. Out of her pale face great midnight eyes that reflected the starlight transfixed him with their mystery and passion. "You liar! You fool!" she went on, her soft voice belying the hard words. "You poor misguided man! To dishonor your name for Hildrith's sake! To tell Stafford he was right! To let Dad hear you say you were a horse thief! . . . Oh! I shall never forgive you!"

"My dear. I did it—for Leale—and perhaps more for your sake," replied Dale unsteadily. "I thought you loved him. That was his chance to reform. He would have done it, too, if—"

"I don't care what he would have done. I imagined I loved him. But I didn't. I was a vain, silly, headstrong girl. And I was influenced. I don't believe I ever could have married him—after you brought back my horses. I didn't realize then. But when I kissed you—Oh, Dale! Something tore through my heart. I know now. It was love. Even then! . . . Oh, I needed this horrible experience. It has awakened me. . . . Oh, Dale, if I loved you then, what do you think it is now?"

"I can't think—dearest," whispered Dale huskily, as he drew her closer, and bent over her to lay his face against her hair. "Only, if you're not out of your mind, I'm the luckiest man thet ever breathed."

"Dale, I'm distraught, yes, and my heart is bursting. But I know I love you . . . love you—love you! Oh, with all my mind and soul."

Dale heard in a tumultuous exaltation, and he stood holding her with an intensely vivid sense of the place and moment. The ragged rim loomed above them, dark and forbidding, as if to warn; the incessant chirp of crickets, the murmur of running water, the rustle of the wind in the brush, proved that he was alive and awake, living the most poignant moment of his life.

Then Nalook glided silently into the glade. Dale released Edith, and stepped back to meet the Indian. Nalook thrust into his hands a heavy bundle tied up in a scarf.

"Me keep gun," he said, and bent over his saddle.

"What'll we do, Nalook?" asked Dale.

"Me stay—watch trail. You take girl Halsey."

"Dale, I couldn't ride it. I'm exhausted. I can hardly stand," interposed Edith.

"Reckon I'd get lost in the dark," returned Dale thoughtfully. "I've a better plan. There's a homesteader in this valley. Man named Rogers. I knew him over in the mountains. An' I ran across his cabin a day or so ago. It's not far. I'll take you there. Then tomorrow I'll go with you to Bannock, or send you with him."

"Send me!"

"Yes. I've got to be here. Strickland agreed to send a posse after me in half an hour—an' later a big outfit of cowboys."

"But you've rescued me. Need you stay? Nalook can guide these men."

"I reckon I want to help clean out these horse thieves."

"Bayne is on *your* trail with a posse."

"Probably he's with Stafford's outfit."

"That won't clear you of Stafford's accusation."

"No. But Strickland an' his outfit will clear me. I must be here when thet fight comes off. *If* it comes. You heard Mason say he was leavin' tonight. I reckon they'll all get out pronto."

"Dale!—you—you might get shot—or even . . . Oh, these are wicked, hard men!" exclaimed Edith, as she fastened persuasive hands on his coatless arms.

"Thet's the chance I must run to clear my name, Edith," he rejoined gravely.

"You took a fearful chance with Reed."

"Yes. But he had you in his power."

"My life and more were at stake then," she said earnestly. "It's still my love and my happiness."

"Edith, I'll have Nalook beside me an' we'll fight like Indians. I swear I'll come out of it alive."

"Then—go ahead—anyway . . ." she whispered almost inaudibly, and let her nerveless hands drop from him.

"Nalook, you watch the trail," ordered Dale. "Stop any man climbing out. When Strickland's posse comes, hold them till the cowboys get here. If I hear shots this way, I'll come pronto."

The Indian grunted and, taking up his rifle, stole away. Dale untied and led his horse up to where his saddle lay. Soon he had him saddled and bridled. Then he put on his spurs, which the Indian had remembered to get.

"Come," said Dale, reaching for Edith. When he lifted her, it came home to him why Reed had not found it easy to carry her.

"That's comfortable, if I can stay on," she said, settling herself.

"Hoofs, old boy," whispered Dale to his horse. "No actin' up. This'll be the most precious load you ever carried."

Then Dale, rifle in hand, took the bridle and led the horse out into the open. The lake gleamed like a black starlit mirror. Turning to the right, Dale slowly chose the ground and walked a hundred steps or more before he halted to listen. He went on and soon crossed the trail. Beyond that he breathed easier, and did not stop again until he had half circled the lake. He saw lights across the water up among the trees, but heard no alarming sound.

"How're you ridin'?" he whispered to Edith.

"I can stick on if it's not too far."

"Half a mile more."

As he proceeded, less fearful of being heard, he began to calculate about where he should look for Rogers' canyon. He had carefully marked it almost halfway between the two lakes and directly across from the highest point of the rim. When Dale got abreast of this he headed to the right, and was soon under the west wall. Then despite the timber on the rim and the shadowed background, he located a gap which he made certain marked the canyon.

But he could not find any trail leading into it. Therefore he began to work a cautious way through the thickets. The gurgle and splash of running water guided him. It was so pitch black that he had to feel his way. The watercourse turned out to be rocky and he abandoned that. When he began to fear he was headed wrong a dark tunnel led him out into the open canyon. He went on and turned a corner to catch the gleam of a light. Then he rejoiced at his good fortune. In a few minutes more he arrived at the cabin. The door was open. Dale heard voices.

"Hey, Rogers, are you home?" he called.

An exclamation and thud of bootless feet attested to the homesteader's presence. The next instant he appeared in the door.

"Who's thar?"

"Brittenham," replied Dale, and lifting Edith off the saddle, he carried her up on the porch into the light. Rogers came out in amazement. His wife cried from the door, "For the land's sake!"

"Wal, a gurl! Aw, don't say she's hurt," burst out the homesteader.

"You bet it's a girl. An' thank heaven she's sound! Jim Watrous's daughter, Rogers. She was kidnaped by Reed at the Halsey horse sale. Thet happened this afternoon. I just got her back. Now, Mrs. Rogers, will you take her in for tonight? Hide her someplace."

"That I will. She can sleep in the loft . . . Come in, my dear child. You're white as a sheet."

"Thank you. I've had enough to make me green," replied Edith, limping into the cabin.

Dale led Rogers out of earshot. "Hell will bust loose here about tomorrow," he said, and briefly told about the several posses en route for the horse thieves' stronghold, and the events relating to the capture and rescue of Edith.

"By gad! Thet's all good," ejaculated the homesteader. "But it's not so good—all of us hyar if they have a big fight."

"Maybe the gang will slope. Mason is leavin'. I heard him tell Reed. An' Reed meant to take the girl. I don't know about the rest of them."

"Wal, these fellers ain't likely to rustle in the dark. They've been too secure. An' they figger they can't be surprised at night."

"If Mason leaves by the lower trail, he'll get shot. My Indian pard is watchin' there."

"Gosh, I hope he tries it."

"Mason had his table loaded with bags of coins an' stacks of bills. We sure ought to get thet an' pay back the people he's robbed."

"It's a good bet Mason won't take the upper trail. . . . Brittenham, you look fagged. Better have some grub an' drink. An' sleep a little."

"Sure. But I'm a bloody mess, an' don't want the women to see me. Fetch me somethin' out here."

Later Dale and Rogers walked down to the valley. They did not see any lights or hear any sounds. Both ends of the gorge, where the trails led up, were dark and silent. They returned, and Dale lay down on the porch on some sheepskins. He did not expect to sleep. His mind was too full. Only the imminence of a battle could have kept his mind off the wondrous and incomprehensible fact of Edith's avowal. After pondering over the facts and probabilities Dale decided a fight was inevitable. Mason and Reed had both impressed him as men at the end of their ropes. The others would, no doubt, leave, though not so hurriedly, and most probably would be met on the way out.

Long after Rogers' cabin was dark and its inmates wrapped in slumber, Dale lay awake, listening, thinking, revolving plans to get Edith safely away and still not seem to shirk his share of the fight. But at last, worn out by strenuous activity and undue call on his emotions, Dale fell asleep.

A step on the porch aroused him. It was broad daylight. Rogers was coming in with an armload of firewood.

"All serene, Brittenham," he said, with satisfaction.

"Good. I'll wash an' slip down to get a look at the valley."

"Wal, I'd say if these outfits of cowboys was on hand, they'd be down long ago."

"Me too." Dale did not go clear out into the gateway of the valley. He climbed to a ruddy eminence and surveyed the gorge from the lookout. Sweeping the gray-green valley with eager gaze, he failed to see a moving object. Both upper and lower ends of the gorge appeared as vacant as they were silent. But at length he quickened sharply to columns of blue smoke rising above the timber up from the lower lake. He watched for a good hour. The sun rose over the gap at the east rim. Concluding that posses and cowboys had yet to arrive, Dale descended the bluff and retraced his steps toward the cabin.

He considered sending Edith out in charge of Rogers, to conduct her as far as Bannock. This idea he at once conveyed to Rogers.

"Don't think much of it," returned the homesteader forcibly. "Better hide her an' my family in a cave. I know where they'll be safe until this fracas is over."

"Well! I reckon thet is better."

"Come in an' eat. Then we'll go scoutin'. An' if we see any riders, we'll rustle back to hide the women an' kids."

Dale had about finished a substantial breakfast when he thought he heard a horse neigh somewhere at a distance. He ran out on the porch and was suddenly shocked to a standstill. Scarcely ten paces out stood a man with leveled rifle.

"Hands up, Britt," he ordered, with a hissing breath. Two other men, just behind him, leaped forward to present guns, and one of them yelled, "Hyar he is, Bayne."

"Rustle! Up with 'em!"

Then Dale, realizing the cold bitter fact

of an unlooked-for situation, shot up his arms just as Rogers came stamping out.

"What the hell? *Who . . .*"

Six or eight more men, guns in hands, appeared at the right, led by the red-faced sheriff of Salmon. He appeared to be bursting with importance and vicious triumph. Dale surveyed the advancing group, among whom he recognized old enemies, and then his gaze flashed back to the first man with the leveled rifle. This was none other than Pickens, a crooked young horse trader who had all the reason in the world to gloat over rounding up Dale in this way.

"Guess I didn't have a hunch up thar, fellers, when we crossed this trail," declared Bayne in loud voice. "Guess I didn't measure his hoss tracks down at Watrous's for nothin'!"

"Bayne, you got the drop," spoke up Dale coolly, "and I'm not fool enough to draw in the face of thet."

"You did draw on me once, though, didn't you, wild-hoss hunter?" called Bayne derisively.

"Yes."

"An' you told Stafford he was right, didn't you?"

"Yes, but—"

"No buts. You admitted you was a hoss thief, didn't you?"

"Rogers here can explain thet, if you won't listen to me."

"Wal, Brittenham, your homesteadin' pard can explain thet after we hang you!"

Rogers stalked off the porch in the very face of the menacing guns and confronted Bayne in angry expostulation.

"See here, Mister Bayne, you're on the wrong track."

"We want no advice from you," shouted Bayne. "An' you'd better look out or we'll give you the same dose."

"Boss, he's shore one of this hoss-thief gang," spoke up a lean, weathered member of the posse.

"My name's Rogers. I'm a homesteader. I have a wife an' two children. There are men in Bannock who'll vouch for my honesty," protested Rogers.

"Reckon so. But they ain't here. You stay out of this. . . . Hold him up, men."

Two of them prodded the homesteader with cocked rifles, a reckless and brutal act that would have made the bravest man turn gray. Rogers put up shaking hands.

"Friend Rogers, don't interfere," warned

Dale, who had grasped the deadly nature of Bayne's procedure. The sheriff believed Dale was one of the mysterious band of thieves that had been harassing the ranchers of Salmon River Valley for a long time. It had galled him, no doubt, to fail to bring a single thief to justice. Added to that was an animosity toward Dale and a mean leaning to exercise his office. He wanted no trial. He would brook no opposition. Dale stood there a self-confessed criminal.

"Rope Brittenham," ordered Bayne. "Tie his hands behind his back. Bore him if he as much as winks."

Two of the posse dragged Dale off the porch, and in a moment had bound him securely. Then Dale realized too late that he should have leaped while he was free to snatch a gun from one of his captors, and fought it out. He had not taken seriously Bayne's threat to hang him. But he saw now that unless a miracle came to pass, he was doomed. The thought was so appalling that it clamped him momentarily in an icy terror. Edith was at the back of that emotion. He had faced death before without flinching, but to be hanged while Edith was there, possibly a witness—that would be too horrible. Yet he read it in the hard visages of Bayne and his men. By a tremendous effort he succeeded in getting hold of himself.

"Bayne, this job is not law," he expostulated. "It's revenge. When my innocence is proved, you'll be in a tight fix."

"Innocence! Hell, men, didn't you confess your guilt?" ejaculated Bayne. "Stafford heard you, same as Watrous an' his friends."

"All the same, thet was a lie."

"Aw, it was? My Gawd, man, but you take chances with your life! An' what'd you lie for?"

"I lied for Edith Watrous."

Bayne stared incredulously and then he guffawed. He turned to his men.

"Reckon we better shet off his wind. The man's plumb loco."

From behind Dale a noose, thrown by a lanky cowboy, sailed and widened to encircle his head, and to be drawn tight. The hard knot came just under Dale's chin and shut off the hoarse cry that formed involuntarily.

"Over thet limb, fellers," called out Bayne briskly, pointing to a spreading branch of a piñon tree some few yards farther out. Dale was dragged under it. The loose end of the rope was thrown over the branch, to fall into eager hands.

"Dirty bizness, Bayne, you _____!" shouted Rogers, shaken by horror and wrath. "So help me Gawd, you'll rue it!"

Bayne leered malignantly, plainly in the grip of passion too strong for reason.

"Thar's five thousand dollars' reward wrapped up in this wild-hoss hunter's hide an' I ain't takin' any chance of losin' it."

Dale forced a strangled utterance. "Bayne —I'll double thet—if you'll arrest me . . . give . . . fair trial."

"Haw! Haw! Wal, listen to our ragged hoss thief talk big money."

"Boss, he ain't got two bits. . . . We're wastin' time."

"Swing him, fellers!"

Four or five men stretched the rope and had lifted Dale to his toes when a piercing shriek from the cabin startled them so violently that they let him down again. Edith Watrous came flying out, half dressed, her hair down, her face blanched. Her white blouse fluttered in her hand as she ran, barefooted, across the grass.

"Merciful heaven! Dale! *That rope!*" she screamed, and as the shock of realization came, she dropped her blouse to the ground and stood stricken before the staring men, her bare round arms and lovely shoulders shining white in the sunlight. Her eyes darkened, dilated, enlarged as her consciousness grasped the significance here, and then fixed in terror.

Dale's ghastly sense of death faded. This girl would save him. A dozen Baynes could not contend with Edith Watrous, once she was roused.

"Edith, they were about—to hang me."

"*Hang you?*" she cried, suddenly galvanized. "These men? . . . *Bayne!*"

Leaping red blood burned out the pallor of her face. It swept away in a wave, leaving her whiter than before, and with eyes like coals of living fire.

"Miss—Watrous. What you—doin' here?" queried Bayne, halting, confused by this apparition.

"I'm here—not quite too late," she replied, as if to herself, and a ring of certainty in her voice followed hard on the tremulous evidence of her thought.

"Kinda queer—meetin' you up here in this outlaw den," went on Bayne with a nervous cough.

"Bayne . . . I remember," she said ponderingly, ignoring his statement. "The gossip—linking Dale's name with this horse-thief outfit . . . Stafford! . . . Your intent to arrest Dale! . . . His drawing on you! His strange acceptance of Stafford's accusation!"

"Nothin' strange about thet, Miss," rejoined Bayne brusquely. "Brittenham was caught in a trap. An' like a wolf he bit back."

"That confession had to do with me, Mister Bayne," she retorted.

"So he said. But I ain't disregardin' same."

"You are not arresting him," she asserted swiftly.

"Nope, I ain't."

"But didn't you let him explain?" she queried.

"I didn't want no cock-an'-bull explainin' from him or this doubtful pard of his here, Rogers. . . . I'll just hang Brittenham an' let Rogers talk afterwards. Reckon he'll not have much to say then."

"So that's your plan, you miserable thick-headed skunk of a sheriff?" she exclaimed in lashing scorn. She swept her flaming eyes from Bayne to his posse, all of whom appeared uneasy over this interruption. "Pickens! . . . Hall! . . . Jason Pike! And some more hard nuts from Salmon. Why, if you were honest yourself, you'd arrest them. My

259

father could put Pickens in jail. . . . Bayne, your crew of a posse reflects suspiciously on you."

"Wal, I ain't carin' for what you think. It's plain to me you've took powerful with this hoss thief an' I reckon thet reflects suspicions on you, Miss," rejoined Bayne, galled to recrimination.

A scarlet blush wiped out the whiteness of Edith's neck and face. She burned with shame and fury. That seemed to remind her of herself, of her half-dressed state, and she bent to pick up her blouse. When she rose to slip her arms through the garment she was pale again. She forgot to button it.

"You dare not hang Brittenham."

"Wal, lady, I just do," he declared, but he was weakening somehow.

"You shall not!"

"Better go indoors, Miss. It ain't pleasant to see a man hang an' kick an' swell an' grow black in the face."

Bayne had no conception of the passion and courage of a woman. He blundered into the very speeches that made Edith a lioness.

"Take that rope off his neck," she commanded, as a queen might have to slaves.

The members of the posse shifted from one foot to the other, and betrayed that they would have looked to their leader had they been able to remove their fascinated gaze from this girl. Pickens, the nearest to her, moved back a step, holding his rifle muzzle up. The freckles stood out awkwardly on his dirty white face.

"Give me that rifle," she cried hotly, and she leaped to snatch at it. Pickens held on, his visage a study in consternation and alarm. Edith let go with one hand and struck him a staggering blow with her fist. Then she fought him for the weapon. Bang! It belched fire and smoke up into the tree. She jerked it away from him and, leaping back, she worked the lever with a swift precision that proved her familiarity with firearms. Without aiming she shot at Pickens' feet. Dale saw the bullet strike up dust between them. Pickens leaped with a wild yell and fled.

Edith whirled upon Bayne. She was magnificent in her rage. Such a thing as fear of these men was as far from her as if she had never experienced such an emotion. Again she worked the action of the rifle. She held it low at Bayne and pulled the trigger. Bang! That bullet sped between his legs, and burned the left one, which flinched as the man called, "Hyar! Stop thet, you fool woman. You'll kill somebody!"

261

"Bayne, I'll kill *you,* if you try to hang Brittenham," she replied, her voice ringing high-keyed but level and cold. "Take that noose off his neck!"

The frightened sheriff made haste to comply.

"Now untie him!"

"Help me hyar—somebody," snarled Bayne, turning Dale around to tear at the rope. "My Gawd, what's this range comin' to when wild women bust loose? _____ the luck! We can't shoot her! We can't rope Jim Watrous's girl!"

"Boss, I reckon it may be jist as well," replied the lean gray man who was helping him, "cause it wasn't regular."

"You men! Put away your guns," ordered Edith. "I wouldn't hesitate to shoot any one of you. . . . Now listen, all of you. . . . Brittenham is no horse thief. He is a man who sacrificed his name—his honor for his friend—and because he thought I loved that friend. Leale Hildrith! *He* was the treacherous spy—the go-between—the liar who deceived my father and me. Dale took his guilt. I never believed it. I followed Dale to Halsey. Hildrith followed me. There we found Ed Reed and his outfit selling Watrous horses. I recognized my own horse, Dick, and I accused Reed. He betrayed Hildrith right there and kidnaped us both, and rode to this hole. . . . We got here last night. Reed took me before Bill Mason. Big Bill, who is leader of this band. They sent for Hildrith. And Mason shot him. Reed made off with me, intending to leave. But Dale had trailed us, and he killed Reed. Then he fetched me here to this cabin. . . . You have my word. I swear this is the truth."

"Wal, I'll be _____!" ejaculated Bayne, who had grown so obsessed by Edith's story that he had forgotten to untie Dale.

"Boss! Hosses comin' hell bent!" shouted one of Bayne's men, running in.

"Whar?"

A ringing trample of swift hoofs on the hard trail drowned further shouts. Dale saw a line of riders sweep round the corner and race right down upon the cabin. They began to shoot into Bayne's posse. There were six riders, all shooting as hard as they were riding, and some of them had two guns leveled. Hoarse yells rose about the banging volley of shots. The horsemen sped on past, still shooting. Bullets thudded into the cabin. The riders vanished in a cloud of dust and the clatter of hoofs died away.

Dale frantically unwound the rope which

Bayne had suddenly let go at the onslaught of the riders. Freeing himself, Dale leaped to Edith, who had dropped the rifle and stood unsteadily, her eyes wild.

"Did they—hit you?" gasped Dale, seizing her.

"No. But look!"

Rogers rushed up to join them, holding a hand to a bloody shoulder. "Some of Mason's outfit," he boomed, and he gazed around with rolling eyes. Pickens lay dead, his bloody head against the tree. Bayne had been shot through the middle. A spreading splotch of red on his shirt under his clutching hands attested to a mortal wound. Three other men lay either groaning or cursing. That left four apparently unscratched, only one of whom, a lean oldish man, showed any inclination to help his comrades.

"Lemme see how bad you're hit," he was growling over one of them.

"Aw, it ain't bad, but it hurts like hell."

"Edith, come, I'll take you in," said Dale, putting his arm around the weakening girl.

"Britt, I've a better idee," put in Rogers. "I'll take her an' my family to the cave where they'll be safe."

"Good! Thet outfit must have been chased."

"We'd have heard shots. I reckon they were rustlin' away and jest piled into us."

The two reached the cabin, where Dale said, "Brace up, Edith. It sure was tough. It'll be all right now."

"Oh, I'm sick," she whispered, as she leaned against him.

Rogers went in, calling to his wife. Dale heard him rummaging around. Soon he appeared in the door and handed a tin box and a bundle of linen to Dale.

"Those hombres out there can take care of their own wounded."

Dale pressed Edith's limp hand and begged earnestly, "Don't weaken now, dear. Good Lord, how wonderful an' terrible you were! . . . Edith, I'll bear a charmed life after this. . . . Go with Rogers. An' don't worry, darlin'. . . . The Mason gang is on the run, thet's sure."

"I'll be all right," she replied with a pale smile. "Go—do what's best—but don't stay long away from me."

Hurrying out, Dale found all save one of the wounded on their feet.

"Wal, thet's decent of you," said the lean, hawk-faced man, as he received the bandages and medicine from Dale. "Bayne jist croaked an' he can stay croaked right there for all

265

I care. I'm sorry he made the mistake takin' you for a hoss thief."

"He paid for it," rejoined Dale grimly. "You must bury him and Pickens. I'll fetch you some tools. But move them away from here."

Dale searched around until he found a spade and mattock, which he brought back. Meanwhile the spokesman of Bayne's posse and Jason Pike had about concluded a hasty binding of the injured men.

"Brittenham, we come down this trail from Bannock. Are there any other ways to get in an' out of this hole?"

"Look here," replied Dale, and squatted down to draw an oval in the dust. "This represents the valley. It runs almost directly north an' south. There's a trail at each end. This trail of Rogers' heads out of here almost due west, an' leads to Bannock. There might be, an' very probably is, another trail on the east side, perhaps back of Mason's camp. But Nalook didn't tell me there was."

"Thet outfit who rid by here to smoke us up—they must have been chased or at least scared."

"Chased, I figure that, though no cowboys appear to be comin' along. You know Stafford an' Watrous were sendin' a big outfit of cowboys up from Salmon. They'll come down the south trail. An' I'm responsible for two more, raised by a rancher named Strickland over at Halsey. They are due an' they'll come in at the lower end of the hole. The north end."

"Wal, I'd like to be in on thet round-up. What say, Jason?"

"Hell, yes. But Tom, you'd better send Jerry an' hike out with our cripples. They'd just handicap us."

"Reckon so. Now let's rustle to put these stiffs under the sod an' the dew. Strip them of valuables. Funny about Bayne. He was sure rarin' to spend that five thousand Stafford offered for Brittenham alive or dead."

"Bayne had some faults. He was some previous on this job. . . . Hyar, fellars, give us a hand."

"I'll rustle my horse," said Dale, and strode off. He had left Hoofs to graze at will, but the sturdy bay was nowhere in sight. Finally Dale found him in Rogers' corral with two other horses. He led Hoofs back to the cabin, and was saddling him when he saw Rogers crossing the brook into the open. Evidently he had taken the women and children somewhere in that direction. Dale's keen eye approved of the dense thicket of brush and trees leading up to a great wall of cliffs and caverns and splintered sections. They would be safely hidden in there.

Then Dale bethought himself of his gun, which Pickens had taken from him. He found it under the tree with the weapons, belts and spurs of the slain men. Dale took up the carbine that Pickens had held, and which Edith had wrenched out of his hands. He decided he would like to keep it, and carried it to the cabin.

Tom and Pike, with the third man, returned from their gruesome task somewhere below. The next move was to send the four cripples, one of whom lurched in his saddle, up the trail to Bannock with their escort.

When Dale turned from a dubious gaze after them, he sighted Nalook riding up from the valley. The Indian appeared to be approaching warily. Dale hallooed and strode out to meet him.

The Indian pointed with dark hand at the hoof tracks in the trail.

"Me come slow—look see."

"Nalook, those tracks were made by six of Mason's outfit who rode through, hell bent for election."

"Me hear shots."

"They killed Bayne an' one of his posse, an' crippled four more."

"Ugh! Bayne jail Injun no more!" Nalook ejaculated with satisfaction.

"I should smile not. But, Nalook, what's doin' down in the hole?"

"Ten paleface, three my people come sunup. No cowboy."

"Well! Thet's odd. Strickland guaranteed a big outfit. I wonder . . . No sign of Stafford's cowboys on the other trail?"

"Me look long, no come."

"Where's thet outfit from Halsey?"

The Indian indicated by gesture that he had detained these men at the rim.

"You watch trail all night?"

Nalook nodded, and his inscrutable eyes directed Dale's to the back of his saddle. A dark coat of heavy material, and evidently covering a bundle, had been bound behind the cantle. Dale put a curious hand on the coat. He felt something hard inside, and that caused him to note how securely and tightly the coat had been tied on. Suddenly a dark red spot gave him a shock. Blood! He touched it to find it a smear glazed over and dry. Dale looked into the bronzed visage and somber eyes of the Indian with a cold sense of certainty.

"Mason?"

The Indian nodded. "Me watch long. Big Bill he come. Two paleface foller. Top trail. Me watch. Big powwow. They want gold. Mason no give. Cuss like hell. They shoot. Me kill um."

"Nalook, you just beat hell!" ejaculated Dale, at once thrilled and overcome at the singular way things were working out. He had not forgotten the sacks of gold and pile of greenbacks on Mason's table. To let the robber chief make off with that had been no easy surrender.

"Me beat hoss thief," replied the Indian, taking Dale literally. "Big Bill no good. He take Palouse girl away."

"Aha! So thet's why you've been so soft and gentle with these horse thieves. . . . Na-look, I don't want anyone, not even Rogers, to see this coat an' what's in it."

"Me savvy. Where hide?"

"Go to the barn. Hide it in the loft under the hay."

Nalook rode on by the cabin. Dale sat down on the porch to wait for his return and the others. He found himself trembling with the significance of the moment. He had possession of a large amount of money, probably more than enough to reimburse all the ranchers from whom cattle and horses had been stolen. Moreover, the losses of any poor ranchers over on the Palouse range would have to be made good. That, however, could hardly make much of a hole in the fortune Mason had no doubt been accumulating for years.

The Indian came back from the barn, leading his horse. He sat down beside Dale and laid a heavy hand on his arm.

"No look! . . . Me see man watchin' on rock," he said.

"Where?" asked Dale, checking a start.

Nalook let go of Dale and curved a thumb that indicated the bare point on the west rim, in fact the only lookout on that side, and the one from which he had planned to get Rogers' signal. On the moment Rogers returned.

"Rogers, stand pat now," said Dale. "The Indian sighted someone watchin' us. From the bare point you know, where I was to come for our signal."

"Wal, thet ain't so good," growled the homesteader with concern. "Must be them cusses who busted through here, shootin'. By thunder, I'd like to get a crack at the feller who gave me this cut in the shoulder."

"I forgot, Rogers. Is it serious?"

"Not atall. But it's sore an' makes me sore. I was fool enough to show it to my wife. But I couldn't tie it up myself. Blood always sickens wimmen."

"What do?" asked the Indian.

"We won't let on we know we're bein' watched. . . . Rogers, could any scout on thet point see where you took your wife an' Edith?"

"I reckon not. Fact is, I'm not sure."

"Well, you stay here. It's reasonable to figure these horse thieves won't come back. An' if any others came out of the valley, they'll be stretchin' leather. You keep hid. I'll take Nalook an' these men, an' see what's up out there."

"Couldn't do no better. But you want to come back by dark, 'cause thet girl begged me to tell you," replied Rogers, earnestly. "Gosh, I never saw such eyes in a human's face. You be _____ careful, Britt. Thet girl is jist livin' for you."

"Rogers, I'm liable to be so careful thet I'll be yellow," rejoined Dale soberly.

Soon Dale was jogging down the trail at the head of the quartet. In the brush cover at the outlet of the canyon they had to ride single file. Once out in the valley Nalook was the first to call attention to horses scattered here and there all over the green. They evidently had broken out of the pasture or had been freed. Dale viewed them and calculated their number with satisfaction. Not a rider in sight!

Dale led at a brisk trot. It did not take long to reach the lower trail. Here he sent Nalook up to fetch down the ten white men and four Indians that Strickland had been able to gather together. After an interval of keen survey of the valley Dale voiced his surprise to Tom and Jason.

"Queer all right," agreed the older man. "Kinda feels like a lull before the storm."

"I wonder what happened to Stafford's outfit. They've had hours more time than needed. They've missed the trail."

The Indian was clever. He sent the men down on foot, some distance apart. They made but little noise and raised scarcely any dust. Dale looked this posse over keenly. They appeared to be mostly miners, rough, bearded, matured men. There were, however, several cowboys, one of whom Dale had seen at the horse sale. The last two to descend the trail proved to be Strickland with the Indian.

"By jove, you, Strickland!" ejaculated Dale, in surprise.

"I couldn't keep out of it, Brittenham," returned the rancher dryly. "This sort of thing is my meat. Besides, I'm pretty curious and sore."

"How about your cowboys?"

"I'm sure I can't understand why those outfits haven't shown up. But I didn't send for my own. I've only a few now and they're out on the range. Sanborn and Drew were to send theirs, with an outfit from the Circle Bar. Damn strange! This is stern range business that concerns the whole range."

"Maybe not so strange. If they were friends of Mason!"

"Thick as hops!" exclaimed Strickland with a snort.

"We'll go slow an' wait for Stafford's cowboys," decided Dale ponderingly.

"Hoss thieves all get away mebbe," interposed Nalook, plainly not liking this idea of waiting.

"All right, Nalook. What's your advice?"

"Crawl like Injun," he replied, and spread wide his fingers. "Mebbe soon shoot heap much."

"Strickland, this Indian is simply great. We'll be wise to listen to him. Take your men an' follow him. Cowboy, you hide here at the foot of the trial an' give the alarm if any riders come down. We've reason to believe some of the gang are scoutin' along this west rim. I'll slip up on top an' have a look at Mason's camp."

Drawing his rifle from its saddle sheath, Dale removed his coat and spurs. Nalook was already leading his horse into the brush, and the Indians followed him. Strickland, with a caustic word of warning to Dale, waved his men after the Indian.

"Come with me. Throw your chaps an' spurs, cowboy," advised Dale, and addressed himself to the steep trail. Soon the long-legged cowboy caught up with him, but did not speak until they reached the rim. Dale observed that he also carried a rifle and had the look of a man who could use it.

"Brittenham, if I see any sneakin' along the rim, shall I smoke 'em up?" he queried.

"You bet, unless they're cowboys."

"Wal, I shore know thet breed."

They parted. Dale stole into the evergreens, walking on his toes. He wound in and out, keeping as close to the rim as possible, and did not halt until he had covered several hundred yards. Then he listened and tried to peer over the rim. But he heard nothing and could see only the far part of the valley. Another quarter of a mile ought to put him where he could view Mason's camp. But he had not gone quite so far when a thud of hoofs on soft ground brought him up tight-skinned and cold. A horse was approaching at some little distance from the rim. Dale glided out to meet it. Presently he saw a big sombrero, then a red youthful face, above some evergreens. In another moment horse and rider came into view. Leveling his rifle, Dale called him to halt. The rider was unmistakably a young cowboy, and as cool as could be. He complied with some range profanity. Then at second glance he drawled, "Howdy, Brittenham."

"You've got the advantage of me, Mister Cowboy," retorted Dale curtly.

"Damn if I can see thet," he rejoined, with a smile that eased Dale's grimness.

"You know me?" queried Dale.

"Shore, I recognized you. I've a pard, Jen Pierce, who's helped you chase wild hosses. My name's Al Cook. We both ride for Stafford."

"You belong to Stafford's outfit?" asked Dale, lowering his rifle.

"Yep. We got heah before sunup this mornin'."

"How many of you an' where are they?"

"About twenty, I figger. Didn't count.

Jud Larkin, our foreman, left five of us to watch thet far trail, up on top. He took the rest down."

"Where are they now?"

"I seen them just now. I can show them to you."

"Rustle. By gum, this *is* queer."

"You can gamble on it," returned Cook as he turned his horse. "We got tired waitin' for a showdown. I disobeyed orders an' rode around this side. Glad I did. For I run plumb across a trail fresh with tracks of a lot of horses. All shod! Brittenham, them hoss thieves have climbed out."

"Another trail? Hell! If thet's not tough . . . Where is it?"

"Heads in thet deep notch back of them cabins."

"They had a back hole to their burrow. Nalook didn't know thet."

"Heah we air," said the cowboy, sliding off. "Come out on the rim."

In another moment Dale was gazing down upon the grove of pines and the roofs of cabins. No men—no smoke! The camp site appeared deserted.

"Say, what the hell you make of thet?" ejaculated the cowboy, pointing. "Look! Up behind the thicket, makin' for the open grass!

There's Larkin's outfit all strung out, crawlin' on their bellies like snakes!"

Dale saw, and in a flash he surmised that Stafford's men were crawling up on Strickland's. Each side would mistake the other for the horse thieves. And on the instant a clear crack of a rifle rang out. But it was up on the rim. Other shots, from heavy short guns, boomed. That cowboy had run into the spying outlaws. Again the sharp ring of the rifle.

"Look!" cried the cowboy, pointing down.

Dale saw puffs of blue smoke rise from the green level below. Then gunshots pealed up.

"My Gawd! The locoed idiots are fightin' each other. But at thet, neither Nalook or Strickland would know Stafford's outfit."

"Bad! Let me ride down an' put them wise."

"I'll go. Lend me your horse. You follow along the rim to the trail. Come down."

Dale ran back to leap into the cowboy's saddle. The stirrups fit him. With a slap of the bridle and a kick he urged the horse into a gallop. It did not take long to reach the trail. Wheeling into it, he ran the horse out to the rim, and then sent him down at a sliding plunge. He yelled to the cowboy on guard. "Brittenham! Brittenham! Don't shoot!" Then as the horse sent gravel and dust sky high, and, reaching a level, sped by the cowboy, Dale added, "Look out for our men above!"

Dale ran the fast horse along the edge of the timber and then toward the thicket where he calculated Nalook would lead Strickland. He crashed through one fringe of sage and laurel, right upon the heels of men. Rifles cracked to left and right. Dale heard the whistle of bullets that came from Stafford's outfit.

"*Stop!*" he yelled, at the top of his lungs. "Horse thieves gone! You're fightin' our own men!"

Out upon the open grass level he rode, tearing loose his scarf. He held this aloft in one hand and in the other his rifle. A puff of white smoke rose from the deep grass ahead, then another from a clump of brush to the right, and next, one directly in front of him. The missile from the gun which belched that smoke hissed close to Dale's ear. He yelled with all his might and waved as no attacking enemy ever would have done. But the shots multiplied. The cowboys did not grasp the situation.

"No help for it!" muttered Dale with a

dark premonition of calamity. But he had his good name to regain. He raced on right upon kneeling, lean-shaped cowboys.

"Stop! Stop! Horse thieves gone! You're fightin' friends! My outfit! Brittenham! *Britt—"*

Dale felt the impact of a bullet on his body somewhere. Then a terrible blinding shock.

When consciousness returned, Dale knew from a jolting sensation that he was being moved. He was being propped up in a saddle by a man riding on each side of his horse. His head sagged and when he opened his eyes to a blurred and darkened sight he saw the horn of his saddle and the mane of his horse. His skull felt as if it had been split by an ax.

His senses drifted close to oblivion again, then recovered a little more clearly. He heard voices and hoofbeats. Warm blood dripped down on his hands. That sensation started conscious thought. He had been shot, but surely not fatally, or he would not have been put astraddle a horse. His reaction to that was swift, and revivifying with happiness. A faintness, a dizziness seemed to lessen, but the pain in his head grew correspondingly more piercing.

Dale became aware then that a number of horsemen rode with him. They began to crash through brush out into the open again where gray walls restricted the light. Then he felt strong hands lift him from the saddle and lay him on the grass. He opened his eyes. Anxious faces bent over him, one of which was Strickland's.

"My Gawd, men!" came to Dale in Rogers' deep voice. "It's Brittenham! Don't say he's—"

"Just knocked out temporarily," replied Strickland cheerfully. "Ugly scalp wound, but not dangerous. Another shot through the left shoulder. Fetch whiskey, bandages, hot water, and iodine if you have it."

"Aw!" let out Rogers, expelling a loud breath. He thumped away.

Dale lay with closed eyes, deeply grateful for having escaped serious injury. They forced him to swallow whiskey, and then they began to work over him.

"You're the homesteader, Rogers?" Strickland queried.

"Yes. Me an' Britt have been friends. Knew each other over in the Sawtooths. . . .

Lord, I'm glad he ain't bad hurt. It'd just have killed thet Watrous girl."

"I'm Strickland," replied the other. "These fellows here are part of a posse I brought up from Halsey."

"Much of a fight? I heerd a lot of shootin'."

"It would have been one hell of a fight but for Brittenham. You see, the horse-thief gang had vamoosed last night. But we didn't know that. The Indian led us up on an outfit that had discovered us about the same time. We were crawling toward each other, through the thickets and high grass. The Indians began to shoot first. That betrayed our position and a lively exchange of shots began. It grew hot. Brittenham had gone up on the rim to scout. He discovered our blunder and rode back hell bent for election right into our midst. He stopped us, but the other outfit kept on shooting. Brittenham went on, and rode into the very face of hard shooting. He got hit twice. Nervy thing to do! But it saved lives. I had two men wounded, besides him. Stafford's outfit suffered some casualties, but fortunately no one killed."

"What become of the hoss thieves?"

"Gone! After Reed and Mason had been killed, the gang evidently split. Some left in the night, leaving all their property except light packs. Sam Hood, one of Strickland's boys, killed two of them up on the rim, just before our fight started below."

"Ha! Thet ought to bust the gang for keeps," declared Rogers, rubbing his big hands.

"It was the best night's work this range ever saw. And the credit goes to Brittenham."

"Wal, I'll go fetch the wimmen," concluded Rogers heartily.

When, a little later, Dale had been washed and bandaged, and was half sitting up receiving the plaudits of the riders, he saw Edith come running out from under the trees into the open. She ran most of the way; then, nearing the cabin, she broke to a hurried walk and held a hand over her heart. Even at a distance Dale saw her big dark eyes, intent and staring in her pale face. As she neared the spot where he lay surrounded by a half-circle of strange men, it was certain she saw no one but him. Reaching the spot where he lay, she knelt beside him.

"Dale!"

"Hello—Edith," he replied huskily. "I guess I didn't bear such a charmed life— after all. I sure got in the way of two bullets. But my luck held, Edith."

"Oh! You're not seriously injured?" she asked composedly, with a gentle hand on his. "But you are suffering."

"My head did hurt like h— sixty. It's sort of whirlin' now."

"Rogers told me, Dale. That was a wonderful and splendid thing for you to do," Edith said softly. "What will Dad say? And won't I have Mister Stafford in a hole?"

Strickland interposed with a beaming smile. "You sure will, Miss Watrous. And I hope you make the most of it."

"Edith, I reckon we might leave for Bannock pronto," spoke up Dale eagerly. "I sent Nalook to tell your friends of your safety."

"Wal, Dale, mebbe I'll let you go tomorrow," chimed in Rogers.

"Don't go today," advised Strickland.

Next day Dale, despite his iron will and supreme eagerness to get home, suffered an ordeal that was almost too much for him. Toward the end of the ride to Bannock members of Strickland's posse were supporting Dale on his horse. But to his relief and Edith's poignant joy, he made it. At Bannock, medical attention and a good night's sleep made it possible for him to arrange to go on to Salmon by stage.

The cowboy Cook, who had taken a strong fancy to Dale, and had hung close to him, came out of the inn carrying a canvas-covered pack that Dale had him carefully stow under the seat.

"Britt, you sure have been keen about that pack. What's in it?" inquired Strickland with shrewd curiosity.

"Wouldn't you like to know, old-timer?"

"I've got a hunch. Wal, I'll look you up over at the Watrous Ranch in a couple of days. I want to go home first."

"Ahuh. You want to find out why those cowboy outfits didn't show up?"

"I confess to a little curiosity," replied the rancher dryly.

"Don't try to find out. Forget it," said Dale earnestly.

The stage, full of passengers, and driven by the jovial stage driver Bill Edmunds, rolled away to the cheers of a Bannock crowd.

"Dale, what *is* in this pack under the seat?" asked Edith.

"Guess."

"It looked heavy, and considering how fussy you've been about it—I'd say—*gold*," she whispered.

Dale put his lips to her ear. "Edith, no wonder I'm fussy. I'm wild with excitement.

That gang is broken up. An' I have Reed's money in my coat here—an' Mason's fortune in thet pack."

"Oh, how thrilling!" she whispered, and then on an afterthought, she spoke out roguishly. "Well, in view of the—er—rather immediate surrender of your independence, I think I'd better take charge."

Darkness had settled down over the Salmon River Valley when the stage arrived at Salmon. Old Bill, the driver, said to Edith, "I reckon I'd better hustle you young folks out home before the town hears what Britt has done."

"That'd be good of you, Bill," replied Edith gratefully. "Dale is tired. And I'd be glad to get him home pronto."

They were the only passengers for the three miles out to the ranch. Dale did not speak, and Edith appeared content to hold his hand. They both gazed out at the shining river and the dark groves, and over the moonlit range. When they arrived at the ranch, Dale had Bill turn down the lane to the little cabin where he lived.

"Carry this pack in, Bill, an' don't ask questions, you son-of-a-gun, or you'll not get the twenty-dollar gold piece I owe you."

"Wal, if this hyar pack is full of gold, you won't miss thet double eagle, you doggone lucky wild-hoss hunter."

"Thank you, Bill," said Edith. "I'll walk the rest of the way."

Dale was left alone with Edith, who stood in the shadow of the maples with the moon lighting her lovely face. He could hear the low roar of rapids on the river.

"It's wonderful, gettin' back, this way," he said haltingly. "You must run in an' tell your dad."

"Dad can wait a moment longer. . . . Oh, Dale, I'm so proud—so happy—my heart is bursting."

"Mine feels queer, too. I hope this is not a dream, Edith."

"What—Dale?"

"Why, all thet's happened—an' you standin' there safe again—an' so beautiful. You just don't appear real."

"I should think you could ascertain whether I'm real flesh and blood or not."

Dale fired to that. "You'll always be the same, Edith. Can't you see how serious this is for me?" He took her in his arms. "Darlin', I reckon I know how you feel. But no words can tell you my feelins. . . . Kiss me, Edith— then I'll try."

287

She was in his arms, to grow responsive and loving in her eager return of his kisses.

"Oh—Dale!" she whispered, with eyes closed. "I have found my man at last."

"Edith, I love you—an' tomorrow I'll have the courage to ask your dad if I can have you."

"Dale, I'm yours—Dad or no Dad. But he'll be as easy as that," she replied, stirring in his arms and snapping her fingers. "I hate to leave you. But we have tomorrow —and forever. Oh, Dale! I don't deserve all this happiness—kiss me good night. . . . I'll fetch your breakfast myself. . . . Kiss me once more. . . . *Another!* Oh, I am—"

She broke from him to run up the lane and disappear under the moonlit maples. Dale stood there a few moments alone in the silver-blanched gloom, trying to persuade himself that he was awake and in possession of his senses.

Next morning he got up early, to find the pain in his head much easier. But his shoulder was so stiff and sore that he could not use the arm on that side. Having only one hand available, he was sore beset by the difficulty of washing, shaving and making himself as presentable as possible. He did not get through any too soon, for Edith appeared up the lane accompanied by a servant carrying a tray. She saw him and waved, then came tripping on. Dale felt his heart swell and he moved about to hide his tremendous pride. He shoved a bench near the table under a canvas shelter that served for a porch. And when he could look up again, there she was, radiant in white.

"Mornin', Edith. Now I believe in fairies again."

"Oh, you look just fine. I'm having my breakfast with you. Do you feel as well as you look?"

"Okay, except for my arm. It's stiff. I had a devil of a time puttin' my best foot forward. You'll have to do with a one-armed beau today."

"I'd rather have your one arm than all the two arms on the range," she replied gaily.

They had breakfast together, which to Dale seemed like enchantment. Then she took him for a stroll under the cottonwoods out along the river bank. And there, hanging on his good arm, she told him how her father had taken her story. Visitors from Salmon had come last night up to a late hour, and had begun to arrive already that morning. Stafford's outfit had returned driv-

289

ing a hundred recovered horses. Dale's feat was on the tip of every tongue.

"I didn't tell Dad about—about *us* till this morning," she added finally.

"Lord help me! What'd he say?" gulped Dale.

"I don't know whether it was flattering or not—to me," Edith replied dubiously. "He said, 'That wild-horse tamer? Thank God, your hash is settled at last!'"

"He sure flatters me if he thinks I can tame you. Wait till I tell him how you routed Bayne's outfit!"

"Oh, Dale, Dad was fine. He's going to ask you. . . . But that'd be telling."

"Edith, if he accepts me, must I—will I have to wait very long for you?"

"*If!* Dad has accepted you, Dale. And honestly, he's happy over it. . . . And as for the other—just what do you mean, Mr. Brittenham?"

"Aw! Will you marry me soon?"

"How soon?"

"I—I don't know, darlin'."

"Dale, dearest, I couldn't marry you with your head bandaged like that—or your arm in a sling," she said tantalizingly, as her dark eyes shed soft warm light upon him.

"But, Edith!" he burst out. "I could take them off pronto. In less than a week!"

"Very well. Just that pronto."

Watrous came out to meet them as they crossed the green. His fine face showed emotion and his eyes, at that moment, had something of the fire of Edith's. He wrung Dale's hand. But as befitted a Westerner, little trace of his deep feeling pervaded his voice.

"Brittenham, I won't try to thank you," he said in simple heartiness.

"Thet suits me, Mr. Watrous. I'm kind of overwhelmed. An'—so I'd better get somethin' out before I lose my nerve. . . . I've loved Edith since I came here first, three years ago. Will you give her to me?"

"Dale, I will, and gladly, provided you live here with me. I'm getting on, and since Mother has been gone, Edith has been all to me."

"Dad, we will never leave you," replied Edith softly.

"Bless you, my children! And Dale, there's a little matter I'd like to settle right now. I'll need a partner. Stafford has persuaded me to go in big for the cattle game. I see its possibilities. That, of course, means we'll have cattle stealing as we have had horse stealing. I'll need you pretty bad."

"Dad!" cried Edith in dismay. "You didn't tell me you'd want Dale to go chasing cattle thieves!"

"My dear, it might not come for years. Such developments come slowly. By that time Dale may have some grown cowboy sons to take his place."

"Oh!" exclaimed Edith, plunged into sudden confusion.

"Dale, do you accept?" added Watrous, extending his hand with an engaging smile.

"Yes, Mr. Watrous. An' I'll give Edith an' you the best thet's in me."

"Settled! Oh, here comes Stafford. Lay into him, youngster, for he has sure been nasty."

As Stafford came slowly down the broad steps, Dale found himself unable to feel the resentment that had rankled in him.

"Brittenham," said the rancher, as he advanced, "I've made blunders in my life, but never so stupid a one as that regarding you. I am ashamed and sorry. It'll be hard for me to live this injustice down unless you forgive me. Can I ask that of you?"

"Nothin' to forgive," declared Dale earnestly, won by Stafford's straightforwardness and remorse. He offered his hand and gripped the rancher's. "Suspicion pointed at me. An' I took on Hildrith's guilt for reasons you know. Let's forget it an' be friends."

"You are indeed a man."

But when Stafford turned to Edith he had a different proposition to face. She eyed him with disdainful scorn, and stood tapping a nervous foot on the path.

"Edith, you can do no less than he. Say you forgive me, too."

"Yes, of course, since Dale is so kind. But I think you are a rotten judge of men."

"Indeed I am, my dear."

"And you're a hard man when you're crossed.'

"Yes. But I'm a loyal friend. After all, this was a misunderstanding. You believed it, didn't you?"

"I never did—not for a minute. That's why I followed Dale."

"Well, you found him and brought him back." Stafford took a colored slip of paper from his pocket. He looked at it, then held it out to Edith. "I offered five thousand dollars reward for Brittenham, dead or alive. You brought him back alive—very much alive, as anyone with half an eye could see. And no wonder! It seems to me that this reward should go to you. Indeed, I insist upon your taking it."

"Reward! But, Mr. Stafford—you—I," stammered Edith. "Five thousand dollars for *me?*"

"Surely. I imagine you will be able to spend it pronto. We all know your weakness for fine clothes and fine horses. Please accept it as a wedding present from a friend who loves you and who will never cease to regret that he mistook so splendid and noble a fellow as Dale Brittenham for a horse thief!"

Quaking-Asp Cabin

I

Log cabins have played a great part in the history of the West. The lonely deserted ones and those falling to ruin, with which any hunter is familiar, have always fascinated me. Many stories of mine tell the romance and drama of these wilderness homes.

Late one autumn afternoon I found myself lost in the forest. This had happened to me before, but not often enough to make the experience something all in the day's hunt. Hours before, the hounds had trailed a bear down over the Mogollon Rim into a canyon. My companions became separated from me. Probably they had followed the cowboys. Already that day I had had two ringing runs after these range riders. The lowering weather threatened rain. I rode along the Rim listening to the bay of the hounds and looking out over that vast green gulf called the Tonto Basin, the wildest and roughest region in Arizona. In case the pack jumped the bear I stood as good a chance as anyone to get a shot.

A cold wind began to blow from the north and the clouds darkened. It grew hard to hear the hounds or an occasional yell of a cowboy. Eventually all sounds of the chase ceased. I turned back on the trail toward camp, keeping a sharp lookout for deer and turkeys.

The Mogollon Rim is an extraordinary geological fault which zigzags three hundred miles across Arizona into New Mexico. It has an altitude close to nine thousand feet and breaks off sheer down into the Tonto Basin. In the other direction it slopes for sixty miles to merge into the desert. The singular feature is that all water runs away from the Rim. Canyons and ridges, like the grooves and ribs of a washboard, head at the Rim and run down. All this region is densely timbered with spruce, pine and aspen.

A flock of wild turkeys lured me off the trail. I chased them for a mile or more down in the woods, without getting a shot. Then fresh deer signs augmented my excitement and drew me on. When I heard elk bugling below I descended the ridge after them. The piercing bugle of a bull elk is one of the wildest and most beautiful calls in nature.

Once down off the ridge into the canyon I ascertained that the elk were moving to the north, an advantage for me, as the wind was coming from the north. The herd evidently was small, comprising some cows and yearlings, with at least two bulls.

Most of these canyons, some distance down from the Rim, opened out into grassy parks; I rode into one just in time to see a great tawny elk, with antlers like the roots of an upturned stump, glide into the pines.

They climbed the ridge and I followed. I did not need to trail them because every little while the leader bugled. Presently an answer pealed from above, and if I needed any more to whet my hunting instinct that was it.

I pursued this band of elk over the ridge, down into another canyon, up again, and on and on, until I discovered that they had either heard or scented me, and after the habit of elk, were just moving along. But it was not this that brought me up with a start. A fine rain had begun to fall; the sky was dark and gave not the slightest hint of the sun. Under such circumstances it was easy for anyone to become lost. I turned back with some concern, until I ascertained the north from moss on a pine; then I turned east. Back-trailing my own tracks would have been futile, for the day was far spent, and I had traveled miles from the Rim. The thing to do was to head east, up and down the ridges, until I crossed Beaver Canyon, in which our camp was located.

If I did come across a landmark that should have been familiar the rain deceived me. All the parks, trees, slopes and ridges looked exactly alike. I was lost, and as the shadows began trooping down the aisles of the forest I decided to find a place to camp, before darkness overtook me. On the morrow, if the sun shone enough to give me my direction, I could get out easily.

Shortly after that decision I came to the brow of a ridge from which I gazed down into a small park, perhaps a score or more acres in extent. On the far side, at the base of the slope, I could see a log cabin, sitting black and strange against the golden blaze of quaking asps. A vacant and eye-like door peered up at me forbiddingly.

The park, with its lonesome manifestation that someone had lived there sometime, was a welcome sight. I found a dim grass-grown trail leading down. My horse, White Stockings, snorted his approval of the green-carpeted pasture. I heard running water.

It appeared that the old log cabin sat back against a lichened cliff from the tip of which hung wet ferns and scarlet-leaved vines. The roof of split shakes was intact and covered by a thick layer of moss and pine needles. I dismounted and walked around, thrilled by the place. From under the base of the cliff boiled a magnificent spring, ten feet wide and as deep. It was the source of the brook I had forded. One of the most superb silver spruce trees that I had ever seen towered over the cabin with its top above the cliff. To the left and verging right on the west side of the cabin was a grove of quaking asps, that even in the rain and gathering twilight blazed white and gold. Every leaf quaked as if still alive and shuddering in a last agony.

This struck me so singularly, even in that moment of satisfaction at my prospective shelter for the night, that I looked again and gazed long. Aspen trees in the fall are remarkably beautiful. They were my favorites of the high timber belts. But somehow my reaction was not as usual.

Unsaddling my horse, I haltered him with a long lasso to a bush which marked a luxuriant grass plot, and packed my saddle, blankets, canteen and rifle to the cabin. I carried them in and deposited them upon the floor. This proved to be an exception to the majority of cabins I had entered. It had been built of rough-hewn boards and was still solid. A strong odor of bear mingled with the musty scent of dust and pine. The single room was about twenty feet square, with a fireplace and chimney of yellow rock built against the west wall. Here too my quick survey grasped a good job of masonry, still intact except for crumbling corners of the fireplace.

My need was a fire for light and warmth. It behooved me to rustle dry wood while I could see to find it. There was a loft half across the ceiling and a ladder flat against the wall led up to it. I thought I might tear out some of the poles. But I found an old built-in bedstead of peeled poles in a corner, and it was covered with a layer of pine needles. From here the smell of bear emanated pungently. My hand found a round depression where bruin had made his bed. I did not relish the idea of a grizzly returning home to find his bed occupied. But there was no help on it. Only a mean bear would resent my occupancy.

In another corner I found a pile of fagots and pine cones, as dry as tinder.

"All set!" I soliloquized with satisfaction, wondering who had gathered that firewood and how long ago.

Soon I had a fire blazing on the hearth, and it made a vast difference. I went outside and filled my canteen with water from the spring. It was as cold as ice, and like all the water in that wonderful region came from snow water running through granite. I had in my coat a big sandwich—a biscuit with a generous slice of venison. Also I had a piece of chocolate, but this I chose to save for the next day.

Sitting in front of the warm fire, I made my supper and it was sufficient. After that I put on more wood and dried my coat and saddle blankets, upon which I had been sitting. Once more warm and dry, with hunger and thirst satisfied, I felt comfortable. Nevertheless, as one might have supposed, I was neither tired nor sleepy. Furthermore the old cabin intrigued me so thrillingly at first, and then, as I began to study its features and to think, so peculiarly, that I marveled greatly and sought to analyze the reason. It was already a foregone conclusion that I would put this cabin in one of my stories. Strange to record, I never did until now, and I am sure when this one is read my readers will not wonder.

By the light of the fire I made out details. The cabin was very old, but as it had been remarkably well and solidly built, it had withstood the ravages of time. There were many signs of dry rot, of crumbling chimney, of general disintegration. In some places the clay that had been used to fill the chinks between the logs was still there, shrunken and as hard as rock. I found indecipherable lettering on the irregular-shaped flat stone above the fireplace, and the imprint of a bloody hand, and bullet holes in the logs. These, however, could hardly account altogether for the powerful curiosity and emotion that stirred in me. I analyzed it presently as a kind of intuitive realization of the life, the drama, the tragedy that had abided there. No old cabin I ever entered, even those down in the Basin, on the scene of that most desperate and bloody feud, the war of sheepmen and cattlemen fought to the last man, had affected me so poignantly as this one. Surprised and perturbed, I put that down as stress from the excitement of being lost, and I sought to make light of it. But I could not, and in view of what I learned later this was no wonder.

With my saddle for a pillow, and lying between warm blankets, I stretched out to make a night of rest and sleep. While the fire burned I lay awake. The flickering shadows from the changing blaze wrote stories on the gloomy walls of that cabin. When the light waxed dim and failed I shut my eyes. The oppression in my breast persisted. Rain pattered softly on the roof. Alone in that speaking solitude, I surrendered to the phantasms induced by the mystery of what had happened there. It was the prerogative of a writer, but it was not a happy one this night.

I fell asleep. Late in the night I awoke. The radium hands on my watch told two o'clock. Presently I ascertained that the rain had ceased. A wind had arisen and the air was colder. This augured well for my finding my way to camp on the morrow. But the moan and sough and mourn of that wind added to the weird and inexplicable something which pervaded the old cabin. Always as a child I had been afraid of the dark. Even since I had attained manhood, night had always been invested with phantoms, peopled with spirits, full of queer dreams that the sunlight of day dispelled. The conflict between my imagination and my will ended as such conflicts always end, with a victory for the former. Fear of the unknown beset me. I knew perfectly well that I was in no danger physically. But the mind is strange. No scientist or psychologist has plumbed it yet. I was at the mercy of the life, the birth and death, the love and hate and passion, the terror and the ghastliness, of all that had happened in that old cabin. Even if I had never learned what it had all been I would have known it instinctively just the same. Those hours before the gray of dawn were bad ones, from the point of view of peace and sleep.

Day broke at last. I got up to pack my things outside. The morning was clear. Frost whitened the grass of the park. The nipping air had teeth. When I got White Stockings saddled and bridled my fingers stung. A rosy light over the high horizon gave me the east, from which I took my direction, and by sunrise I was up on the ridge. I was lost still, however, until two hours later, when I rode out of the colored forest into the Rim trail, from which I could see the blue haze of the Basin. How good it was to find myself again! But that somber something did not leave me. In two hours and a half I cut off the Rim trail down into Beaver Canyon, and soon rode into camp.

Babe Haught, my old bear hunter, and the Japanese cook, Takahashie, were the only ones in camp. Haught's four sons, the cowboys, and my brother were out hunting for me.

"Wal, I wasn't worried atall," said Babe, his craggy face wreathed in a smile. "Unless you get ketched in a storm, gettin' lost heah don't amount to shucks. All you got to do is foller canyon or ridge up to the Rim."

In some detail I told Haught where I had been and especially about the old cabin.

"Say, you was lost," he replied in surprise. "Thet park's way down, ten miles an' more from the Rim, west of Leonard Canyon. Rough Jasper of a country without bein' lost."

"I'll say it's rough. Babe, do you know anything about that old cabin, who lived there—and what might have happened?"

Haught gave his short dry laugh. "Reckon I do. Quakin'-Asp Cabin, it's known to us. Built long before I come to the Tonto, twenty-four years ago. Haven't hunted thar these last half-dozen years. You know the Apaches used to burn the grass over this woods every fall. That made fine open

307

huntin'. But it's growed up brushy. Them jack-pine thickets are shore tough."

"Quaking-Asp Cabin?" I echoed ponderingly. "Babe, didn't a lot happen there?"

"Hell, yes! . . . It's haunted—that cabin —Suthin' turrible happened to everyone who lived thar."

"All right, old-timer. Get going," I said with elation.

"Wal, first thing that comes to mind," replied Haught reminiscently, as he squatted down to get a red ember from the campfire to light his pipe, "was told me by Ben Kettle, a hunter heraboots. Ben camped at Quakin'-Asp one night with a feller named Bates, a sheepman. Durin' the night Ben was waked up by a squall from his pardner. One of them coyote-bitten skunks—you know, the kind that have hydrophobia—had hold of Bates's nose. Funny how them poison varmints always bite a feller with a big nose. Ben had to choke the skunk to death to make it let go. Wal, Bates didn't go to see no doctor. He wasn't worried none by them civet-cats. Some days after that, over on the Cibeque at a round-up, he was took down with rabies. My brother, Henry, was thar an' helped tie Bates in a wagon. They took him to Winslow, whar he had to be roped to a bed. He went mad. Turned black all over. An' died a horrible death . . . I've knowed of several other fellers bein' bit by hydrophobia skunks. . . ."

"Tell more about Quaking-Asp Cabin," I interposed. "That's got me, Haught, I'm on the trail of something."

"Ahuh? Wal, if you trail all thet's come off at Quakin'-Asp, you'll make tracks till doomsday. . . . Lemme see. Next I remember thet aboot the Hashknife outfit. More'n twenty years ago. Thet outfit, if I never told you before, was one of Arizonie's best cow outfits. Jim Davis owned it, an' was runnin' ten thousand haid of cattle flanked with thet Hashknife brand. Lefty Dagg, son of the Dagg who was first to be killed in thet Pleasant Valley War old one-arm Matt Taylor told you aboot, was foreman of this outfit. Wal, Jim Davis an' his bunch camped thar at Quakin'-Asp one day in the fall of thet year. Jim had been to Pine, where he'd sold a big herd of stock to the Mormons. He had a wad of money on him, an' Dagg with his cowboys was well-heeled. Naturooly they fell to gamblin' an' from thet to fightin'. Dagg killed a cowboy Davis set much store on an' it riled the boss. Nobody ever knowed for shore the truth of what come off. They said on the range thet it was an even break an' they said also thet Dagg murdered Davis. We never got the straight of thet. But we did find out, you bet, thet Dagg an' his outfit went crooked after thet fight. They turned rustlers. In the years thet follered the Hash-knife earned a hard name. They fought other cattle outfits. But it was fightin' among themselves thet snuffed thet outfit out. Thar has been a dozen Hashknife outfits since, an' all of them took on two or three gun-toters from the older outfit, which I reckon worked like a few rotten applies on a barrel of good ones. No Hashknife outfit has ever outlived thet heritage."

"Babe, that's good—a whole story in it-self. But not the one I'm on the track of," I replied eagerly. "Go on."

"Wal, the first time I rode down to Quakin'-Asp Cabin I had a jar," resumed Haught. "Thar was a feller livin' thar alone, a lean, dark-browed man with 'range rider' stamped all over him. Thet was twenty-three years ago, but I remember as well as if it was yestiddy. 'Cause thet hombre threw his gun on me an' I had a hell of a time talkin' him out of borin' me. But I con-vinced him thet even if he was on the dodge he needn't fear me. I stayed all night with him an' he waxed friendly. Before I left he omitted tellin' me his name but he did tell me that there was a price on his haid. The next summer when I rode in thar again he was gone. I never saw him again. But years afterward a rich an' respected cattleman told on his deathbed a story that went the rounds heah in Arizonie. I figgered thet he an' the ootlaw I had met at Quakin'-Asp had been pards, ridin' together in the same outfit. They both fell in love with the ranchman's daughter. He hisself had pulled the crooked deal thet his pard took the guilt for an' he couldn't die with it on his conscience. He told his old friend's name an' begged him to come an' stand free before the world. But the outlaw had long gone crooked of his own account. If he ever heahed of his pard's confession no one knowed. He was shot in a road-agent hold-up in New Mexico."

"Babe, you're hot on the track of what I felt that night in haunted Quaking-Asp Cabin," I declared forcibly. "Come on. Come on."

"Wal, I dunno aboot that," replied the old bear hunter dubiously. Then he told me the story of Tappan and his great burro Jenie.

Tappan had been a giant prospector, a wanderer of the wasteland, a lonely hermit whose young manhood and maturity had been given to the naked shingles and rocky fortresses of the desert, to the lure of gold. One time, way down on the barrens at the base of the Chocolate range in California, his burro gave birth to a little one that Tappan feared he would have to kill. But it chanced that when he was about to rid the mother of her encumbrance he stumbled upon the richest pocket of gold he had ever found. He spared the life of the baby burro and called her Jenie. She grew to be the largest and finest and most intelligent burro that Tappan had ever owned. She became famous on the desert from Picacho to Death Valley. Other prospectors tried to buy her and steal her. But Jenie grew to be more than gold to Tappan.

Once Tappan was caught in one of the terrible storms of flying poison dust, and torrid blasts of heat, that prevail in Death Valley in summer. At midnight the hellish furnace winds began to blow. Blinded, lost, Tappan clung to the tail of his faithful burro, and she led him up and out of the valley of death and desolation. After that Tappan loved Jenie more than all the burros he had ever owned.

Tappan's peculiar thirst for gold led him

in quest of all the lost gold mines that the desert fact and legend had left to torture prospectors. The day inevitably came when he took the trail of the famed and elusive Lost Dutchman Mine somewhere far into the wilds of the Superstitions in Arizona.

One night into his camp rode a group of riders, four men and one woman. They were not welcome, because Tappan had bags of gold and he preferred to be lonely, but the fair-spoken leader, who claimed his band were lost and hungry, and the persuasive offices of the handsome young woman, prevailed upon Tappan to be hospitable.

There had been no woman in Tappan's life. This one contrived to win his sympathy. She claimed to be virtually a prisoner and she hated her captivity. She worked upon the mind and heart of the simple prospector.

The leader of the band talked about the ranch he had up in the timbered canyons of the Tonto Basin, and what a contrast the shady cool retreat, the singing brook, the richness of verdure and toothsomeness of venison and turkey, made to this ghastly desert of cactus and rock, down upon which the pitiless summer sun had begun to burn. Before Tappan lay down to sleep that night the woman had won him to go with them. She hinted that he might save her.

Ten long days Tappan rode with the range, on one of their horses, while Jenie plodded on behind, loaded with his pack. They climbed to a canyon up under the gold rim of the Mogollon. The ranch and cattle did not materialize, but all the other features the leader had lauded to Tappan were there in abundance. Tappan reveled in all the rich attributes of that timbered canyon, so different from his desert. Then he fell in love with the woman Bess. It was a malady that he could not resist nor cure. Not until afterward did it occur to Tappan how strange that the men left him so much alone with Bess! And when she confessed her love he lived in his first fool's paradise.

Bess confessed that her associates were rustlers and she begged Tappan to save her from them, to take her far away and make her happy. Tappan consented to that in the only transport of his life. They planned to ride away early one night, but it would be impossible to take Jenie. To part with his faithful burro, to betray her for this woman, to leave her alone, knowing she would wait there for him until she died, filled Tappan's heart with anguish. But it had to be done.

They escaped one night on horseback, with only one pack animal, carrying Tappan's bags of gold, some food and bedding. They rode south all night and all the next day before resting. Tappan believed they were safe, but Bess showed fear of pursuers. While they were eating at their campfire, something stampeded their horses. Tappan went to hunt them and succeeded in catching only one. Upon his return to camp he found Bess gone with his bags of gold. She left a note swearing she loved Tappan and would have gone to hell for him, but this was the only way she could save his life.

Tappan tracked that gang out of Arizona, down through California into Mexico. The blue-eyed woman and the swarthy leader who gambled and drank at every town made them easy to trail. One by one the other members of the gang disappeared. At length Tappan stood bowed over Bess's grave and he buried his love and heart there with her. And soon after that he got his great hands on the villain who had murdered her—the suave leader of the rustler gang—to break his bones and wring his neck.

Tappan retraced his steps. A year and more had passed. He remembered Jenie and he journeyed across the desert wastes, far up into Arizona, to the green-and-gold canyon where he had deserted her. To his everlasting relief and joy he found her there, waiting for him, as she had waited a thousand and more mornings on the desert. Tappan took her to the nearest hamlet and there spent his remaining gold for an outfit. Packing her more heavily than ever before, Tappan turned his back forever on the desert and climbed up over the Rim to wander down into the shady canyons and shining parks until he happened upon Quaking-Asp Cabin. There he took up his abode for the summer and fall.

But he lingered late, loath to leave this verdant, colorful retreat, the only one that had ever wholly satisfied him.

Then one day a man on foot strode upon Tappan as he sat in his doorway. This intruder claimed to be lost and hungry. Tappan guessed him to be a bad man, hunted surely, and not to be trusted. But as Tappan now had nothing to lose he arose to take the fugitive in and feed him, hoping he would be on his way next day. But Blade, as he called himself, did not leave. He stayed, day after day, though Tappan offered to see him off with a share of his diminishing store of food. Blade feared he could not find his way

316

out of that wilderness alone, and always he tried to persuade Tappan to go. His argument was that they must start before the snow fell. If they were snowed in there they would starve to death.

But Tappan, grown surly and resentful, stayed on, until a great howling blizzard blew down upon the park. When the storm passed there was four feet of snow on the level. Winter had set in. Tappan saw the peril he would not think of before. While waiting for a crust to harden on the snow, he fashioned snowshoes. The day came. Blade raged at Tappan's intention to take Jenie with them. He argued in vain. Then in a passion he snatched up Tappan's rifle to kill the burro.

"We'll need the meat," he yelled.

"Wha-at! *Eat* my burro! My Jenie!" roared Tappan, and made at this man.

A terrific fight for the rifle ensued. Blade was big and powerful, but no match for the giant prospector. They fought to and fro in front of Quaking-Asp Cabin, trodding the snow down, while Jenie watched meekly. At last the rifle broke in their hands, Blade getting the stock and Tappan the barrel. Tappan warded off blows until he had his opening. He brained his opponent. Blade fell back in a snowbank, his boots sticking out grotesquely.

"Huh! You would eat my burro!" Tappan grunted, and binding his wounds he strapped a tarpaulin and his meager remnant of food upon Jenie. Then on snowshoes he set out leading the burro.

Jenie's sharp little hoofs broke through the snow crust, but not all four at once. Tappan climbed up on the ridge when the crust was harder. He headed downhill. That night he ate and slept under a spruce. All day he led Jenie, plodding along, zigzagging the slopes. Night passed and another day and another night. His food gave out. Jenie nibbled at the buckbrush and other greenery. Tappan lost track of time. When the snow began to thin out and soften he put Jenie on the tarpaulin and dragged her along. Tappan passed out of the spruce, down out of the pines, down into the cedars. At sunset one day he gazed down upon the open range, bare of snow in spots. Spent and tottering, Tappan fell upon the tarpaulin and covered himself. The night down at the edge of the open desert was bitterly cold. Tappan slept. In the morning when Jenie welcomed the sunrise with a long-drawn "Hee-haw, hee-haw, heehawee," and waited for Tappan, he did not awaken.

"Thet's the way it always seemed to me," concluded the old backwoods storyteller. "Shore I cain't prove it all happened thet way. But Blade's skeleton was found, his skull split. An' then aboot the same time, next summer, the riders found all the coyotes had left of Tappan. Jenie roamed thet sage an' cedar range for years, wilder'n any wild deer. Men who knowed Tappan's story an' who're still livin' saw Tappan's burro after she grew wild. But I never saw her."

"Great stuff, Babe!" I exclaimed, shaken to my depths. "But still that's not it. That's not *all*. *Who* built Quaking-Asp Cabin? *What* happened there first, before all these things you tell of?"

"Wal, I reckon thar's only one man left in these parts who can tell you if anyone knows. Thet's old one-arm Matt Taylor. Mebbe you can get him het up to talk, like you did aboot the sheep war."

After our hunt ended and we got down to the little Tonto settlement I went to call on Matt Taylor. But he was away somewhere. The following fall on the way in I tried again, with like result. Then twice during that hunt I endeavored to find Quaking-Asp Cabin, once alone, and another time with Haught's son. We failed to locate the park. All this vain oblation only whetted my appetite for that story. The longer I had to wait the bigger it loomed.

The third season after my discovery of Quaking-Ask Cabin I met a half-breed Indian, an intelligent fellow, and a great hunter, and invited him to my camp. It turned out that my bear hunters had no use for him. They were jealous no doubt, as he was the most unerring rifle shot in that region, and I had taken a decided fancy to him. The fact that he had killed a couple of men and was a sort of desperado did not influence me greatly. He was the grandest fellow to hunt with that I ever had with me. He rode a mule that could hear and scent and see game quicker than any hunter—But that is another story.

This half-breed led me straight across country, over ridge and down canyon, to Quaking-Asp Cabin. Early in October the park and wooded slopes presented a glorious blend of autumn colors. It was without doubt the most idyllic and lovely spot I ever encountered in any forest.

I rode down ahead of my guide, and along the edge of the park, where isolated pines and spruce and aspens straggled out toward the open. A troop of deer trotted away under the trees, and turned to watch me, with long ears erect. Quick as a flash I piled off my horse, and picking out a four-point buck I let him have it in the breast. Making a prodigious leap, with front feet doubled under him, he crashed down into the brush. His action indicated a mortal wound. In my hunter's excitement at downing so fine a buck, the first in two seasons, I ran forward. Coming upon him I stood my rifle against a sapling, and drawing my hunting knife I was about to step to him when he gave a bound right at me.

His hindquarters were down and he had leaped upon me on his front feet. Surprise checked me and then horror rooted me to the spot. My bullet had gone through the deer, destroying the power of his hindquarters. He presented a bloody and terrible sight. With his last power of movement he meant to kill me. All dying beasts of the wild at bay exhibit eyes almost too appalling for the gaze of man. I was sick, frozen, paralyzed. That buck lowered his sharp antlers to rip me asunder when a rifle cracked and he fell in a heap. My guide had come upon me in my predicament and had shot from his horse.

"Never go close to a dying deer!" he admonished.

I pulled myself together, but the incident spoiled my return to Quaking-Asp Cabin. It fit in with all the rest I had felt about that lovely strange place. I rested while the Indian cut out two haunches of the deer and packed them in his slicker. Then we walked on to the cabin, leading our horses. A reluctance to enter the cabin held me back. But my guide glided around with a somber mien that struck me most singularly. It dawned upon me that he knew the place—that it meant a great deal to him—but the effect upon him was far from happy. This slowly stirred my old curiosity. My thirst for the romance or tragedy, whatever haunted the spot, returned stronger than ever.

He came at length to sit beside me in the golden shade of the aspens. For a man who was half Indian his strong face appeared less bronze than usual. Beads of sweat stood out upon his brow, and his dark eyes burned with a somber and inscrutable fire.

"Haven't been here for nigh on twenty years. Same as ever!" he muttered, as if to himself.

"You must have been only a kid then?" I queried, feeling my way.

"No, I was a man then. . . . How old do you reckon me?"

"About twenty-eight, maybe thirty," I ventured.

"I'm close to fifty. . . . Do you know, sir, I wouldn't have come here for any man in the world but you?"

"Indeed! Well, thanks very much, my hunter pard. I sure appreciate that," I replied feelingly. "But why such reluctance? It's such a wonderful place to me."

"I was born here," he said, huskily, and hung his dark hawk-like head.

It was not that astounding information which shocked the blood back to my heart, but a flash of intuition that at last I was on the heels of the tremendous secret of Quaking-Asp Cabin.

"Born here?" I ejaculated wonderingly. "Haught didn't tell me that."

"He doesn't know it."

"Oh! . . . Look here. . . . For three years I've been trying to find out all about this Quaking-Asp Cabin. Old Matt Taylor, who told me the story of *To the Last Man*, is the only one, Haught says, who knows what happened here. I've been trying to meet him again. . . . But, maybe now, I won't need to, if you . . ."

"Old Matt worked here when I was a boy. He's over eighty now and his memory is failing. . . . I'll tell you who built this cabin—what happened in it—why a shadow hangs over it."

"You'll never be sorry," I rejoined with deep gratitude.

"I was born here—played and roamed and hunted—worked here and loved until *she* died."

"Friend, I'm primed for a great story. I've waited years. But before you start, tell me . . . how does it come that you speak so fluently and well, if it's true, as you told me, you're half Apache, and lived here in this wilderness till you were twenty years old?"

"Sounds queer, but it's simple enough. *Her* mother was from the East. She was educated—taught us both."

"Was *her* mother yours, too?"

"No, mine was Apache. I never was sure which of the brothers was my father. But when my heart broke and the devil came up in me and I drifted from hunter to a hard-nut cowboy, to rustler, and gunman, then I suspected my father was he—the brother who cast the evil spell over this homestead."

Then for hours this somber-eyed white Apache talked, living over the past. What he related would have filled a volume. From all he saw and heard and felt and suffered there I embodied, with the privilege and license of the writer, my own tragic tale of Quaking-Asp Cabin.

Among the passengers on the first Santa Fe train to reach Flagerstown, Arizona, in the seventies, were Richard Starke, his young wife Blue, and his brother Len. They left the train at this town because the wildness of the black timbered mountains all around appeared a refuge for an eloping girl under age and the erring brother, Len, who had fled to escape prison.

The frontier town, with its Indians and cowboys, its brawling streets and noisy gambling hells, was thrillingly new and strange to the Easterners. A vast contrast to conventional Boston! The brothers felt the leap of primitive blood and that the life of adventure they had read and dreamed of as boys was to become a reality.

Richard Starke had been ten years old when his only brother, Len, an unwanted child, had come into the world; and all of Len's nineteen years Richard had loved him, shielded him, and had at last saved the weakling from jail, if not from disgrace. Len was a handsome stripling, careless, lovable, too weak to curb bad instincts. Blue was pretty and spoiled, wild as any schoolgirl, mad with love and freedom from restraint. Richard had converted considerable property into cash, which he carried with him, and which must be carefully conserved to last for years. Long before Richard reached Flagerstown the West had called deeply to him and had claimed him forever. What life he chose must necessarily be Blue's and Len's. There they stood, then, on the wide dusty street of this unlawful frontier settlement, like so many thousands of Easterners and Southerners who had journeyed toward the setting sun, many of them keen to put their shoulders to the wheel of empire, many of them fugitives, outcasts, adventurers, all of them a part of this great movement of an expanding people.

Richard left wife and brother at the hotel and went up to mingle with the men of Flagerstown. A stranger among a crowd of strangers, he excited no notice, and his queries were the natural ones of a newcomer. The upshot of this contact was that under cover of the darkness of the spring night he drove a team and heavily laden wagon down the lonely road to the south, headed for the wildest section of Arizona. Blue sat beside him, speechless from excitement and rapture. Len lounged at the back, dragging three horses by their halters.

In eight days' travel down toward the Tonto Basin the Starkes passed but two homesteads. The road passed through a virgin forest, its green and brown solemnity broken here and there by grassy parks, where game abounded. At last on the rim of a vast blue basin the homeseekers encountered a road, cut through the forest toward the east. They camped at that intersection, undecided whether to venture along this wild rim, or follow the main road down into this deep mountain-encompassed valley of green and gold.

A caravan of three wagons caught up with them at this camp, and the leader made friends with Richard. He said he was a Mormon and belonged to the little settlement of Pine, down in the basin. It was plain that any new homesteaders traveling this way would be welcome among the Mormons. Richard acknowledged no creed, nor did he frown upon the proselyte's kindly advances. Richard said to him, "Lead me to a secluded place deep in the wilderness. Help me build a log cabin. Sell me stock and things to plant."

Next day the Mormon sent his wagons on, and mounting a horse he led the Starkes all day along that rim road, with the silver-green wall of forest on one side, and the ragged rim and dim blue basin on the other. This road had lately been cut through the forest by General Crook and his soldiers, in their campaign against the Apache Indians.

From that camp on the rim the guide drove Richard's wagon zigzagging down a ridge until the windfalls made further progress on wheels impossible. Then he packed the horses, except the one that Blue was to ride, and led miles and miles down into an ever-increasing wilderness of giant trees and swales and rocky fortresses, at last to come out into an open park, level as a lake, shining like a gun, dotted with wild game, and surrounded by slopes of tufted pine crests and fern-festooned cliffs. A solitude and silence such as these Easterners had not dreamed of lay heavily and sweetly upon the park.

"Here we will live!" said Richard in deep elation.

"Oh, Dick . . . it's paradise!" cried Blue.

Len gazed from a survey of the lovely spot

to turn a grateful light of tear-dimmed eyes upon the brother who had saved him.

They pitched camp under the great spruce that shaded the spring. The Mormon took the rest of this day packing down the remaining supplies from the wagon. On the following morning he said, "I will go. My sons and I will fetch what you need, and cut timber and throw up your cabin and plant your grain. God abide with you here!"

The days that came passed like magic. They made a pioneer out of Richard Starke. Strong and shapely, skillfully designed and built, the homestead of yellow peeled pine logs went up, back wall against the cliff, stone chimney rising sturdily, at length to send its column of blue smoke lazily aloft to mingle with the green foliage. The brown tilled park, rich with its many fallow years, grew green with beans and maize and cabbage and turnips, and with the orchard and vineyard transplanted from Pine. Calves bawled in the white aspen-pole pens; chickens learned to run from the shadows of swooping hawks; the bray of burros mingled with the bugle of elk.

Blue was rapturously happy despite the housewifely duties so difficult for her. Richard had encouraged an Apache family to stay and live in the canyon at the head of the park. And the Mormons left one of their number, Matthew Taylor, a young farmer and experienced hunter, to help the Starkes. Len Starke hated work and he ran wild in the woods, along the trout brooks. The frosty autumn days, with their colored falling leaves, saw Len roaming the forest with the buckskin-clad Taylor, and that season brought up the one unplumbed strong instinct in him.

When snow fell Taylor and the Indians went back down into the basin for the winter. But for the Starkes, to be snowed in meant only a climax to their adoption by the wilderness. With cords of firewood, meat hanging under the eaves, stored fruit and vegetables, books and light and warmth, they welcomed the roar of the north wind in the pines and the white drifting clouds of snow.

Winter passed and spring returned. Matt Taylor came back with the Apaches. That summer saw Letith, the daughter of the Apache squaw, develop from a child to a slim, voluptuous creature, dusky-eyed, wild as a deer, restless at her work, shy before the bold-eyed Len, ever running from him only to be pursued.

Richard worked in the fields. He had

grown to love this park and cabin. His cattle had begun to multiply. He would prosper here. And as the months passed, dread of that reaching hand from out the East gradually folded its sable coat and faded away.

Another golden-scarlet Indian summer merged into white winter. At nineteen Blue had outgrown her girlish frailty. Outdoors three-fourths of the year, she had grown strong and brown and beautiful. Richard reached the summit of his fullness of joy. His sacrifice had been rewarded. Blue seemed to be changing, growing. Len was content with his lonely fishing, hunting, dreaming. The future held prospects beyond a lonely seclusion. The snow fell and melted, and again it was summer.

While Richard was absent, having gone to Pine to pack up supplies, during one of Taylor's frequent trips to the railroad, the Indian girl Letith gave birth to a baby boy. This happened in Richard's cabin, where Blue had kept the girl for her confinement. Len swore that the baby was not his. Letith did not betray him in words, but her great dusky eyes, fixed upon Len with the strange worship of the savage maiden for the white man, appeared to be conclusive evidence for Richard.

Blue repudiated his opinion with a passion that amazed him. But presently when Letith's father dragged her away, leaving the baby there, Blue took it to her heart, and seemed all at once to blossom into a woman. When Blue's daughter, Hillie, was born the following summer, Richard accepted the idea of adopting the Apache maiden's boy.

Then the threatening shadow that had revived in Richard's mind, to haunt him again with its mocking inevitableness, retreated with a subtle and welcome change in Len. The boy seemed to be growing into a man, and up until the hunting season that year he worked hard around the ranch. What with these precious truths, and the multiplying cattle and the mounting grain, Richard was too busy working and being happy to count the months until they had grown into years. Also these same things, added to his loving faith, blinded him to what he came bitterly to learn.

One day in midautumn he was up in the woods with Matt Taylor rounding up calves that had become too numerous to brand. Something, he forgot afterward what, gave him occasion to make a short cut on foot down the slope to the park, at a point near the cabin. As he was about to emerge from the wooded slope to enter the straggling spruces and aspens he heard Blue's high sweet laughter ringing out, with a rich bell-like note he had never heard. She came in sight running, looking back, her eyes wide and dark, her breasts shaking under her thin garment. She hid behind a tent-shaped spruce that spread its lower branches on the ground. Then Len appeared, flushed of face, his hair disheveled, his eyes shooting ardent flames everywhere. He found Blue. She had only run to be pursued, only hidden to be found. Len seized her with a low exultant cry, and as he enveloped her tightly her arms slid up his shoulders to clasp round his neck. That moment, so shockingly fraught with amaze and panic, froze Richard in his tracks. And the next, when his brother's handsome rosy face bent to his wife's, and their lips came together, and she stood tense, her eyelids closed heavy and rapt, was one in which Richard's heart broke, and a horrible hell bellowed into his soul.

It was Len who broke that embrace, not Blue. She clung to him as they wended a slow way back to the cabin. The children were playing and shrieking around the door. Richard watched the lovers enter and stood stricken until he saw Blue's scarlet face

flash against the blackness of the open doorway. She peered out into the park, then disappeared.

Richard plunged up the slope like a mor-
tally wounded bull and at length slunk under
a dense spread of spruce to lie like a log.
When, hours or minutes later, his mind
awoke to clear thought again, he saw the
catastrophe. He understood then the change
in Len—his staying at home, his frenzied
labors, his unusual gaiety. He understood
Blue's glamorous beauty, the pale glow of
her face, the silver music of her laughter,
the moods that alternated in her. He re-
called now the look he had seen in Len's
bold eyes, across the cabin room, in the
firelight. He recalled his wife meeting him in
the door, at his return from work, too
innocent-eyed, too sweet and loving to be
true. Len and Blue had fallen in love, terribly, not as boy and girl, but as man and
woman.

The husband reasoned that they had only
recently discovered their love, that they
had just begun to surrender to the ecstasy
of it, and not yet wholly and shamelessly.
Richard had to save them. But how? He
could not send Len adrift, after all these
years of protection, to become an outcast

among the vicious characters of the Basin. He would have to hide from Blue his knowledge of her duplicity, if that were possible. Still, was it duplicity? Could she help falling in love with his brother, younger, handsomer, wilder? Richard blamed himself. This was the penalty of eloping with a sentimental girl, of forcing her into womanhood. This was the price he had to pay for taking his brother from the world, which would have made him pay for his weaknesses.

Richard plodded down toward the park. It was the hour of sunset in which the golden rays of light shone down upon the manifold autumn hues with a beauty and glory that made this lovely place all-satisfying. Richard saw it once more—and saw it die and become transformed with an appalling shadow.

He changed as had the aspect of nature. He went back to the cabin with a gnawing rat in his heart, a burning jealousy, a clouded mind, all at bitter war with his better self. Blue thought he was tired; Len spoke of Matt returning alone from work, and he gave Richard a strange glance. Their gaiety went into eclipse. It never pealed out again in that cabin.

From that hour Richard confined himself to labors in the fields close at hand. He never left the park. And as the fineness of him disintegrated under this wreck of love, so the reaction upon Blue and Len was correspondingly great. The shadow deepened over that household. Len knew that his perfidy had been discovered—that he was permitted to stay on there through the incredible loyalty of his brother. He ceased to work; he roamed the forest; he lay idle and brooding under the spruce; he rode to Pine and came back smelling of rum.

Blue's bloom left her, and so did the dancing light of her violet eyes. She tried to remedy the evil, to get back to Richard, but there was a stronger will than hers at work, a power that dragged her down. Richard divined it was Len's love and Blue's mad response to it that had enslaved her. They never realized, these two misguided and fated lovers, that when Richard plodded the furrows of the fields or stood leaning on his hoe, or sat brooding before the fire at night, that he was fighting himself, his baser physical side, to beat it down and go away forever, leaving them to a possible happiness. But that was what obsessed him. Greater love hath no man! This was triumphing in Richard's soul.

One day in early fall he had gone to the

upper end of the park, taking his shotgun with him to kill a grouse or wild turkey. Len had gone hunting early that morning. Taylor was picking beans with Hillie and the Indian boy Starke. Richard avoided passing them. Of late the Mormon had watched him with covert sympathy.

In the aspen swale where the park converged there was a huge pile of dead hardwood that Richard had snaked down to chop up for winter cooking fires. Day after day he had labored at this task, finding mental relief in physical violence. But today, which was to see the fruition of his struggle, he never lifted up the ax. For hours he sat in the melancholy forest, his soul naked to his inner gaze. All around him were the amber and purple blaze of leaves, the passing brown rumps of elk, the frisky gray squirrels, the drumming grouse and scratching turkeys, to which sights and sounds he was oblivious.

Toward sundown he arose like a giant casting off a burden and bent his stride toward the distant cabin, with his mind made up. He would give Blue to his brother with enough money for them to make a new start in life, far away somewhere. But the mother must part with Hillie.

The trail kept to the straggling spruce

and pine trees along the edge of the park. Richard had not gone far when a rustling in the brush reminded him that he had not thought of the meat Blue had importuned him to hunt.

His quick glance caught a movement of parting leaves. Then not ten steps distant he saw two round black holes, and he looked along the brown barrels of a shotgun, into eyes that blazed murderous hate and hell. Len!

The gun belched smoke and fire. A terrific shock knocked Richard flat and his ears clapped with a crash. His faculties sustained a stunning check, but instantly rallied. He lay still, expecting his brother to emerge from the brush to see if he was dead. He heard rustlings and retreating steps.

Richard's effort to sit up ended in a fall. He had tried to use his right arm. It had been blown off with part of his shoulder. Blood poured down his side in a red deluge. He feared part of his lung had been shot away. Something hot and salty welled up into his mouth.

Using his left arm, he got to his knees and began to crawl along the trail toward the cabin. He met the imminence of death with an appalling supremacy of spirit. He would not die. He would face this perfidious brother who had meant to destroy him. He must look into Blue's eyes to see if she was a party to this lecherous crime. On he crawled. And the colored maple leaves along the trail were the redder for his passing. He reached the corner of the cabin and struggled erect, holding to the logs. Children's mirth struck Richard incongruously. Taylor at the woodpile with ax aloft saw him and stiffened. Richard got to the door—held to the lintel.

Blue appeared inside, her face set, white, strained. Her starting eyes saw first his bloody boots—traveled upward—over his dripping garments—to the gory side with its missing sleeve and arm. They met Richard's gaze. Conscious and insupportable truth gleamed in them. They betrayed the intelligence that he was not dead, but alive. Then they protruded and fixed in horror. She shrieked and fell back into the cabin.

Richard staggered inside. As he lurched for the chair his hand left a perfect crimson imprint upon the yellow stone over the fireplace. Then Taylor rushed in, panting, mute with fright.

"Shot—myself," gasped Richard, and strangling, he succumbed to faintness.

When he recovered consciousness he

found himself on the couch along the wall where the light from the door fell. Either his body was bound so tightly that he could scarcely breathe or the excruciating agony made it feel so. Matt Taylor knelt beside him, feeling his pulse.

"Dick," he said hoarsely. "I reckon you'll die—pronto."

Richard's lips framed an almost inaudible "No!"

"Your arm's gone—shoulder—top of your lung! Man, tell me what to do when—when—"

"Matt . . . I'll . . . not die."

"I hope not. But I reckon you will. Did all I could, Dick. . . . Listen, man! What'll I tell—do? . . . I trailed you—found your gun. It hadn't been fired!"

"Tell—do—nothing."

"Ahuh!" The Mormon's dark and grim glance rested wonderingly upon Richard. "Shall I pray for you?"

"Yes—that—I live."

This religious Mormon bowed his head over Richard and prayed in husky fervid whisper, the last of which grew intelligible: "And damn their cursed souls to hell!"

"Yes!" whispered Richard, echoing that in his own soul. "Where—are they?"

"Outside. Waiting for me to tell them you've passed on."

"Matt—stay by me. . . . Give me whiskey—water. . . . I shall not die!"

Richard knew that nights and days passed, because his consciousness registered light and dark through his closed eyelids. His senses were in the grip of a transcendent and superhuman will. He refused to die. His mind must conquer his body. A terrible and insupportable revenge upon these traitors would be to live. Agony was nothing. Time was nothing. Love would have let him die. But hate would save his life.

The days passed. If Richard could have looked at himself lying prostrate there he would not have seen any perceptible improvement in his condition, but his inward eye told him differently. His spirit swore and his mind believed that it had known beforehand he could have been killed outright and yet would have come back to life.

Often he felt the children near him, and the time came when he opened his eyes and whispered to them. Violet-eyed Hillie, with her curly nut-brown hair, was six years old. The Apache boy Starke, Len's son, was seven, a tall lad, inscrutable, fated to tragedy. They both were that. Richard could not resurrect the love he had felt for his little girl.

But when Blue was in the cabin Richard never opened his eyes. Often he heard her and Len whispering outside. They were waiting for him to die.

One night in the gloaming at the end of this belated fall, when the children were asleep, the low voices of the lovers floated to Richard on the still air.

"Matt says Dick will live."

"Oh, I hope to God he will, but I fear he won't," cried Blue poignantly.

"I can't stay here longer, Blue. . . . I'm tortured."

"*You* are tortured! For God's sake, what am I?"

"Let us run away, Blue. You can't stand it either. When you come out of this cabin you look like—like death. . . ."

"Yes. Death! There is death in there. All that Dick was! Love, home, child, happiness—dead!"

"But it's too late, Blue. . . . *We* might find those things—somewhere—after we forgot. . . . Come. Let's take Hillie and go."

"Oh, how can you? . . . Len, I loved you—love you still. I gave you the best of me—what he never had. I share your guilt.

. . . Oh, God—help me! My eyes were wide open. If Dick had died I'd have been his murderer, equally with you. . . . But *now* —it's all different. While he lives I must stay here—and suffer—and work my fingers to the bone for him . . . and never dare to look him in the face again!"

"What will become of me?"

"That doesn't matter, any more than what becomes of me. Go away. Leave me peace in retribution. . . . But if you have any manhood, you will let this terrible deed —this fruit of our passion—be a turning point in your life."

"Manhood! Am I my brother's keeper? I want *you*, Blue. You, my woman, else I'll go to hell!"

"Len, if you stayed here, you'd make me loathe you. Leave—while I still love you! Leave me to give my life to him."

"I'll go, you white-livered cheat!" he cried in bitter passion. "It's the end. I knew—I always knew this lonely hole would be our ruin. We were not savages. But we became savages—like that bastard son of mine in there. . . . This wilderness cabin is accursed. If it were not cursed by nature, by a primitive something as raw as these yellow logs we threw up, then *I* cursed it—my crooked,

343

rotten, selfish self—and *you* cursed it—with your pretense of wifehood and motherhood —with your damned sweet lure—with the female in you that couldn't be satisfied. . . . Good-by, Blue Starke!"

Matt Taylor stayed at the cabin until winter set in and then went out on snowshoes. Richard lay on his couch, sleeping, mending, his mind warped in one narrow orbit. He never spoke to Blue—never looked at her when she might observe it. But he saw her carry water, chop wood, bake and cook and mend, and use what hours these tasks left her to teach the children. What little communication there was between her and him was carried by Hillie, and sometimes by Starke. The Indian boy revealed a somber affection for Richard, and through that long solemn winter Hillie grew to worship him. Richard saw this, marveled that it made no change in him. But he was dead to all save hate. He survived to make this woman suffer, and the days were as moments.

Spring came, and with it Matt Taylor with a pack train of supplies. He said his prayers had been answered. That summer Richard arose from his couch to walk about, a shell of a man, ghastly of visage, marvelously and imperceptibly gaining.

Summer and fall went by, and winter, similar to the preceding one, except that Richard read and brooded before the fire. There was never a moment, waking or sleeping, in which he was not conscious of the tragic presence of his wife. She seemed sustained, too, by a spirit that neither hard work nor misery could break. The measure of her sin was a faithfulness and repentance that came too late. Her beauty augmented, but it was no longer the bloom and freshness of a girl. At twenty-five all that she had lived, all the havoc she had wrought, all the soul that anguish had burned to gold, showed under the marble of her face, in the terror of wide-open, staring eyes.

When planting season came again Blue worked in the fields, with Hillie and Starke to help. They were springing up like the weeds they had to pull. Taylor came once more with supplies, for which this time he received no recompense. During the succeeding years he visited the cabin every summer, as if the place haunted him, as he said it haunted Len Starke. It was rumored, Taylor said, that Len lived in the forest like an Indian, and cattlemen of the Tonto called him hard names. More than once he had been seen by riders in the vicinity of Quaking-Asp Cabin, by which Richard's home had become known. It was conceivable that the man found an irresistible urge to return to the scene of his great crime, to take a hidden look at the spot which had so fatally influenced his life. Richard did not allow Matt to tell Blue of Len's visits, and in his own mind he sustained a surprise that Len showed character enough to make them. Blue should have no sympathy. There might have been solace in the proof of Len's remembrance, perhaps in the thought that he wanted to see her.

Then Matt Taylor did not visit the park for five years. Sometimes forest riders rode down and in the fall hunters blundered in there, or came out of curiosity. Richard saw that the mystery of Quaking-Asp Cabin was guessed at if not known.

His cattle were rustled or they wandered down into the dense thickets and canyons to be killed by lions and bears, or to become as wild as the beasts that preyed upon them. The once fertile fields of maize and beans returned to grass and weeds again. Richard, like a ghost of his old self, worked desultorily in the little garden that Blue, with Hillie and Starke, planted each summer. Prosperity had long departed and poverty came in the gloomy cabin door.

The Mormon friend rode down again, after his long absence, and stayed in the park awhile. But it was evident that despite his interest in Richard and Blue, and his affection for Hillie and Starke, he could not endure to stay long.

The white winters succeeded the brown autumns, as the summers fled on the heels of spring. Such was the peculiarity of Richard's malady that he did not see the swift flight of time, nor the development of the children. He saw only this woman who had laid waste his heart and his life; and in proportion to the wretchedness she evinced, his vitality survived.

In the spring of the tenth year after the catastrophe, Hillie died. This thing wedged thought and feeling and realization into the almost impenetrable sepulcher of Richard's mind. Death, in a strange flash, brought back his love for his child. She had grown to be a frail girl of sixteen, lovely as one of the columbines under the cliff, and like them shadowed by the mystery of Quaking-Asp Cabin. She had never known the secret of her father's deadness to her worship. He divined now, with terror gathering in a heart which had harbored only hate, that his insane passion for revenge had struck the child of the mother down.

All at once he saw Starke, a fine upstanding lad who adored Hillie, as the one to whom his starved heart had gone. And the Apache, stony-faced and sloe-eyed over her grave, buried his heart there, and left the homestead without farewell to the couple who had raised him. Richard never saw him again.

Richard was left alone with Blue. And hate, the fierce consumer, turned to ashes. It died without a flicker. Perhaps for long it had been unconsciously cooling. But the habit of silence abided with him. At the moment of death he could forgive Blue and Len. And he had strange inward tremors and loosenings, as if the knotted cords of life had been untied. His hate, his passion might have kept him alive indefinitely. But these had perished and he saw himself as hideous of soul as he was deformed in body. If he relinquished this hold on life he would not last long.

When Matt came up again that spring Richard took him out to Hillie's grave, which was near the babbling brook, out of sight of the cabin. The Mormon did not hide his grief.

"Gone—that lovely child—without love or God!" he exclaimed at length. "Dick, you failed in fatherhood. . . . And Blue will be next to go."

"Friend, if I had it to live over . . . but no matter. I am a broken vessel. . . . Do you ever see my brother?"

"Only seldom. But I can find him if you—"

"Fetch him, Matt. Then your loyal service to me will be ended. It bears this fruit. I shall ask you to pray to your God, as you prayed over me ten years ago, for mercy in the beyond."

Richard's decision seemed a letting go of the terrible force that had sustained him. If he let go utterly he knew that would be the end. He bade the Mormon depart and make haste on his errand.

That night, when the early twilight of autumn darkened the park, Richard looked out of the door. There were deer grazing with the cows. Frost breathed down from the heights. The moan of the pines, eternal it seemed to him, spoke of the long years, the travail, the end, the ways of the inscrutable. It was good that this lovely park and

Quaking-Asp Cabin should go back to the wild. He would invest them with the shadow that had hovered over him, and which would deny this place to an abiding love of men.

Richard turned away from the door. Blue had just put a light upon the table, which was her mute signal that his supper was ready. But he approached his old armchair and sank into it.

"Blue!" How strange—how hollow— mocking—the sound of that name on his lips—the first time in ten years! "I shall not eat tonight. . . . Come here."

She fell upon her knees beside him, and her hands like steel, clutched at his one arm.

"I have sent Matt to fetch Len."

"Oh, my—God!" and the strength to go on seemed shaken out of her. White as it would ever be, her face dropped to his shoulder.

"I forgive you, Blue—and him. I should have forgiven long ago. But jealousy and hate have the power of hell. . . . I might not last till he comes. For I have let go— and the fire that heated my heart is growing cold. . . . Tell him what I say. . . . And this I leave you—not my wish, but my due —that you go away from Quaking-Asp Cabin forever. My doom has fallen upon it. . . .

See that bloody hand—there on the chimney stone? By that Len marked this cabin—and I have fostered the shadow. It would blight any lives here—much more yours and Len's —who still have your great battle. If he has repented, as you have, my Blue, then there surely will be . . . But if he has sunk low— lift him up. He had a terrible strength of love for you. . . . There is money left that I hoarded—enough for you to go far away —as we all did once before—and begin life— over again."

All day Richard had sat in his chair as if holding on to a taut and stretching cord, waiting for the clip-clap of hoofs. Blue flitted to and fro in the calm—silent, hovering back of him, peering out the door. In the silence he could hear her heart beat. But he could not even feel his own. Dusk stole in at the door and with it a cool sweet tang of the pines and the smell of burning leaves. That dusk darkened the room, accentuating the flickering sparks of the hearth. Or was it the creeping shadow that had darkened his mind? The old phantasms trooped back, de- tached, illusive. And on the moment when Blue's poignant cry rang out and the beat of hoofs pierced Richard's ear, a darkness came before his eyes to obliterate the mark of a spread hand on the chimney stone. And he thought it presaged the mantle of time— the generous years—the alchemy that had worked in him—the thing which lifted his failing heart to piercing gladness at the sound of the hoofbeats coming—faintly—fainter— lost.

Ohio's Writer of the Purple Sage

By Erwin A. Bauer

There are still a few old-timers around Ohio that remember a certain bright young ball player who almost made the major leagues around the turn of the century. They knew him as "Pitchin' Pearl" Grey because he had a fast ball that "fairly smoked." It seemed certain that stardom was in his future. But somehow, somewhere, he was sidetracked.

You might say that Pearl Grey was fortunate to be sidetracked. Most baseball players are forgotten as soon as they can bat and run no more, but Pearl's achievements will be remembered as long as America and adventure are synonymous. As Zane Grey, writer of the purple sage, he became world famous. More people read his books and stories than those of nearly any other American author.

Before he died in 1939 Grey composed more than five million words for publication, including seventy-one books which were translated into nearly every modern language. These printed works were made into countless movies and eventually into a television series. America has been depicted to readers throughout the world by this man who first saw the light of day in 1872 in Zanesville.

Psychologists nowadays make much of a man's heritage and background. They like to point out the obvious effect of early years on a man's entire life. Well, Zane Grey's early years were spent in the rolling blue-green hills along Ohio's Muskingum River. Evidently this was a good training ground for a life that raced through sixty-seven years and touched some of the strangest places on the face of the earth.

Grey's ancestors were of genuine pioneer stock. His father's family came as Irish immigrants to Pennsylvania, settled there, but eventually pushed on to the greener pastures of Ohio. An adventuresome, pioneer spirit was even stronger on his maternal side. His mother, the former Alice Josephine Zane, was a direct descendant of Colonel Ebenezer Zane.

Ebenezer was the defender of Fort Henry

through many a siege, and later he conceived the idea of building a wilderness road—Zane's Trace—to open the Ohio River valley for settlement when hostile Indians still lived there. After the road was a reality, he received a land grant from Congress which included the present site of Zanesville.

Zane's boyhood in Zanesville was lively and largely unrestrained. His home was at 363 Convers Avenue in a part of town called The Terrace. Young Grey didn't spend much time indoors. With a gang of boys known as the "Terrors of the Terrace," he dug secret caves, organized clubs with mystic rites—became something of a nuisance in the community. He also authored his first story during this period on a strip of wallpaper, but his father destroyed the "manuscript" as a punishment.

Young Grey's father, "Doc," had taken up dentistry late in life, but his heart wasn't in it. He was really a rough-cut backwoodsman, hunter, farmer and preacher—all of which appealed to Zane except the last. At a tender age Doc taught him to hunt and fish.

Young Grey spent his boyhood climbing in hardwood hills thereabouts, swimming in the steamboat locks, or fishing in the murky

Muskingum and Licking rivers, which join at Zanesville. On other occasions he'd raft down the Muskingum to Duncan Falls where giant catfish were available.

Since he was christened (unaccountably) Pearl, he at first had to defend his unusual name to be accepted by his contemporaries. A "terror" as a boy, he became one of Zanesville's outstanding athletes and a lifelong outdoorsman.

Although fishing was his first love, Pearl was far better at baseball. During his high school days the Grey family moved to Columbus, and it was there he developed into a star. One summer afternoon in the sleepy village of Baltimore, just south of Buckeye Lake, Grey almost lost his scalp, but got the biggest break of his young life.

Baltimore and a nearby town took their baseball seriously—and their teams were intense rivals even though the other town always won. One day Grey appeared in the Baltimore lineup as a "ringer" and both pitched and batted the team to victory. But the opponents found out he was a "furriner" and started collecting tar and feathers. Somehow Grey escaped to Columbus, where a University of Pennsylvania scout who had seen the game was waiting for him with an athletic scholarship.

After graduation from Penn, where he earned a degree in dentistry, Pearl had offers to sign with several big-league teams. But relatives convinced him that, in the long run, pulling teeth was more profitable than pitching. As a result he opened up an office in New York City.

Business was slow and dreary from the beginning. But it must have been a balmy, springlike afternoon when existence in the big city suddenly became unbearable. Many years later Grey recalled thinking that the hills would be light green, and dogwoods would be blooming back in Ohio. Without further ado, he snuffed out the gaslight in his drab office and walked out. He never filled another tooth. Instead he kept going until he reached the Lackawaxen River in Pennsylvania, which reminded him of home. There he stayed to fish and relax.

While living on the Lackawaxen, Grey began to put some of his experiences and his thoughts on paper. He did so laboriously, in longhand, a practice he was to continue all his life. *Field and Stream* magazine bought one of his first writings.

But fame and fortune didn't come immediately to Grey. His first full-length novel, *Betty Zane*, a frontier story about his great-great-aunt, sold well later, but initially he had to have it published at his own expense. Mostly he received rejection slips in wholesale quantity, an unhappy experience that many writers frequently share. Some are discouraged, and some only become more tenacious. Grey was one of the latter.

His wife Lina, whom he married in 1905, encouraged him in his work even though it meant personal sacrifice. He credited her determination with keeping him going during the discouraging early years.

Then Grey met a lecturer called Buffalo Jones who talked him into traveling West. A week later he stepped off the train at a desert whistle stop in Arizona's Tonto Rim country. It was like landing in a new world.

For several months Ohioan Grey mingled with cowpokes, Indians, sheriffs, and prospectors. Farther north, in Montana, Teddy Roosevelt was doing the same thing for the first time. It was still the unadulterated Wild West that both of them saw. Grey roped wild horses, hunted lions, helped find a herd of lost buffaloes in the Tonto Basin. Once, as the victim of a practical joke, he rode an unbroken stallion and was almost trampled in a stampede.

It was a rough, dirty and saddlesore existence, but it was inspiration for *Heritage of the Desert*, his first successful novel. *Riders of the Purple Sage* soon followed and sold two million copies, an unprecedented sale at the time. Zane Grey's reputation was made.

Beginning in those first novels, Grey set a pattern for his heroes that never varied and, in a sense, described the author himself. Always these men were hard-bitten and resolute, extremely moral, square-jawed and blue-eyed. Invariably they toiled on the side of law and justice.

The villains were stereotyped, too. They were contemptible, with no respect for law, order or women. Almost without exception, the women were steadfast, virtuous and shining inspirations to their men. Heroine after heroine in dozens of novels that cascaded from the presses suffered, persisted and was finally rewarded with lasting happiness.

Many men set out to acquire a fortune and in the process forget why they wanted it in the first place. Grey was different. One of his editors and closest friends pointed out that Zane just wanted to travel and go fishing wherever he pleased. Anyway, that's surely what he did.

The man who at first caught bullheads and bass on the Muskingum bought a 190-foot three-masted schooner and visited the far corners of the globe. He fished around the bleak and lonely Perlas Islands and rocky Galápagos, off the coast of Ecuador. He trolled off New Caledonia, Australia, New Zealand, and Tahiti, catching giant marlin and sharks which remained as world records until modern advancements in tackle made it possible to catch bigger fish. At one time Zane Grey held nearly every deep-sea fishing record.

He was especially interested in young people and often wrote that an outdoor background early in life would mold them into happy, useful citizens. His *Zane Grey's Book of Camp and Trails* was one of the first volumes on camping written especially for boys.

Zane Grey was a conservationist when few people knew what the word meant. He attacked water pollution in an era when it was officially ignored. He was alarmed as he saw more and more of primitive America disappear.

Zanesville—and Ohio—had one last chance to see Zane Grey in 1921. World

360

War I was finished, and the famous man who had left his birthplace as a boy returned at the invitation of Zanesville's Rotary Club. A worldwide wanderer was coming home. Nearly everyone in town turned out for Zane Grey Homecoming Week.

Grey spoke at a vast banquet in the Masonic Temple, attended a Rotary luncheon, walked again the streets he had roamed as a boy. But Zane was most touched, he revealed, when he appeared before 3,000 cheering children, free from school for the day, in the then-new Weller Theater. Grey spoke briefly; then a film adaptation of his novel *The Desert of Wheat* was shown. Movies based on Grey's novels have been Saturday matinee fare ever since.

When Zane Grey died of a heart attack in 1939, both he and his books had become symbols of a type of rugged, outdoor adventure that is part of the tradition of the American frontier. But somehow, whether he was writing of frontier days in the Ohio Valley or the rolling plains of the West, he always seemed to see them through the eyes of a tow-headed boy clambering along the banks of the Muskingum River. And through his eyes millions of others have seen them since.

The publishers hope that this
Large Print Book has brought
you pleasurable reading.
Each title is designed to make
the text as easy to see as possible.
G.K. Hall Large Print Books
are available from your library and
your local bookstore. Or, you can
receive information by mail on
upcoming and current Large Print Books
and order directly from the publishers.
Just send your name and address to:

G.K. Hall & Co.
70 Lincoln Street
Boston, Mass. 02111

or call, toll-free:

1-800-343-2806

A note on the text
Large print edition designed by
Bernadette Montalvo.
Composed in 18 pt Plantin
on a Xyvision 300/Linotron 202N
by Marilyn Ann Richards
of G.K. Hall & Co.